Andy Rigley,
Belper Rd,
Stanley Common.

The Lost Dark
Copyright: Andy Rigley
Published: 14th February 2013
Publisher: Andy Rigley

The right of Andy Rigley to be identified as author of this work has been asserted by him in accordance with the Copyright, Designs and Patents Act 1988. All rights reserved. No part of this publication may be reproduced, stored in retrieval system, copied in any form or by any means, electronic, mechanical, photocopying, recording or otherwise transmitted without written permission from the publisher. You must not circulate this book in any format.

Published by Andy Rigley
Edited by Kathryn Koller

Find out more about the author and upcoming works online at www.andyrigley.co.uk or @andyrigley

For Brandon, Kealan, and Nat.

With thanks to Kathryn, Tim, and Paul.

Chapter One

"Hey, you. I'm down here. At your feet."

Jake looked down, even though the voice was in the centre of his skull.

"That's you?" he said.

"Yeah. Hello."

Walking home in the dark, Jake noticed two shadows at his feet. He didn't pay too much attention. It wasn't the first time he'd seen a second shadow, dancing off at a strange angle. It was, however, the first time it had spoken to him.

"Wow," he said. "I noticed you before, but thought it was the street lights or something. You know the way you see it on football matches?"

"No. Not at all," the voice replied. "I'm real. Well, about as real as a shadow can be anyway."

Jake tilted his head side-to-side and watched as one shadow, his shadow, did the same.

"But I already have a shadow," he said.

"Hmm. Sorry. Are you annoyed?"

"Er, well. No. I don't think so. It's just a little odd having more than one shadow. How long you been there?"

The shadow sighed, then said, "About two days. I think. It's hard to tell. I don't really know time the way I used to."

Jake stopped walking.

"So, you've been with me for two days?" he said. "You've seen everything I did over the last two days?"

"Yes. I didn't mean to. I've not done this before."

"But...I came home really drunk and..."

"Yes, that. Made me squirm a little."

"But you're a girl."

"Yes, I... How do you know that?" The girl sounded genuinely surprised.

"I can hear you."

"You can hear me? Like a real voice?"

Jake wiggled a finger into one ear.

"Yeah," he said. "Quite clearly. Very clear in fact."

"Oh wow that's great," the girl said. "I thought maybe you just *thought* you could hear me. Like imagining me. Wow. This is great."

"Is it?" Jake asked, examining the finger he'd just removed from his ear. He looked around, aware that anyone watching him talk to himself would think he was weird. He walked on.

"Well yes," the girl said. "I thought I was completely lost." She lowered her voice to a whisper. "Gone apart from being."

Jake laughed. "You're not lost. You're probably the opposite of lost. My shadow is still down there and he's going where I'm going, and I'm not lost. So we all know where we are. How did you get there?"

"I was detached," the girl said. She sighed.

"Detached?"

"It's what happens to us when our host dies."

Jake stopped walking again. He raised his hands,

5

palms up, in front of him, "What? You're the shadow of a dead person?"

"Sometimes our host dies so quickly, so," she paused as if searching for the right word, "unexpectedly, that they forget to take us with them. It happens more than you might think."

Jake shook his head.

"You're a ghost? What's your name?"

"No, we're not ghosts. We're very much shadows. The Lost Dark."

"I don't know what's worse," Jake said. "Knowing it happens, or knowing you have a collective name. So ghosts do exist?" Watching the shadows at his feet, Jake was sure he saw the girl's shoulders slump.

"You know how the whole ghost thing works when you try to communicate with them?" the girl said.

"Ouija boards and EVP and séances and all that 'is there anybody there' nonsense?"

"Yes. Well it *is* nonsense. You call out for a person, a name, a famous person from the past. It's ridiculous. When you are detached, you lose your name. Ghosts do too. It's why the living have so much trouble communicating with them. And us."

"So you have no idea who you are?"

"Oh I do. I have every idea of who I once was. I can still feel the warmth around my outline. And the smell. Oh, that sweet smell, drifting into me at every shift of the air around us. It's hard to tell I really have gone." She paused, and Jake thought he heard the quietest of sobs. "If I had eyes I think I'd also have tears right now," she said.

"Oh, God," Jake said. "That sounds horrible. I'm sorry."

"Please don't be sorry. It's okay."

Jake wasn't sure what to say. He scratched his cheek.

"Can I ask you a really big favour?" the girl said.

"You can ask," Jake said.

"Can I stay with you?"

"Can you what?"

"Can I stay with you? The three of us together. Just for a while, until someone comes to collect me. Until the lights go out forever."

"Oh. I, er..."

"It's okay. I understand."

"Hang on," Jake said, watching the way his own shadow moved as he did. "I don't see why not. Maybe my shadow could do with the company."

"Wow. Thank you," the girl said, her voice high-pitched and excited. "Thank you so much. I promise not to intrude."

"Ha. Don't worry," Jake said, shaking his head. "Next time I come home really drunk, I'll just turn out all the lights."

Chapter Two

I'm writing this with the lights out. I can read it again tomorrow, when the sun comes up. I don't trust myself to let go any more. I don't want to write, but I have to. It's getting harder to recognise my own writing. I can only write when I'm drunk. Only feel when I'm drunk. I drink to get drunk. I'm scared. I hope that at least stands out. *Scared*.

My shadow. *Me*. It's gone. Days ago. I don't know where. It just went away. Not like it faded or cracked. I just looked down and it wasn't there. I don't want to ask the girl about it right now. I don't have the guts.

Jake folded the faint-ruled A4 sheet in half and dropped it beside his chair. He took a swig from an almost empty bottle of whiskey. He'd only been home a few hours.

"I saw that," the little girl said.

"What I just wrote?" he said.

"Yes."

"How? I thought you couldn't see?"

"I *can* see. I can't cry. I can't blink. I can't stop images. Do you know what that's like? To never shut anything out, to see everything for too long. It's only in the dark that I can see nothing."

"Then I won't write anymore," Jake said, swirling

the drink around the base of the bottle.

"You will," the girl said. "You have nobody else to tell."

"That's not true," he said, watching the way the liquid clung to the inside of the bottle before sliding back down.

"It is true," the girl said. "It's me and you against the world."

"I'm tired."

"You're resting."

"What? No. I've had enough."

"I don't think you have. There's more to come."

"I want my old shadow back. Okay? My shadow."

"It's not about what you want," the girl said, her voice flat. "It's about what *we* want."

"Me and you? Or you and them?"

"Why are you being mean? I'm your friend, Jake."

Jake finished the bottle and let it drop onto the carpet between his bare feet.

"You're a monster," he said.

"Don't."

"I don't care anymore."

"I'll tell you why you should care," the girl said. Her voice was clearer, closer somehow, than it had ever been. "They're here. They listen. And they know about you. And me."

Jake pushed the bottle over with his big toe. "Are you trying to scare me?" he said.

"You can't walk away now. I won't let you."

Jake raised his voice. "This has to stop." He kicked the bottle across the floor.

"It will stop. At the end. When the lights go out forever."

"All the lights?"

"All of them. All at once. In a blinding flash."

"My head hurts."

"I know. I can feel it. Just let go. It's...inevitable. Go to sleep now. I'll see you in the morning."

The bright glow from the clock raged into Jake's eyes. He turned it around, but its pale reflection on the wall continued to mock him. Even with it facing the other way, he could still see the time change, the night ending one minute at a time.

Every time he closed his eyes, he saw a different girl. Her hair a different colour, her face a different shape, eyes wide or narrow or blue or green. When he opened his eyes, she was still there for just a moment.

For Jake, there was no awake and no asleep, just a thin strip of daylight through the curtains, illuminating creases in the wall.

At work he started drawing lines in notebooks, on pristine bright white copier paper, on Post It notes, on the yellow Error Report sheets that he should have been filling in with reported errors. Tiny lines, each one adorned with a dot. A forest of tiny shadows. At the end of the day his faint ruled, margined notepad was awash with them. His Error Report sheet pad was full. All those lines, he realised, at a perfect angle to the sun as it passed around the office windows. As the pen scribed and tracked, he drew them all.

He tried to ignore the girl during the day. He spoke to her whilst making coffee, when the kitchen was empty.

"There are so many," he said.

"Yes. I told you. We are the Lost Dark."

"I have pages full of them. Pages for every day. Why?"

"You're getting closer now. Your stupid little pen draws a map of us. If I could still draw, I'd fill a whole book in a heartbeat. A book you wouldn't understand. A pattern of the days passing that only a few of you could read."

"I doubt that."

"You doubt that? Or us?"

"Stop it with the *us,*" Jake said, slamming his mug down. "I'm sick of hearing about them. Sick of drawing them. I have one thing right now, and I'm torn between you and them. Can't you see? I hate *them* with a passion. But I need you."

"You can't *need* me," the girl said. "I'm beneath."

"You know what I mean. You're all I have and you're not even my shadow. What if I want my own shadow back?"

"What do I do? Tell them to come now? Bring your shadow back? Tell them I want to move on? To detach again?"

"No. I don't want that. I still want you. Beneath *me.*"

"Do you really love me?"

Jake felt a flush of anger. "Fuck you," he said.

"Jake. Stop that," the girl squealed. "You're not

lying are you? You only get angry when you're sure about something."

"Yes, I'm angry. And yes, I am sure."

"It hurts doesn't it? Your head hurts."

"Yes. Yes it does."

Jake turned off the TV, stared over at the dirty pots in his kitchen, then sat back in his chair. He took a swig from his tumbler.

"I have a surprise for you," he said.

"A surprise? How can you have a surprise for me?" the girl said.

"You've been with me for so long now. I want to do something for you."

"What can you possibly do for me?"

"I want to give you something. Something special. I've been having dreams when I can't even get to sleep," he said, staring through the bottom of his empty glass.

"I know."

"And, well, I think that if I can do this one thing for you, then maybe I can just get to sleep for real."

He refilled his glass.

"So it's for you," the girl said. "Not for me."

"A name," Jake said, smiling.

"No," the girl said.

"I want to give you a name."

As the girl spoke, her voice swirled in Jake's head. "Please, no," she said. "You can't. I won't let you."

Jake shook his head and drank. "I thought you'd be happy," he said.

"I *am* happy."

"No. You're not. There's something missing that needs replacing. You need a name."

"You can't. They won't let you."

"It's all I can think about right now. It's what stitches my thoughts together from one moment to the next, the momentum in my head. I have to give you a name. Then maybe things can get better."

"You'll be hurt."

"I wrote it down on the back of this receipt when it all made sense."

"Stop!" the girl screamed.

"No! You need a name," Jake screamed back.

The blurred outline of the midday sun rippled around the edges of Jake's vision as he tried to open his eyes. He knew he was hurt, but he couldn't feel anything. It was more a knowledge that his body had been raked with fire.

A grunt. A cough. A guttural noise in the centre of his head. All his own sounds that seemed dislocated and distant.

He tried to raise his head, but his cheek was stuck to the carpet's weave, blood and flesh binding him to his resting place. His arm felt like a tightly bound length of rope as he reached up to his face, to his nose. Through a dark squint he saw blood. Dark black and red sinews hung from his fingertips like dead matter, and he knew that he had been bleeding.

The little girl spoke. "I told you not to. I pleaded with you to give it up, but you just can't help yourself can you? I tried to help you."

His lips stung as he whispered, "I tried. For you."

"Then don't try. You can't give me a name."

A moth flitted its way over the carpet inches from his face, scuttling back and forth in a frenzy.

"What did you do?" Jake said.

"Me? It wasn't me," the girl said. "It's just the way it is. The way it's always been. We don't have names that you can give us."

Jake felt the cool tracks of a tear roll across the bridge of his nose and wondered what colour it might be by the time it hit the carpet. Pink? Red? Black? He pushed his fingers between his cheek and the carpet, flecks of dried blood pushing up under his fingernails, and managed to free his face. He lifted himself up like a wounded dog and stared down at the mess that had recently been his free-flowing blood.

He went into the bathroom to clean himself. The mirror showed him what had happened. Tears of blood had flowed down his face, around his mouth and chin. For a moment he wondered if he actually had flesh beneath the mess of red. He ran the tap as hot as he could bear and rubbed his skin in small, circular motions, marvelling at how the dried, caked on blood could become so compliant again, at how much it could cover. The sink looked like an abattoir drain.

"I feel sick," he said.

"You swallowed a lot of blood. You were so determined," the little girl said with a hint of sadness.

"I had to try."

"You could have died."

The little girl let out a shrill laugh that echoed around the bathroom. Jake thought his mind was playing tricks on him, and at the same time, pain came back into his eyes and the base of his skull.

In his bedroom, he closed the curtains on the midday sun and lay on top of his bed, sweating and cold. Then he drifted into the first full sleep since the little girl had been with him.

At work, Jake looked at his computer screen and closed his last support call report. He ran his pen across his yellow pad from corner to corner, removed his headset, and looked out over the office at all the other people taking support calls.

"They keep asking me what's wrong," he said, clicking the pen in one hand and scratching sticky grey fluff off his desk with the other.

"Do you care?"

"About them, no. About me, yes. I'm coming apart, and it seems that only everyone else can tell me. They all keep asking if I've been out all night. And they laugh. Apart from Emma."

"Emma?"

"My girlfriend." Jake looked out over the office to where Emma sat with her back to him.

"You don't *have* a girlfriend, Jake," the girl said.

"I meant ex-girlfriend," he said, flicking a grimy ball of fluff away. "It was a long time ago."

"Did you love her?"

"Of course I did. Back then. We had a house. Lived together. Were going to get married. She wanted a dog. Kids. All that..." he pulled the ball of fluff back towards him and flicked it away again, "shit." He shook his head. "Don't worry about it."

"*I'm* not worried. You have been drinking a lot."

"It's not the drinking."

"They think it is. If all they think is that you're drinking too much, what's the problem?"

"We only talk in questions," Jake said, fed up with the way the conversation was going.

"Me and you?" the girl asked, sounding surprised.

"There. Me and you. Questions and answers. Riddles and rhymes. Why?"

"Why? That is a question."

"I know. I can't help it. I need answers. I just keep chipping away at something bigger that's not there. There is no answer. Emma asked me if I'm okay and if I want to talk to someone. She seems concerned."

"She's not concerned. She doesn't love you."

Jake shook his head and sighed.

"Maybe you're right," he said. "Interested. She seems more interested in me now than she has for, well, I can't remember how long. You *are* right. She's not concerned. She's probably laughing at me with everyone else. "

"Maybe she knows about shadows."

"Could she?"

"There are so many of us out there. You've already seen them. Even before I was here. You just didn't know it. Some people will see it in you as well. In your eyes. In the way you walk. In your very being. People you pass in the street. The girl who served you coffee in the shop, or the man on the train with the tired eyes and his hands shaking over his laptop. You know how to be alone in a room full of people. To be a small part in a bigger army."

"Yes. Part of an army."

"You want to feel the pain because it makes you what you think you are. Flesh and blood. You're more than that, Jake. You all are. It just takes time to understand."

"I know," Jake said. "Deep down I know. Hey, I had this dream. I was up in the clouds moving about. I could reach out and pull them towards me, collect them on my arms like a bee collects pollen. I pulled so many clouds together and wrapped my arms around them all. As I squeezed, the rain came, and I just felt like no one understood what had happened. People on the streets looked into the sky. Umbrellas opened and hoods went up. Car headlights and wiper blades came on. The streets went dark and empty. And it was all because of me."

"And you enjoyed it."

"And I was God..."

"An army..."

"The lightning was my pulse..."

"You still think it was a dream?"

"A thundercloud alone and terrible in a blue sky..."

"Do you understand now?"

"Everything I ever knew before didn't make sense..."

"That we're moving..."

"I was so alone..."

"That a whole new world exists at your feet..."

"And powerful..."
"And that you only have to look down to see us."

Jake stood waiting for the train doors to open. He stared hard at the plastic disc of the open button. He thought that if he could just get on the train and sit down, then his head would stop hurting.

There was a shrill bleep, and the disc flashed orange. Jake raised his hand and poked out a finger that didn't quite connect with the button. Something inside him clicked. There was a knotting in his bowels and pain in his lower spine. An arm brushed past his and into the button. He felt something deep down inside him that he didn't quite recognise. A feeling, a thought, an idea. People started to push past him, jostling and bumping his body from side to side, but Jake was concentrating on holding on to that raw emotion that he couldn't quite figure out. He didn't dare move in case he lost that something forever. Someone asked if he was okay, then moved onto the train without waiting for a reply. His eyesight narrowed and white globes of light pricked his vision.

"Get on or move," someone said.

He ignored all those bodies against his, the movement of the tide, the flood spreading to either side and into the train.

At Derby, Jake got off the train and followed the crowd along the platform. At the steps to the rail bridge, the crowd slowed. One side of the steps was blocked by a station guard, his left hand palm out, his right ushering the crowd to the steps on the other side. The trail of commuters slid slowly up the steps, their heads craned sideways.

Jake saw a man lying face down on the steps. An old, black man, his tight curled hair grey and dull. His feet were at the top step, his head lay a few steps down. One arm was beneath him, the other flung out and bent. A beaten and worn Head bag lay on one side, a first aid box on the other. Green staff crouched beside him, not moving.

How many other people, Jake thought, knew he was dead? How many of that slow-moving line of people actually felt their insides convulse at the sight of a dead man? How many went home wondering if the dead guy had made it home and was wearing his cream and brown paisley pyjamas, sipping a cup of sweet tea? How many clawed through the next morning's paper for a 'Hey. *I* saw that dead man.' story? How many would have noticed, in the glare of the fluorescent down-lights, that the dead man had no shadow?

"He was dead," Jake said to the little girl.

"Does that make you unhappy?"

"I'm not sure. I never saw a dead person before in real life."

The girl laughed, then said, "In real life you never saw death. That's funny. How did you know he was dead?"

"Same way I know I am alive I guess. Same way I know when my electric toothbrush will stop working. Same way I know I'm gonna have a shit day at work. Sometimes I just know stuff."

"Wow. You know so much," the girl said.

"Don't. I'm not in the mood."

"No. I mean it. How many people actually realise that at any moment their toothbrush will stop working or that their cat will die? Or that the next phone call will be to inform them that their parents were in a car crash. Most people only shrug it off after it's happened. You always seem to be waiting for it. Watching for it and expecting it."

"I'm just realistic. That's all."

"You're open to it. Did you notice?"

"Yes."

"He had no shadow."

"Don't. I don't want to know."

"But you already know."

"No. I don't. I know what I saw, but not why. I need to leave it at that."

"Then you're not realistic, Jake. You're hiding. When a shadow is detached, the host dies. It's like the opposite of you dying then your shadow detaching."

"You're my final shadow aren't you?"

"I'm still here, Jake. And I want to be."

Chapter Three

Jake didn't know it, but two whole weeks of daytime TV had taken their toll. He'd slipped into a routine of hard drinking and closed curtains, waking up in his armchair with an empty tumbler of melted ice-cube water gripped in his hand.

Every day was exactly the same. Every morning there was pain in his head, throbbing in his bladder. Walking to the local shop, when he could be bothered, for fresh milk or apple juice became a strange and dizzying experience. Whenever he moved around, he felt like he was in a house of fun on a cushioned, tilted walkway with tilted walls and tilted exits.

He heard the letterbox clap shut then shuffled over to check what had been delivered. It was a rental DVD. He stared at the grubby off-white label on the front of the garish blue envelope and laughed.

"Picked by Maximov," he said to himself.

He ripped off the front flap and threw it into a drawer where he kept all the other torn off flaps with amusing names.

He sat back in his chair, closed his dry, aching eyes and felt like he was floating, then sinking.

If someone were to walk in now, the smell would be of a diseased man. Alcohol and sweat,

...Ding....

damp and mould,

...dong...

heat and ozone from the TV.

...dingggggg...

Jake opened his eyes and looked up to where the doorbell hung from its yellowing cable. He looked at the curtains and at the sun on the other side of them, knocking and ringing and burning to get in.

...Knock knock...

...doonnnngggg...

The tired doorbell had become as hungover as he was. It started its digital Westminster chime with gusto only to slur into a long, drawn out note that never quite finished.

...Knock...knock...

"Hmm," Jake murmured as he lifted the tumbler and sipped at the musty warm water. It was enough moisture to lubricate his lips and mouth. He glanced at the fridge, thinking about how he must still have some fresh, cold apple juice and thinking about how he had no bacon or eggs.

"Just a, hang on," he called out, pulling his stiff body out of a sodden patch of sweat and spilled drinks that had been him for two weeks.

Jake is running through woods, chasing a squirrel. The deep musty smell of old leaves. Fresh grass brushes his legs and cools them as his body surges through the undergrowth, bare feet slapping into grass, mud, and flowers. When the squirrel scrambles up a tree Jake stops, watching the thing jump across to another tree. His body is awake and his eyes fill with daylight that splashes through gaps in the leafy canopy and his nostrils fill with clean, fresh air. He shouts that the squirrel is up this tree. His friends all shout back from somewhere else that there's one up this tree.

Between breakfast and tea, when their bare legs are brown with dirt and red with nettle stings and bramble scratches, Jake and his friends chase squirrels through sunlight and green but never catch a single one.

Jake opened the door, the muscles in his forearm tense and slow. As the sunlight hit him, he closed his eyes. But the light didn't go away. Pink and blue flashed in his head. He felt warmth on his face. Smelled baking concrete in the back of his throat.

"Jake. Hi."

With his eyes still closed he replied and opened the door some more, "Emma. Hi."

"Jesus, Jake? Can..."

"Yeah, sure. In. Come on. Emma."

Even with his eyes fully closed and his brain slow, he knew it was Emma. The smell. The voice. The tingle in his scrotum. Emma.

Between opening the door and Emma walking in, Jake was sitting down again, his left hand swirling an empty glass. *To what do I owe this?* his brain turned over as his mouth refused to make the words.

"Jake. Shit. You *are* a mess." Emma hunched down and grabbed his clammy hands into hers. "Jake. You in there?"

He shook himself down, shivering from head to

toe. "Emma." He rolled the sunlight from the door over his body and dropped his tumbler. "Shit. Emma."

Then he cried. Every ounce of moisture that was inside his body fell from his eyes, down his face and into his two weeks.

"Hey, Jake. I'm here, sweetie."

He could taste her breath.

There was silence. The only sound he had truly heard for a long time.

Emma ran her thumb across his cheek, pushing his tears around to his hair. Then she was gone.

"Emma," he shouted.

"Hey, Jake. Hey, I'm just here."

Jake stood up. He wanted so badly to move into Emma, to hold her, to touch her, to do something meaningful to her. She was at the window silhouetted against the evening sun, framed by open curtains. Jake wasn't afraid. For the first time that he could remember, he wasn't afraid of the light sheering into his eyes. He could feel her silhouette smiling at him and he moved closer to her.

As she pulled her arms tight across his back, he shuddered. Her neck was warm and smelled sweet. Her bright blonde hair shimmered and refracted the sun as it lay across his aching eyes.

"I need a shower," he said, and pulled away.

In the shower, Jake kept his eyes wide open as water tore into them, pulling at his lower lids and stinging. He watched his smell washing away around his feet. Then watched some more as he applied a second coating of Morning Fresh bath and shower gel that smelled of pine. The steam in the bathroom had blurred his now unblurred vision in the mirror and he smiled. He thought how Emma turning up like that didn't make any sense, but that how, if she hadn't, he might not have smiled that day.

He dried himself as best he could in the humidity then walked into the bedroom and changed into fresh clothes. A clean shirt. Clean underwear. Clean shorts. *Had fresh clothes ever felt this good?* he thought.

He trudged into the kitchen where Emma sat thumbing a cup, staring out the window that for two weeks had not been a window.

"Sorry," he said.

"Hey," Emma said, standing up, staring at him with eyes that he remembered. "Don't worry. It's all good. Except you didn't finish." She walked towards him.

"Huh? Finish?"

"Yeah, your face."

Jake fumbled across his mouth, his cheeks and his neck. His fingers scratched across a patch of beard and he heard and felt every sharp hair in minute detail, tiny shadows crackling. He felt his cheeks flush. Of all the things he'd felt bad about during his daytime TV time, this was the one thing that made him blush.

"Shit," he said into his chest.

"Hey don't," Emma said, her warmth, her smell, moving closer, "It's still all good."

Jake felt her smile on the back of his neck as she pushed him gently to the bathroom, pushed his shoulders up toward the mirror, then reached around him to clear the glass in smears. He stared at a disjointed picture of a happy couple as her hand reached around, a flash of blue in her fingers. He closed his eyes. He felt her left hand on his cheek. Felt her fingers on his skin. He'd never been held this way before, from behind, not even by her. A pink hand and a blue blur moved over his right cheek and scratched away those tiny shadows. He felt her left hand pressing against him, the smell of her wrist close to his nostrils. He pushed his head into her fingers and sniffed hard as the last few remaining flecks of daytime TV hair dropped into the porcelain and were gone.

Jake opened his eyes at the exact moment that Emma began to speak, maybe a fraction before, he couldn't tell.

"You know I love you more now than I ever did?" she said into his neck, her breath pulling away the warmth like a breeze in a rain shower.

"Me too," he said, staring into the mirror, at himself, at Emma and at the shadow behind them both.

That evening, his dinner tasted better than any dinner he could remember. They sat in a pub garden wrapped in the aroma of gammon, eggs, and tobacco smoke. Tied in a bow with sunlight. Jake felt as if a tiny hole inside his body had been filled with warmth. Emma loved him now more than then. And it felt good.

Jake lay down that night with his bedroom curtains fully open, his alarm clock facing him. With both his hands behind his head, he smiled. He felt the muscles in his face pull at his ears and around his skull. Felt his eyes widen larger than their sockets should allow. Love, feelings, friendship. They all worked better when they had been just out of reach for just so long.

Jake woke up to smell of orange. No. His eyes woke up to smell of orange. To the sight of gold. To the feeling of morning—that was it—to the sun. That big-ass hunk of fire burning into his house and onto his skin.

"Fuck, yeah," he said, without knowing he'd said it out loud. He padded barefoot to the fridge. His stomach held the weight of a good night's meal. His bowels the lightness of a good night's real ale instead of the tightness and acidity of spirits knotting his insides. Bloated was good right now and he opened the fridge door to see no bacon and no apple juice.

"Figures," he said. He pulled out a ball of mozzarella and chewed it in the shallow yellow light of the open fridge.

He ripped open a sachet of instant cappuccino. "Mozzarella and coffee," he sang as the kettle boiled.

He swapped the dull brown packet of saccharin laden coffee for a small business card that lay on the worktop, and to the rumbling boil of the kettle, he studied the pure white writing on the pure black background.

> Party in the Dark.
> Miss it. Miss us.

Emma had given him the card. An *are you going to this?* gesture. He said he might, knowing full well he would. She loved him more now than then. And he felt that right down the centre of his spine. She made him feel like everything else was just a joke, and that she was the punchline. That true love was not true love. That true love could be a fairy-tale ending without the price tag. That if two people could feel the exact same raindrop at the exact same time then the world would end in a good way.

Jake and Emma sat in the dusk watching pints of Pedigree slowly melt away against the background of a round aluminium table. They talked nonsense. They watched the outdoor Big Screen TV showing its usual Big Screen news. They talked about some things that made sense but that soon drifted back into comfortable nonsense. Then the Big Screen changed. The news flicked off then back on, as if someone had changed channels and then changed their mind.

"You got any change?"

A man stood so close to the table that Jake worried he might lose his precious pint, and he was asking for spare change. Jake looked him up and down, his mouth open, his eyebrows high.

The man was tall, his shoulders square and large and...

Padded? They're blocking the whole Big Screen TV, Jake thought.

He wore a smart, charcoal grey suit with faint, red lined squares all over it. *Like a math book. No a drawing book*, Jake thought.

Jake is sitting in his bedroom and has given up trying to glue the top of a grey plastic Spitfire wing to the bottom of a grey plastic Spitfire wing. He has a faint blue lined book that he bought from the Post Office with money from his paper round that he doesn't like spending in the newsagents. He's spent hours finding different ways to fill a thousand squares all in different ways. Blocks, lines, dots, stripes, circles. Each square has a different pattern.

His favourite is to draw two slightly elliptical lines from corner to corner inside each square like some kind of leaf. Then he draws another one and another and another, until his leaves, they kind of form a square of leaves in four squares. He fills a whole page with those things. No reason. Just that he has a pad different to most pads that needs filling differently to most pads and his Spitfire model doesn't look like the Spitfire painting on the box.

The man stretched out his hand and his charcoal grey, red squared suit sleeve rustled across the table as if it was made from dry leaves or burnt paper, burnt notepads, burnt plastic aeroplane models crinkling into balls of black plastic on the garden path.

"Just a few quid will do," the man said. His hand, palm up, was brown and leathery like he'd been in a dirty bath too long. It smelled of decay. Emma and Jake both placed their palms over their drinks to stop their beer from becoming contaminated. The man leaned in. His face was the same dirty brown as his hand, flecked with stubble that, in the backlight of the Big Screen, seemed to have grown at different speeds on either side of his chin. His lips were cracked and pale, like two fat worms dried out on a parched pavement. His breath stunk of strong tea and day old pet food. But his suit was smart. Tidy and only slightly creased, the kind of creased it might be if this man had just come home from working on the top floor of an air-conditioned, blue tile floored, white box-cell computer stationed office that Jake was all too familiar with.

His breath was hot and sticky and Jake felt it flowing around his face like a molten glove, over his chin and cheeks and right up around his ears.

"No, I don't have any change," Jake said.

"No change?" the man said, adding layers of hot sticky breath to Jake's face. Suffocating. Rank.

"No I..."

The man's eyes seemed the exact same blue as a coconut centred sweet wrapper that has a torch shining through it. Japanese cartoon eyes the way a girl's eyes would look drawn in a comic.

Jake was confused and angry. He was torn between the acts of covering his pint and holding his nose. Emma had a tight hold of his right hand and was squeezing it so that he was suddenly aware of just how many bones there were in it, grinding and threatening to crack. Whether she was scared, or embarrassed that Jake wouldn't give in to the man's demands, he wasn't sure. He wasn't sure of anything.

"Look. Just fuck off," he said, staring hard into

those sweet-wrapper eyes. "Just fuck off."

The man moved his hand away, ran it through his oily black hair and sniffed back what sounded like a dead animal rolling down his throat. Then he smiled. His lips rolled back, and his teeth were perfect. Perfect white. Perfect straight. It was the smile of a male model in a black and white aftershave advert on a glossy back page of a magazine. He spun slowly around on his heels and walked away towards the screen. Jake stared at his shoulders, at the way his arms moved rhythmically, like a soldier's. He noticed that he was wearing dark brown cowboy boots, steel heels glinting purple in the fading light. The man didn't stop at any other tables to ask for money. He didn't even look towards any other people in the crowd. He just walked away.

"Jake, what was *that* about?" Emma said.

Jake stared at the palm of his free hand. "Just some tramp. I guess."

"You could've given him *something*," Emma said, releasing her grip on his right hand. "Some change."

Jake sipped at his pint, stared into its shining white surface and said, "He asked for spare change. Spare, Emma." He looked up hoping he might see the man again, pleading with some poor mother while she clutched her child into her hip. "I don't have any fucking spare fucking change," he said to Emma whilst still staring out. There was no mother clutching her child and no man. He was gone.

Emma sighed one of those sighs that was meant to be heard, and Jake was filled with a rage so tight and balled up that his vision became a blurred graph-paper picture of leaves.

"Spare change," he hissed. "Spare. And his suit. He was wearing a goddamn suit Emma. A suit better than any I've ever worn. Why don't I have a fucking suit with red squares on it like that? Eh? Emma? Why?"

Emma didn't seem bothered by his sudden outburst. She sipped at her pint, put it down, then turned close into Jake's face and smiled. "Just saying. You could have give him *something*," she said.

Jake felt empty. But a good empty. Like he'd just purged his guts of a particularly rancid, long building fart. His shoulders sagged and he shook his head, cracking his neck.

"Yeah. I guess. Something." he said, grabbing Emma's hand into his, careful not to let her know how many bones she had in it.

Sky News flicked off. And stayed off.

"Plastic cup time," Emma shouted, then ran off into the bar.

By the time she returned with two full plastic pints of Boddingtons, Jake was on his feet and edging toward to the throng of excited people in the centre of the cobbled market square.

"This is quite cool," he said, grasping the plastic glass into an oval and sipping before the beer could escape.

"Yeah. A rave." Emma flicked an inappropriate rock and roll devil horns hand and whooped at the TV.

The market square was packed solid. Jake and

Emma guarded their drinks while drinking to avoid any loss. Even in the cool air, Jake was beginning to sweat, and he felt the heat and moisture of every single person he moved past. The Big Screen TV had never looked so bright and was blaring out an industrial-Goth-synth rock-futurepop anthem that no one knew but clearly felt. Epilepsy warning did not apply. It was mandatory.

"This is fucking industrial," Jake shouted, thrusting one arm into the air and bouncing with the vertically animated crowd.

The screen blared out in blues and greens. A female screamed vocals through the air in blonde and black. White bodice, glow sticks, red lips with silver piercings. The crowd in front of Jake and Emma bounced and shoved aggressively, circling one another, stumbling and pulling, pushing and throwing. Jake and Emma bounced and waved and whooped. The crowd behind them bounced and shouted on the edges of the boiling ripples.

The music shifted. It stopped for a few synthesised beats of silence, then the blonde black voice spoke over it all.

"Darkness will..."

The image changed to a gently rotating sphere of the sun, solar flares rolling and spitting up its sides, orange and red glow filling the screen. The sound returned as a constant, fluid, rolling rumble.

Then it all flickered out. The screen went black, except for a small, piercing white dot in the exact centre. The noise rolled into a single monotone bass note that blipped like a scratched record heartbeat.

The crowd stopped seething. The air felt fresh but close. Behind Jake and Emma, a single loud *whoop* went up from somewhere in the crowd. A *come on* shouted from the front and a *hell yeah* from the left. Then a *get below the screen*, from inside.

At the front of the square, on either side, a pair of lights popped in tandem, went out and shattered. Jake felt the whole crowd shrink down as one, every single living person ducking at the violence of the light's explosion.

"Go now. Please."

Jake could feel the energy of the crowd. They expected something big.

The tiny light in the centre of the screen pulsed and ebbed to the drone of that single deep note. A crackle like a too close lightning strike accompanied the explosion of the second set of lights that were further back as their cast iron casings smashed into shards of metal, glass, and filament that rained down on the crowd in bright shimmering sparks.

Above the low rumble came a single piercing scream. The third row of lights exploded and fell onto the heads of the crowd. Above the piercing scream of that first scream came more screams as people scattered.

"Please. Go. Now," the little girl told him. Begged him.

From front to back as each set of lights shed themselves, darkness pounded into the crowd as a brutal, angry tide. Screams were drowned out by an aggressive, high-pitched squeal of something else.

"Emma?" Jake shouted. "The screen, Emma."

As the dark wave of unforgiving rolled across the square, new sounds rose into the air and wrapped around the bodies of people. The lights of the surrounding bars blinked out under the onslaught of the blackness. Jake was on his knees, staring at shoes and the occasional forearm as he scrambled to the front, still shouting for Emma.

He could not see where he was going, only glimpses of flesh, of his hands and of a face to his left carved from anguish. A stench crawled into him, through his nostrils, eyes, and mouth. It was the smell and taste of thick stagnant pond water and decay, of a festival toilet full of shit, of rotten leaves, of flecks of food teased out with dental floss.

He crawled over the soft body of a child, and his feet pushed its limp body backwards as he dug for purchase. His head was filled with screams. Filled with gargling and fluid sounds. Glass smashed and guttural, panicked shouts engulfed everything. He imagined a scene behind him of pure hate. Of pure fear. Of pure loss. He managed to pull his body underneath the Big Screen TV and its loud hum. He hunched back against a cold metal support and pulled his knees into his chest as the sounds filled his right ear. To his left he could hear the river, rushing and whispering over the weir. To his right he heard the crowd rushing and whispering over some other weir.

Jake flung himself through his front door and slammed it behind him with both hands. He stood with his palms flat on the thick green paint and stared out through one of the mottled squares of glass. Outside was all layers. A layer of black for the road, a smudge of grey for the hedges, and a line of blurred orange street lamps. His eyesight matched his hearing, dull, distant.

He turned away from the outside world and, with his back against the door, slid down it and onto his backside. He pushed the flats of his hands into his closed eyes and breathed in. There was a crack from somewhere between his shoulder blades. Behind closed eyelids, he saw tiny lights whirling and crashing in the deep blackness. He started to track them, his eyes moving manically around in their sockets. Then as he started to count them, he felt something terrible, like a moment of realisation that made him want to throw up. There was something about those tiny globes, about the way they moved and interacted as they bounced off one another that made him uneasy, like he was seeing much, much more than just flecks of matter on the surface of his retina. He opened his eyes, and although the house was still dark, it hurt.

He reached up and locked the door. He even used the bolt at the bottom that he almost never used, cajoling it until it fell fully into place. Then he pushed his back into the door, placed his head once more into his hands, and started to count again. Some of the orbs would rush right out of the distance and make him jump, but he kept his focus on these until they slowly glided back away.

By the time the lights had nearly all gone, his head was a rotating spiral that disappeared into nothing.

He opened his eyes, stood up, and with his forehead resting on the cold glass, he stared out the window again. His crotch and legs were cold, and he knew that between sitting and standing, he'd wet himself. He ran his hand down the inside of one leg, pressing the cold into his thigh. He raised his fingers and sniffed. It was the smell of an ill man: thick, salty, earthy, rotting piss.

Rain speckled the glass and what little definition the outside world had before was being crushed and teased into a murky ball. He tried to unpick the scene, to flatten it back out so that he could see where Emma would appear. But it was hard. His head wasn't working. He just kept repeating the words, Emma. Shit. Emma. Shit. Emma.

"She might be dead," the girl said in a soft, matter of fact, way.

"No," Jake said, loud enough that it surprised him.

"Of course. She's most likely dead. Gone."

Jake spoke softly as if he were trying to get a child to sleep, "Hush. No. She'll be fine."

He pulled out his mobile phone and slid open the silver cover. The screen was blank except for a thin row of blue-white light across its centre.

"Shit," he said.

The phone was cold and wet. Jake wondered whether it was his own piss or the shadows that had stopped it working. He visualised the Big Screen and that single white dot.

"Damn it," he shouted and threw the phone into

the floor.

He unbolted the door and opened it. Rain fell on his hot, flushed face and for a brief moment he felt calm. Then he clenched his fists, his fingernails digging into his palms and, like a kid finally standing up to the school bully, shouted out into the night.

"Bastards."

"Don't," the girl said. "They *will* come."

"Fuck them," he said, then he shouted again. "You can all go to hell."

A passing cyclist stood up and pedalled faster, his tiny, grey dog tripping and scampering to keep up as it was pulled along sideways. Jake and the cyclist exchanged glances, their eyes speaking to each other with hate, fear, surprise and anguish.

Just as Jake was filling his lungs for another barrage of abuse, the girl spoke. "Please don't. Please. They *will* come."

Her voice soothed Jake a little. It wasn't fear but calm that moved him into backing down. He opened his hands. "Shit," he said, as the white crescents his fingernails had made filled back to pink. "Where's Emma?" he asked the girl and the street.

"I don't know. How could I know?"

Jake raised his face to the rain and let it settle on his eyes. "I just thought, you know, you and them. Your army. How could you not know?"

"They're not *my* army Jake."

Jake laughed. From somewhere deep in his stomach, he laughed hard. "I swear to God..."

"To God?"

"Whatever. I swear that if Emma is hurt, or gone,

or..."

"Do you love her so much already?"

"Already? How the hell do you know what already is?"

"It doesn't feel like you do. Like somehow you can't."

"Hmm," Jake said, rubbing the sole of his shoe into the ground and watching the tiny lines it drew there. His mind searched through a list of responses to defend himself but he soon gave up. He'd be lying to himself and a shadow.

"Ah shit," he said. "DVDs."

"You haven't watched them yet?"

"No. I've had them almost a week."

"Good. That's great." The girl sounded genuinely excited. "Then go back inside."

Jake went back inside.

After the fresh air and rain, the room smelled of vanilla, sweat, damp, and...

"Whiskey," Jake shouted.

He switched on the kitchen light and watched as the fluorescent tube struggled then popped into life with a satisfying metallic ping. He opened a new bottle of High Commissioner, marvelling as the metal seal on the lid cracked and scratched in his palm. It was a comforting feeling. He gulped down two large mouthfuls that burnt his throat and chest. His stomach immediately retaliated with a spasm and hot acid. But Jake took another swig whilst running his free hand through his damp hair. Leaving the bottle top rolling back and forth on the Formica worktop, he headed back to his chair, opened up his

LoveFilms envelope, swigged again and said, "Well, well. The Usual Suspects."

"Who was it picked by?" the girl asked.

Jake looked at the white label on the blue envelope.

"Picked by Audrone," he said, smiling. He shovelled the tear off flap with the warehouse picker's name on it into the pile of other tear off flaps of warehouse picker's names, put the disc in the player, sat back, switched on what he needed to switch on, took another swig of whiskey while his free hand pressed play on the remote. "Good film this," he said. "Damn good film."

"I don't know it," the girl said.

"Why would you? Damn good film."

"Can you tell me what happens?"

Jake laughed and swigged again from the bottle until it was half empty. "You've got no chance," he said. Then he fell asleep.

He was back in the square staring at the white light that was the centre of the Big Screen, but he was the only one standing as around him all in black and white were hundreds of bodies head to toe laid out like some sick naked meaty crop circle sweeping out from him at the centre to the edges of where his eyes couldn't see any further and a few where alive and whimpering and trying to raise their faces or their arms to him but just as they did they were smashed back down onto the cobbles by some unseen force and more black blood filled the gaps between the stones and Jake was trying to find a clear path through the bodies to try and get out to the screen where maybe he'd be okay and he and his shadow would be safe under the calm white light that was the centre of everything and he'd be back to plain old Jake with no daytime TV and no talking to shadows or watching dull lifeless faces on trains and in bars then he remembered another dream where he was up in the clouds but he knew he couldn't be up in the clouds because something was clawing at his ankles that felt cold and clammy and bone thin like he was being poked with a dining fork wrapped in seaweed and he looked down to see the boy from before clawing and Jake was screaming except he realised the volume had been turned down and he looked at the Big Screen again and there was a mute sign in its corner so he knew he couldn't scream however hard he tried and the boy looked up at him and the only colour in the whole dream was the red around the boy's eyes and the blue tears streaking down his cheeks and mixing with the black blood of all the other bodies around him as everyone who wasn't dead began to scream and all the mouths were deep black O's open wide and screaming with no sound and the boy just kept on pulling until Jake began to lose his balance and he knew that if he fell he would drown in that sea and no one would help after what he had done to them so he stamped hard on the boy's face and *crack* heard the child's skull split between his boot and the cobbles and the face became slack and lifeless and his tears were no longer blue so Jake ran and as each foot fell there was another *crack* as he broke a bone or *crunch* as his boots dislodged some teeth *pop* a jaw snapped loose and a mother's silent screams as *crunch* her baby was trodden into the gaps between stones *crack crack crack* as ribs snapped and pushed upwards through flesh.

crack

Jake opened his eyes to a room the colour of burning lavender.

crack

He looked around. His TV was blank except for the mute symbol in the top right corner.

tap

Someone was knocking on the door.

BANG, BANG, BANG.

"Emma," Jake said.

He stood up faster than his whiskey filled body would let him. He stumbled to the door then twisted the keys before realising he hadn't locked it.

"Jake," Emma said, and pushed past him straight to the bottle of whiskey as if she knew it would be there and without taking her eyes off him, she swallowed the last remaining mouthfuls, screaming as the drink burnt her throat. For a while she just stood staring, her shoulders heaving up and down, her fingers opening and closing around the neck of the bottle that hung by her side.

"Emma?" Jake said. He was worried by her silence and her eyes, eyes that were glassy and empty of everything except rage.

Emma raised her hand high above her head and flung the bottle hard towards Jake. It whistled past him and as it smashed against the door behind him he pulled his head into his hands.

"Jesus fucking Christ," he shouted.

As Emma spoke spit flicked from her lower lip. "You," she said, jabbing a finger in his direction. "You left me."

"Emma," Jake said. "Please. It was all just a blur. I had to get out. I was told to get out. I looked for you but I, well, Emma, I had to get out."

"Told to get out?" Spit hung from her chin.

"Yes." Jake said. He thought the mood might change in his favour. It didn't.

"By her?" Emma said, wiping her chin and mouth then running her hand through her wet, tangled hair.

Jake saw a flicker in her eyes as if a second set of eyelids had cleared her vision. By the time he could raise his hands to defend himself, Emma had already closed the gap and laid two solid punches. One to the bridge of his nose, the other a sharp thud to his left temple.

"Mother fucker," she screamed into his face. He felt her breath on the blood running down his nose. She grabbed his head in both hands and he thought this was the bit where she would pull him in close to her chest and tell him how much she loved him and how everything would be...

Crack.

She smacked the back of his head against the edge of the open door. After the third thudding impact, as the bright white streaks of pain disappeared, Jake pushed Emma hard. She took two steps away. Jake wiped his face, then felt around the back of his head. Just as she raised her hand again, Jake, fuelled by adrenaline and pain and a sense of self-preservation, lashed out. He struck her on the face and felt her cheekbone between his knuckles. She went down onto her hands and knees.

Jake shook his head to clear it then crouched down in front of her. He took her chin gently in one hand and lifted her face. There was a bright white mark where his knuckles had hit.

"Emma," he said, "if you ever touch me again," he let go of her. "I will kill you. I mean really, properly kill you. Okay?"

Emma's expression didn't change. She looked blank, empty, gone.

Jake reached up and grasped Emma's wrist just as the piece of broken bottle reached his throat.

"Ditto," she said, smiling, pushing the large shard of broken bottle.

With his free hand, Jake grasped the back of her hair and pulled her head in close so that the glass was close to both their throats. Emma's eyes flickered as they had before and Jake felt her grip loosen ever so slightly.

By the time they both dared to let the glass drop to the carpet, the morning light had the colour of embers running through it. The lavender hue was gone.

"Jake," Emma said. "I've lost my shadow."

Jake woke up in his chair and immediately looked around the room for Emma. His eyes were wide but also gelled with sleep. When he knew she wasn't there he looked over to the door. The broken bottle, that significant shard, was still on the floor, pink along its edge with blood. He ran his hands around his throat then checked his palms. Nothing. He knew better than to imagine the whole thing had been a dream. They had both come so close to killing each other.

The back of his head hurt, and he could feel hard lumps underneath his hair. He scratched away a little dried blood that flaked up under his nails. He looked up at the wall clock. 4:30. The second hand twitched manically back and forth. One second on, one second back. Stuck. Spasmodic. He instinctively reached out for his remote control and turned on the TV. It was the usual daytime TV bullshit chat show with the usual bullshit slogan: The baby is mine and I've stopped stealing cars for her. *Could be any time about mid morning*, he thought. He felt safe, secure, and warm. Just as he had been those two weeks when nothing mattered. *Nothing*, he thought. *Did I really feel that back then?*

He stood up. The TV cheered and jeered. His knees hurt and his ankles were stiff. He hobbled to the window and opened the curtains. Outside, the day hadn't decided quite what kind of day it wanted to be. Bright sunshine filtered through the trees and reflected from the windows opposite, but over the roofs, tall black rain clouds ripped the sky apart.

He heard a sound in his bedroom and knew Emma had been woken by the incessant cajoling of the idiots on the TV, each voicing an opinion that made no difference, or an idea that came from another world of thought. A man, tall, lank, and tired looking, was standing and shouting at the crowd, at the camera, his thick gold bracelet swinging from a thin arm that looked like string dipped in pale pink wax. "You don't know, bruv," he shouted. "You lot don't know nuffin'. I *have* changed." The crowd laughed. A girl, clutching a baby in her arms, cried. *There was no answer for any of them*, Jake thought, feeling as much hate for the crowd as he did towards the stereotypically dysfunctional couple who were at least pretending to try.

The brief moment of panic when he'd heard Emma move in his bed, in his own bed, had gone. The thought of her flying into the room holding a kitchen knife, had also gone.

He turned off the TV.

"Turn that shit off," Emma shouted, sounding like she had a hangover.

"Just did," Jake said. Then he said, "Sweetie."

Emma appeared in the bedroom doorway, her head down, shoulders slumped.

"You look like shit," Jake said.

"I know," she replied. "I feel it."

Jake laughed. "Time was you'd have kicked off if I said that."

"Not now."

"When you would have told me how, well, yeah, you look shit most the time too."

"Not today."

"Hey, Emma,"

"Yeah?" Emma raised her head and looked at Jake with a faint expectant smile twitching across her pale sunken features.

"Emma. Look." Jake raised his chin into the air.

"My neck's not cut."

"Fuck you, Jake."

Jake felt an empty pull in his guts and realised that maybe his expectation of a show down and his brutish forwardness was not the punchline to the joke he'd expected. But he didn't apologise.

Emma walked across the room. She was wearing one of Jake's shirts that barely covered her thighs. She leaned in to the window and looked out at the black clouds that didn't move. "Remember what I said last night?" she said.

The part about killing each other flashed across Jake's thoughts, but along with it came a sinking, grabbing feeling in his gut. He simply said, "Yeah."

"Look at me, Jake," she said, her back still to him, her thumbs drawing circles on the windowsill. "How long do you think I've got?"

"I don't know," Jake said.

"I have to get another shadow," she said, turning towards Jake.

"Shit, Emma, I don't know if that's..."

"I can. I know I can. I just need to get another shadow."

"Emma, I'm just not sure you can."

"So you won't help me?"

"I didn't say that."

Jake felt himself sliding down the slope of an argument he'd already lost. Just like old times.

"Then help me," Emma said, stepping closer.

She buried her head in his chest and wrapped her arms around him. Jake stood motionless, his arms pinned to his sides, and stared over Emma's head out the window. *This is what it must be like*, he thought, *to cry on the shoulder of a waxwork dummy*. Out the window, over the house opposite, a faint rainbow was disappearing into the chimney.

"I've got to freshen up," he said, pulling Emma's arms gently away before walking into the bathroom.

Emma sat down in the chair and stared at the reflection of the window in the TV screen for a while before switching it on and muting the volume.

Jake washed away the necessity to bully Emma about their confrontation. As he entered the room, towelling his hair, everything was fresh; his skin, the smell of shampoo and coconut conditioner, the clean dry jogging trousers and the old but clean shirt.

Emma was sitting in the chair. His chair. He smiled. She was watching silent TV as the people on there walked along an aisle of antiques and bric-a-brac, all smiling, all joking, all looking at a small porcelain cat.

"Emma?" Jake said.

"It's okay," she said, "I'm okay."

He sat on the arm of the chair, picked up the remote and switched off the TV. He pushed the remote down the side of the cushion.

"That shit'll kill you," he said, placing a hand gently on the back of her head. They sat there staring at their reflection on the screen. The reflection of the window behind them was their happy couple picture frame. He ran his thumb across her forehead, sliding some wayward hair back behind her ear so that he could see her face; her expression. Her eyes narrowed, and she chewed her bottom lip.

"I need another shadow, Jake," she said, watching her mouth on the TV. She looked up and her eyes were filled with a mix of tears and determination.

Jake rubbed his eyes but no answer came, there was only darkness behind his eyelids. *I just don't know*, he thought.

"How?" Emma said, finishing his thought out loud.

"Yeah. I mean. How? Those things don't just latch on."

The little girl spoke. "I did."

Jake was careful not to answer her. He wanted Emma to tell him. He wanted her to make this feel somehow more of a human problem then an inhuman act of getting another shadow.

Emma stood up and looked at the twitching clock. "I just know I can," she said. "We can." She reached up and tapped the plastic cover of the round, white trimmed clock and the second hand jumped back into motion. "Jake, why is everything you own such crap?" she said, under her breath. "There must be a way we can find a..." she stopped, head down, and Jake could see that she was searching hard for the right words, "...find a spare shadow."

Jake shook his head. "But how? I mean. Jesus. A *spare* shadow? It sounds nuts."

The little girl spoke again. "She knows, Jake."

Again, Jake ignored her. He was getting angry with the little girl, he wanted to accuse her of all this being her fault, but somehow he knew it wasn't. The little girl was right, Emma was never this articulate, she was right about Emma knowing.

"Emma," he said. "Listen to yourself. A spare shadow?"

"Of course," Emma said, sounding too surprised for it to be genuine surprise, "it all makes sense. To me at least." For a moment, her eyes flickered at Jake, a tiny slice of time given over to contempt.

"She's done this before," the little girl said in the back of Jake's skull. "Can't you tell?"

"Hmmm, yes." Jake said.

Emma smiled and pulled her hair into a ponytail. "You see?" she said. "Is it making more sense now?"

"Is it Jake?" the little girl said. "You *do* understand now. Don't you, Jake?"

Jake didn't fully understand. For a moment that lasted the same amount of time that Emma's contempt had lasted, he felt pure hatred towards her. But then he found himself, more now than ever, wanting to be there for her and to help her.

"Jake?" Emma said.

He wanted to protect her.

"Hmm?"

To save her.

"Let's go get another shadow. Now. Together."

He suddenly saw her as lost and broken and weak and afraid.

He had no idea how wrong he was.

Again.

Chapter Four

With his key in the door, Harold Moses Keep was surprised at how steady his hand was. At how clear his sight was and how cold the night breeze was.

He opened the heavy, black door and stepped into the dark hallway. For a tiny instant, he forgot what he was going to say as the smell of incense and damp filled his nostrils and the faint sounds of Beethoven filtered through bare plaster walls. Apart from the traffic, the last thing he'd heard that night was muffled screams. Without turning on the light, he removed his wide-brimmed hat, flung it onto the stairs and rubbed at his static laden black and grey hair.

Moses was tall, even without his hat he was over six feet. He was a large man all over and, although not fat, at forty-two years old, he was showing a little spread around his middle and he had thick wrists the same width as his large hands. He looked into the dusty hallway mirror. Dull green eyes. Large nose peppered with blackheads like an overripe strawberry. Lines in his forehead and around his eyes. Short grey stubble. Thinning black hair slicked back, grey at the temples. He rubbed his hand across the dust, creating a clear line, then stared closer. It was the reflection of a tired man. Even the dust didn't hide that. *At least I look kind and respectful,* he thought. Then he laughed.

In the dining room, Luce was sitting at the faded oak table, its surface soaking up the light of a single shadeless lamp. Moses sat down at the end of that long table and placed his forearms and elbows onto its thick sticky surface.

He sighed.

"Here's one for you," he said, studying Luce.

Her face was perfectly round. She had a tiny nose that sloped ever so slightly up at the end. Her ears poked through her long silver hair. She had thin lips that tonight were dark red. Moses was sure that Luce had more different coloured lipsticks than there were colours in the universe. Her eyes were large and round and so amber that they shone gold. They were surrounded by heavy black eye-liner that ran up and out at the edges making her look more than a little like an Egyptian Goddess. Given all the time in the world, Moses would have sat and stared at that face until every last second ticked away. Even at thirty, Luce looked like a child. A fact that manifested itself in Moses as a dirty pleasure.

Luce rocked back on an old leather chair, running her fingers across the back of her neck.

"Is it good?" she said.

Moses smiled. "I think so," he said.

Luce leaned forward, pulled a Marlboro Light from a packet then rolled it the full length of the table to Moses. With his left hand, he placed the cigarette in his lips, and with his right, in one single, faultless motion, pulled a gold lighter from his dirty brown duffel coat, flipped the lid, lit the Marlboro, inhaled, paused, inhaled then said, "It feels right." His words pushed the cigarette smoke into the incense floating above the table.

Luce's face stopped being blank as, one by one, her features moved toward interest. Her eyes widened, catching the lamp light like pennies shining under water. Her lips twitched and pulled to one corner. A smile of sorts. *Jesus*, thought Moses, *Luce is smiling. Kind of.*

Moses rubbed at the side of his head with his cigarette fingers, flicked ash onto the table and pushed it down with his thumb making tiny, circular, precise, thoughtful movements. He sniffed hard making a snorting, gumming noise that broke through the sounds of Beethoven and of Luce clicking earthen beads around her pale neck.

In his head, Moses said the words over and over until finally he spoke them out loud. "I got you a girl," he said.

Luce laughed, a laugh that got stuck and tried to go back down, interrupted by excitement. She slammed the sides of her fists into the table. The lamp rocked. The unused stone ashtray thudded.

She stood up, fluffed out her black feather boa and said, "Man. That is *so fucking cool*."

Moses stared at her. At her dress, all reds and greens and purples and blacks. Luce looked like she'd been drawn in thick pencil then coloured in pastel. She looked as if she was stepping out of the pages of a graphic novel. Moses grinned and his face hurt.

"You look like death," he said. "Only way, *way*

cuter."

"Me and you against the world," she said.

She walked over to the CD player and turned the volume down so that it was barely audible, then walked behind Moses, placed her hands around his face from behind and pulled his head back gently. All Moses could see were those eyes, and that hair floating down around him as she kissed him on the forehead leaving a cold circle on his already cold skin.

"Me and you against the world," she whispered into his ear. As she walked back around to her chair, she lifted her shoulders up to her ears and shuddered, letting out a high-pitched squeal. She pulled the boa out to one side then flung it around her neck.

Moses felt an empty hollow in the pit of his stomach. *I hope to God I'm right*, he thought. He felt warmth rise in his neck and in his hands. *Shit, I hope I'm right.*

Luce sat down and placed her hands flat on the table. "Let's do this," she said.

She closed her eyes and breathed in through her nose so that her chest lifted up. She breathed out, and even at the opposite end of the table, Moses could smell her breath: sweet, alcoholic. Tobacco, spit, and absinthe. He slumped his shoulders into the back of his chair, stretched his legs out under the table and tried to relax as much as he could.

As the first wave of cold bit into the souls of his feet he shuddered.

"Moses," Luce whispered.

No matter how many times she had done this to

him, he never got used to the cold creeping into his bones.

"He's coming," Luce said, giggling.

"Like I don't know."

"Then stop squirming and just let him in."

"Okay. Okay," Moses said. He felt the cold move up his shins and into the gaps behind his kneecaps like electrically charged needles. This was usually the point at which the pain really kicked in. And this time was no different. Moses clenched his teeth and dug his fingernails into the arm of the chair.

Luce stretched her shadow further into him.

She had kept hold of her shadow for nearly three years. She nurtured it. Played with it. She shaped it into what it was now.

It even told her its name.

Abe.

When she first chose Abe, he was weak and faint, like a shadow across damp concrete on an overcast day. He could only speak to her about other shadows when he moved over them. Luce would stand in shops, watching other shadows pass over hers. Waiting for words from Abe.

"Six months," he would say, or, "Girl." "Boy." "Tree." "Sports."

Abe was a child back then, a slow, retarded infant. But Luce had a feeling, a closeness, something she could nurture from nothing. Unlike her other shadows that came with so much emotional baggage, Abe was a blank slate, and over time he came to understand what he was about, what he was for. His meaning. Luce taught him a meaning. He could reach out further into the darkness, unhindered by emotion or fear, and Luce began to hear the words she had waited so long to hear. "Young girl. Seven or eight. Car crash. Four years ago."

Moses hissed.

Abe crept up his spine and into his shoulders and neck. Not long now and Moses would succumb to the cold and sleep and be warm again.

Abe spoke. "It's a young boy, Luce."

"A boy? Go on," Luce said, watching as Moses's head tipped sideways like an overburdened sack.

"There. Is. A car."

"Good. Yes. Come on, Abe."

"But no."

"No?"

"No. It's a young boy, six and a half years old. His father slapped him across the face. Just once. Just one slap. He keeps telling me about the scratch on Daddy's telly, and he's holding up a bright blue metal car. It's a sports car. The boy doesn't even know what sort. It's blue. He never woke up."

"Shit," Luce said, running her hands through her hair.

"I'm sorry, Luce," Abe said.

"It's okay, Abe. Come back to me."

Luce looked at Moses. He was breathing through his open mouth and a thin line of spit hung down, stretching and swaying.

"Fucking *idiot*," she yelled at the sleeping man.

"Luce?" Abe said. "It's not his fault. He tried."

"He always tries," she said. She stood and turned up the stereo that was now playing Chopin Nocturne no 20.

"But he was so close this time, Luce."

"I know, Abe. I do know he was close." She crouched down next to Moses and placed her hand on his. "Look at him, Abe. He's a mess."

"He's weak, Luce. You're pushing him so hard."

"I don't care, Abe," she said, removing her hand and looking at it like she might have caught some disease. "I'm losing patience."

"Would you rather do it the old way? Wait for his shadow to become fully attached and find out that way?" Abe was being sincere.

"No. I really don't have the patience for that. I feel like I'm running out of time."

"Then he'll become weaker and weaker. He never holds onto a shadow for more than a few days, Luce. Sometimes he goes for weeks without one becoming fully attached. You're killing him, Luce. And it's all for you."

"No, Abe. He's doing it for himself. To be with me. It's a simple exchange of services. That's all."

"Don't I know it," Abe said. "You get all the shadows you need and Moses gets to fuck your brains out."

Luce laughed. "Sometimes I think he gets the better end of the bargain. On days like this, I think I should break *my* end of the bargain and pay him with magazines and a box of tissues."

Abe laughed. Luce felt him shaking around her feet.

"I've spoiled him, Abe," she said, wiping away the spit from Moses's mouth then licking it from her fingers. She took off her boa and placed it around his neck. "When he wakes up, I'll repay my end of the bargain like a good little girl."

"Luce?"

"Abe?"

"Will you please, for me, please, for once, turn out the lights when you do?"

Chapter Five

"Get your car keys, Jake," Emma said, grinning like they were about to go shopping. Like they were back when they'd go out and spend money they didn't have and worry about it later.

"My keys?" Jake said. "For the car?"

"Yes for the car. Come on. Hurry."

"But the car. My car?"

"Just get the keys huh, sweetie?"

"But my car is knackered, Emma. It's a death trap. I don't even know if it will start, let alone..."

"It'll be fine. I'm not worried about it."

Jesus, Jake thought, *she really isn't worried.*

Jake's ten-year-old brown Mondeo started first time after almost four months of not being used, and he looked out across the bonnet as if he might see an angel sitting there.

"Ha. See?" Emma said. "It's fine."

Jake looked into the side of her smiling face and noticed how her hair was becoming greasier by the hour, and how her skin was dull. But her eyes, whether it was just the morning sun or something else, her eyes were brighter than he remembered.

"Let's go," she shouted, pointing forward.

The car grumbled out of the drive. *God it feels rough*, Jake thought. *I've not driven this pile of crap for so long, maybe I just forgot how it felt. Maybe it always felt like this*. He shook his head. *This thing had been getting slowly worse and I never realised how bad it had become until I took a break.*

He laughed.

"What's so funny, Jake?" Emma said, playing with the air vent on her side.

"Nothing," Jake said. "It's all good. Just having a thought, that's all. Where we going?"

In a flat tone, Emma said, "The old ironworks."

"What? The old ironworks? Why? That place is all shut down and derelict."

"Just drive."

"Not to mention dangerous."

"I'll tell you why on the way."

"And guarded. Big dogs probably."

"You still scared of little doggies, Jake?"

"No. Big dogs. Guard dogs. You know. Great big fucking Doberweilers or whatever."

"Just drive."

Jake shook his head. He could feel himself trying to back out of helping Emma, but at the same time, he wanted to know what was going on, how far this would go. He decided to just drive.

"You got a tyre lever?"

"Yeah. Here," Jake said, pulling the bent metal rod from the driver's door pocket and turning it in front of him.

"Good," Emma said. "You might need it."

"Yeah. Figures," Jake said. He felt light headed, drunk, and as he put the tyre lever back, he couldn't think any further ahead than the road directly in front of him. His mind had gone grey.

There were a few minutes of nothing more than engine and road noise as Jake drove in what he hoped was the best way to the ironworks.

"Jake," Emma said. "This is what we're going to do."

Engine and road noise.

Emma talked.

Jake's heartbeat grew louder in his ears and his hands stuck to the steering wheel with sweat.

Emma stopped talking.

"Are you out of your fucking mind?" he shouted.

The car sat motionless at a crossroads. The traffic lights were on red. Again. A horn blared behind him, but it sounded muted and distant.

"It'll be fine," Emma said. "I have no choice."

"Well neither..."

The horn blared. Jake turned around, shouted fuck off, then spoke to Emma again. "...do I."

Red and amber.

Horn.

Green.

A screech of tyres.

Amber.

Silence.

Red.

A car screeched up beside them and stopped, blocking traffic. Jake gazed across at the driver. He was just another generic face. Clean shaven, neatly cropped black hair that shone. Below a pair of raised sunglasses stared very wide, very red eyes. The window of the black Honda Civic rolled down and the driver's face exploded into a foul mouthed, muted tirade. His finger waved manically at Jake so that his gold cufflinks wagged side to side on his neatly pressed lilac shirt.

Jake wound down his window and cupped a hand behind his ear. The man in the Honda, his face red, shouted across, "Have you got a fucking problem, pal?" He raised his palms to the sky, waiting.

Jake spoke quietly back, "Yes. Several. You want to give me another?" His face was blank. It was not a question that he wanted an answer for.

"You are a fucking spaz," the man shouted. He reached down to unbuckle his seatbelt.

Jake lifted the tyre iron then hung it out of his window, tapping it against his door.

"Yes," he said, his face still devoid of emotion. "I am a *spaz* and I do have a list of problems as long as your unbroken arm. But," he lifted the tyre iron back into view then slammed it hard against the brown paintwork, lifted it, looked at it, looked at the shiny black passenger door of the Honda, looked at the man, smiled. "If you want to jump right on ahead to the top of the list, feel free. Go ahead. Right up to the top of my list of problems."

Jake saw dilemma flicker across the man's face. He saw his tongue working away behind his lips. He wondered if the man would actually get out of his car. He didn't give a shit if he did.

Red and Amber.

Green.

With his free hand, Jake gestured politely to the road ahead and the Honda burst through a gap in the stalled traffic and was gone. In his rear-view mirror

Jake looked into the eyes of an old lady who stared right back at him and smiled a perfect white smile. Jake put the tyre lever back, raised his hand out the window, mouthed sorry into the mirror then drove on.

After the crossroads everything was calm. The roads were quiet, hedge lined and sedate. The ironworks nestled in a valley that followed the river and a canal, and the whole of the surrounding area was picturesque English countryside in Autumn. The fields stretched away in a patchwork of recently cut corn stubble. Rolling across the higher areas were huge green mounds, like sea monsters gliding over crests of waves.

As the road levelled, Jake saw another sea creature lying in the folds of the valley, a huge hulking collection of grey spines and brown warts and black eyes and silver teeth. The ironworks had given up and lay dead on its back, power lines and rail tracks exposed like vulnerable arteries.

"Hey, Jake," Emma said. "There's our tree."

"Yeah, I noticed," Jake said. "Wow. It's still there."

"Remember?"

"Yes. Of course I do."

"Of all the places to make out. We used to come up here at night and just sit behind the hedges under the lightning tree and smoke and drink and fuck. I can't believe the tree lasted longer than we did."

Jake pushed his finger and thumb into the bridge of his nose. "I used to think that at the time," he said.

Emma stared out the window, her breath on the glass, as they drove slowly past the smooth white tree.

Jake laughed. "I used to wonder if we'd outlive that dead tree. I mean look at it. It was already dead back then. Had nothing to hang on for. No bark, no leaves, its branches all split and reaching out like broken fingers."

"And it's still there Jake. It clung on."

"Yeah. It clung on."

As they drove into the valley, Jake watched the dull grey fingers of the tree disappear in his rear view mirror. *God*, he thought, *we used to have so much fun sitting under a dead tree that outlasted us. If I was going to make a time machine*, he thought, *I'd make it out of a dead tree*.

The ironworks slid behind a hill then reappeared as a huge grey mouth that swallowed them into it; Jake, Emma, the car, everything. It seemed to grow around them like a rigid fog, crushing them into a tiny ball of brown painted aluminium and flesh.

"I'd forgotten how big this place was," Jake said.

"Yes," Emma said.

From where they were parked, the factory looked like the bottom of a forgotten toolbox, a collection of random metal bits stuck together by orange rust and wire. A narrow railway line cut left to right, forking and fading away behind a pale yellow, corrugated warehouse. Just over the tracks sat a row of randomly shaped wagons. Some were boxes with ridges running up their sides. Others, square funnels sitting precariously on massive wheels. To the far right of the line of wagons, one was filled with dark black, fat metal discs that looked like crashed UFOs. Behind those, the shell of another warehouse, its roof a lattice work of triangular metal, with not quite vertical struts, holding it up. A line of telegraph poles, devoid of wires. Steel drums, piled, stacked, scattered on the black earth.

The whole place was more than desolate. It was a man-made black hole.

Drizzle hung in the air like cold steam, and the smell from the valley was of metal and earth and oil.

"I don't know about this," Jake said as he leaned on the roof of the car, his eyes narrow.

"Bullshit," Emma said. "We're here now. It's all good."

Jake stared at two huge towers. They had solid, grey-green concrete plinths and on top of each one was a cylinder, each the size of a house. Steps and railings and pipes tangled their way around the plinths like optic nerves feeding into two large eyes.

"I just feel odd. Like we're being watched," he said.

"No one can see us from down there. And I don't see anyone anyway. Not yet."

Jake ruffled his hair and blinked.

"No," he said. "I don't mean people. The place. It feels like it was slashed and burned and there are these little green shoots waiting to creep through the black soil. Like it wants to wake up."

Emma sounded angry. "Jake. Stop fucking about and let's go. This place has been derelict for years.

Which is precisely why we're here." She walked off down the hill towards the rail tracks.

Jake lifted his hands and made a rectangle with his forefingers and thumbs. He framed the two monolithic sentinels and, *click*, took the picture.

The little girl giggled. Jake waited for her to say something. She didn't.

He picked up his tyre lever and caught up with Emma who was pushing back the chain-link fence like she was peeling a scab. On some of the fences were dull yellow signs warning of CCTV, or 24hr Surveillance, or Dogs, or Private Property, or Sunny Day Rainbow Night Time Securities.

"They're just signs, Jake," Emma said from the other side of the fence. She turned her back and walked towards the warehouse. She followed the tracks, stepping on the sleepers.

Jake felt the weight of the tyre lever in his hand then lifted it to his face. *Of all the places to bring a tiny bent bit of metal bar*, he thought and stepped through the gap.

The ground was like damp, black sand, and he stepped on the sleepers, afraid he might leave footprints.

As they reached the huge rusted doors of the warehouse, Emma's pace didn't slow. She reached up, put her hair into a messy ponytail, stepped into the foreboding doorway and was gone.

"Emma," Jake hissed, looking around him then up and down the corrugated face of the warehouse that had just swallowed Emma. He followed.

Inside, the smell of oil and earth was stronger.

The feeling of damp on Jake's neck was colder and there was stillness in the air. The ceiling was at least three houses high and was a lattice of metal similar to the skeletal remains of the one he had seen before, only this one actually had a roof. The breezeblock and corrugated metal walls were held up with massive vertical girders, each one straddled with crossed beams so that they resembled railway bridges that had been upturned and rooted into the ground. Off to the right were three large structures cradling cylindrical tanks that appeared to be more rivet than plate, each with a huge valve wheel attached. Jake could make out embossed lettering on the nearest one, but couldn't read it.

There was a constant wind-chime sound of metallic plinks and pops as moisture dripped from high up and crashed onto iron and steel and spars and barrels. He could see the drops falling everywhere, flashing, disappearing, flashing, disappearing, plinking, popping, thudding. A drop hit him above his left eye, cold and fresh, and he wiped it away with the back of hand then gently kissed the wet skin between his thumb and forefinger.

Peach-gold sunlight filtered through huge horizontal slats in the walls giving the whole area a subdued carnival look, a painting of a fairground left out in the rain. The various girders were all the colour of glazed pastry. The cylinders and walls were the grey-blue colour of battleships in a green ocean. And the green ocean was...

"Wow," Jake said.

Where the sunlight cut through the air, it lit up ribbons of green moss and grass and stalks that clung to the structures and barrels. Clumps of tiny purple flowers oozed from the sides of rivets. Thin rows of brilliant blue forget-me-nots lit up where the sun caught them. The entire area was covered with tiny fragile plants and flowers like a long-forgotten garden.

Jake walked over to the cylinder nearest. He ran his hand across the firm moss and watched as the stalks, each with a pale luminous yellow bobble on the top, folded then sprang back up. He breathed in a deep lungful of air that smelled of woodland. Two bright yellow butterflies, their wing-tips blue, fluttered around each other, skimming the moss.

"This is amazing," he said. "It's like a greenhouse." He looked up and squinted into the light then looked back down and watched the shadow that was the little girl across the purple petals and vivid green leaves of a clump of flowers. "You know, Emma," he said. "If I ever had my own secret garden, I think this would..."

"Shhh," Emma hissed.

Through the tiny plinks and plops of water, and the occasional groan of the building's structure cooling, there was a rustling, scratching noise. Jake pointed the tyre lever up to the far corner of the warehouse, high up where a walkway led around the entire perimeter. He shrugged. "Up there?" he said.

"Yeah," Emma whispered.

"Rats?"

"Let's go."

Emma walked up a set of rusting metal steps that led to the second of three levels, then she made her way across the second level walkway, looking up at the corner where the noise was, then back down to Jake. She motioned for him to stay put and he motioned back with his hands and mouth, *what the fuck?*

Emma was halfway across the second walkway, but even from where he stood, he could see and feel her glaring at him. He screwed his face into a ball. Emma started up the second set of metal steps, her hand resting on the metal rail.

By the time she had reached the third level, she was out of sight, obscured by the walkway, and Jake had a moment to survey his secret garden again. He imagined himself as a tiny person running through the thick mosses, pushing huge lilac petals aside with his hands. He was stepping side-to-side, dodging fat heavy raindrops. The luminous globes on the stalks reflected his face.

From above there was a muffled thump, the clang of metal on metal and a loud groan and Jake felt his legs get hot as he pushed his feet hard and fast one in front of the other onto the concrete then onto the steps then onto the mesh floored walkways and his eyesight was narrow and black and the edges were a blur of railings and steps and he stopped running and his eyesight spread out like an old camera shutter opening.

He was on the top level breathing hard. In the distance ahead, he heard Emma scream, an almost masculine exhalation of breath, of power. A dark figure that was hunched over her lifted into the air then crashed down hard onto the walkway. Jake felt the thud of impact through his feet. The figure stood up fast and must have turned around as it did so because Jake could see its eyes burning white like oncoming headlights. Jake felt more tremors through his legs as the thing lurched towards him, the tremors coming faster, the figure becoming larger the eyes brighter, larger, closer, wider. This huge, hulking thing was carrying something under one arm. Something large, white, and by the way it was being cradled, important. Just as the face became a pink smudge, Jake swung upwards hard with the tyre lever and felt the force of impact run up his arm and into his elbow. The thing grunted and gasped but its momentum carried it into Jake and he fell back onto his shoulder blades, bright lights in his eyes and hissing in his ears.

"Jake," Emma called out, woolly, distant.

Jake got to his feet and stared past the figure of a man leaning heavily on the railing. He could see Emma walking towards them, her shoulders down, her footfalls slow. She was holding one hand inside the other. The figure leaning over the railing pushed himself up and his head snapped first towards Emma then towards Jake, his eyes were full beam. This figure, swaying, was just a man. His hair lank and greasy, his forehead a red smudge of blood, his mouth a pit of black inside a brown and red beard.

With his eyes still fixed on Jake the man reached down and scooped up the thing he had been carrying.

He spoke, panting and croaking, "Tatty," he said.

"Come here, Tatty." He clutched the limp thing to his chest and Jake could see it more clearly.

It was a large stuffed toy. A white and brown dog with huge flapping ears, a snub pink nose, shining black eyes and dangling legs. The man's face was pure anguish. He licked his dirty fingers then ran them across the dog's head. The dog was cleaner than him.

"Fucking kill him," Emma shouted. She was close and within reach of Jake and the man.

"Don't," said the little girl. "I feel sick."

The man continued to mumble about Tatty being okay, about cleaning Tatty right up. He was swaying more with each breath.

"Now," Emma shouted.

Jake shouted back, "Emma, just shut the fuck up a minute."

The man rubbed hard at a few spots of blood on the dog's head, then rubbed his own head and looked at his fingers. His eyes grew larger and brighter and bluer and fiercer than the sun through the windows of the warehouse. His mouth had become a thin red slit, curled up in pain and disbelief.

"She won't be happy," he said, lisping and spitting.

Emma spoke quietly. "Now, Jake."

"No. Emma, just wait."

The man spoke again to his dog. "Tatty was supposed to save me. To look after me. He's okay. We'll be fine."

"Jake," Emma said. "He hurt me, Jake." She uncovered her hand and lifted it in front of her face.

"He broke my fingers, Jake. He bent my fingers. Bad." Emma's two middle fingers jutted out at right angles in opposite directions like snapped pink twigs.

Jake's belly filled with pain, and fire, and rage, and acid. There was electricity in his spine and needles in the back of his skull. He brought the tyre iron down hard onto the socket of one of those bright blue eyes and it was extinguished. Blue and white became black and red and crunching noise. Jake stamped his foot into the side of the man's knee and heard, and felt, a thick pop, then he lifted up both hands, clasped them together and brought them down on the back of the man's head. There was another crack as the man's teeth smashed into the metal railing.

The man screamed, high-pitched but gurgling. As he lifted his hands to his face to poke and prod at the sharp pieces of broken red and white teeth, Tatty rolled over the edge and was gone. The man had only a few tiny meaningless seconds to look like all the hate in the world before Jake grabbed him by the shoulder and the top of his trousers and rolled him neatly over the railing. A pair of blue running shoes flashed past Jake's face then the man was gone.

Emma smiled and the shafts of sunlight suddenly looked brighter around her.

Jake leaned on the railing and looked down. The man was dead. Laid out like a question mark. His blue trainers a full stop, his hair spread out on the moss like a drop of red ink in green water. As Jake stared, his shoulders heaving up and down, his lungs filling and emptying, he saw two small yellow butterflies lift into the air near the man's face and spiral upwards into the light.

Emma nudged into his side and reached her arm around his waist. She leaned her head into his neck and whispered, "Thank you."

As Jake's blood cooled, as the hissing in his ears subsided, he could hear a voice becoming clearer, repeating in the back of his skull.

"That was stupid," said the little girl. "Stupid." Over and over.

Now that he could hear her words more clearly, he felt an emptiness deep in his stomach and bowels, as if he'd just escaped falling over the railing himself.

"I feel sick," the little girl said. "So stupid, Jake."

Jake pulled away from Emma.

"Hey, sweetie. It's okay," Emma said.

"Don't *sweetie* me, Emma," Jake said. "Just don't..."

The little girl interrupted. She sounded anguished, her voice quiet, her tone high.

"Someone's watching," she said.

"What?" Jake said.

"Huh?" Emma said.

"Someone beneath. I can feel someone beneath," the girl said.

"Beneath?" Jake said, staring hard at the body below for signs of movement.

"Lower," the girl said. "It's hard to say. Beneath us both somehow. Beneath me and you and *her*." She spoke the last word with childish spite.

"What's wrong?" Emma said.

"I don't know," Jake said. "Just be quiet a minute."

"But, *Jake.*"

"Shut *up.*"

Emma hissed.

Jake pressed his thumb and forefinger into the bridge of his nose. He closed his eyes. "Who's there?" he whispered to himself. "Who's down..." He opened his eyes and saw a figure in the door of the warehouse, a silhouette that shifted side to side like smoke in a calm breeze. "There you are," he said.

"Jake. Who?" Emma said. She followed Jake's gaze to the doorway. "Oh God, Jake. Is that the shadow?"

"No," Jake said, trying to see the shape in the bright square of light. "She said it was something else."

"*She.* Well that's okay then. As long as *she* says so."

Jake ignored Emma's attempts at a confrontation. His eyes flicked between the dead body and the figure in the doorway. Whoever it was could see as clearly as Jake what was lying dead and bleeding on the moss.

"Hey," Jake shouted.

The silhouette shimmered, and tiny dust motes lifted around its feet like a cloud of fine diamonds.

"You," Jake shouted, surprised at how non-threatening he sounded. His heart and stomach felt like they'd swapped places as the figure stepped out of view. All that was left was that bright square of light and the flickering dust settling onto the black earth.

Emma sounded frantic. "Jake. We need to get him. Stop him."

"Get him?" Jake said, showing no intention of going anywhere.

"Yes, Jake. Get him. Stop him. He must have seen everything. He'll know."

Know what? Jake thought, *That I just killed a man, or that me and Emma were out hunting for a spare shadow?* Probably both, he decided.

"Did he look like he gave a shit, Emma. Did he run away screaming into the sky, calling for help?"

"No," Emma said. "But..."

"But nothing, Emma." He turned towards her and stared right into her eyes that looked different somehow. "Are we done here?" he said.

The only sound was the musical plinks and plops of the water. Emma looked down at her feet then at the body below. She looked up into the roof and breathed in deeply as if sniffing for something.

"Yes," she said. "I'm done here." She looked over to the empty square of sunlight. "I guess we won't see whoever that was again anyway."

"She's wrong, Jake," the little girl said.

Wouldn't be the first time, Jake thought.

Chapter Six

William Edward Teach was dead and still couldn't quite grasp the concept. The first thing that struck him was that all he could think about was what his headstone would look like. God, he hoped they didn't put his middle name on it. An 'E' maybe. But please, not the whole thing. Surely a lifetime of ridicule wouldn't continue after his death. Even his beard was ginger. Okay? G. i. n. g. e. r. The only time that being ginger came to his defence was in defending his name. He was not a damned pirate, just an unfortunate child whose parents didn't consider that a name is for life, not just the result of a Christmas party!

He was expecting someone to fetch him. An angel perhaps or a pixie. His grandparents maybe. But no. He was utterly alone.

Just as he was wondering, if he did get the chance to see his own headstone what his response would be, Billy Teach watched two tiny yellow butterflies lift away into the air and he ceased to exist entirely as his shadow detached.

Chapter Seven

Luce had repaid her end of the bargain like a good little girl, and as she sat at the table reading a week old copy of *The Evening Telegraph*, Moses came into the room humming *Oranges and Lemons*.

Luce shook her head. Yesterday had taken its toll on Moses, and in the evening Luce had taken even more toll. He looked twice as old, his cheeks sagged, pulling down the bags beneath his eyes. His hair was flat on one side and sticking out on the other like it was caught in a permanent breeze. But his eyes sparkled, and today, there wasn't a fleck of bloodshot in them.

He was wearing one of Luce's pink nightdresses that hugged his arms and threatened to break its buttons around his chest and belly.

"Could you honestly not find anything else?" she said, lifting a cup of tea to her lips, staring up over the rim.

"Nothing clean, no," Moses said. "All my clothes smell of death. I'm running out."

Luce stood up, still sipping her tea. She was wearing a tight green T-shirt with a white 4Kit logo across the chest. A pair of grey jogging bottoms with a thin pink stripe down each side. White and green running shoes.

"Been running?" Moses said.

Luce stared at him, then at the clock on the mantelpiece next to the photo frames, then back.

"It's one thirty," she said. "In the afternoon." Her mouth stayed open, her eyebrows raised. She blinked. "I'm going to get another cup of tea," she said. "You look through that newspaper again." She walked into the kitchen and shouted over her shoulder, "And get *dressed*."

Moses sat down where Luce had been and stared at the black and white photos on the front of the newspaper.

He stared at each tiny, pixelated face in the crowd for a second each. Some were smiling, some laughing, their arms raised, dancing. Some faces were obscured by drinks. Other faces were obscured by other faces as they kissed.

He stared at the picture below that one. The same scene. The morning after. He stared at each, tiny pixelated face in the small groups of people standing outside the police tape. Some were crying. Some stared out over the cobbles at forensic tents, discarded cups and bottles, overturned chairs and tables, glittering glass, bent and broken lamp posts, discarded shoes. Most of the faces were obscured by hands over their mouths, or nestled into the chests of loved ones.

He sighed then opened the newspaper to the next page where he ran his finger down the list of names. He leaned in closer struggling to see the features of the dead and missing.

In colour:

A young girl with bright copper hair in a straight

bob, green eyes, scar above her left eyebrow.

A teenage boy, wearing a grey top and a Jagermeister cap, his blurred face looking into the camera and laughing as a friend leers over his shoulder with crossed eyes and tongue out.

In black and white:

An old man, maybe late fifties, sitting at one end of a long table full of people in suits, leaning back, looking off to one side behind a pair of black sunglasses. Neat black hair. Thick bushy eyebrows. His mouth drawn down at the sides in a gesture that said: *another god-dam wedding party.*

A young boy, maybe ten, sitting on a motorbike and leaning forward holding a trophy.

Moses smiled. "Who picks these pictures?" he said, as Luce walked back in.

"Parents? Loved ones? Friends?" she said. "Depends how far they got themselves in life." She sat at the side of the table and looked at the paper sideways.

"I mean," Moses continued, "who sits down and thinks, 'Well, this one looks great.' or 'Let's put this one in of him at someone's wedding'? They're stupid these folk."

"Hmm," said Luce, pulling the paper towards herself for a better look.

"They're putting in pictures of people all happy but they're dead. This guy at a wedding. This is the best one. He's clearly not enjoying himself. He was probably glad when he realised he was going to die. If you can't be happy at a wedding with free food and stuff, then," he paused. "Unless it was his *own* wedding of course. Then, I mean, well..."

"Moses. Please shut up," Luce said. "I'm not interested in them, at the moment. I'm interested in the ones that *aren't* dead." She closed the paper and tapped her finger up and down on the photo on the front page.

Moses hissed through one side of his mouth, scratched at the back of his ear, then examined his fingers, clicking his nails back and forth across each other.

"Moses!" Luce shouted.

The room seemed to shake, and the light dimmed. Then he felt the cold in the soles of his feet.

"Okay," he said, raising his palms in genuine surrender. He leaned forward, serious and resolute, and placed his finger just above a small photo of a young girl. "This one," he said. "Laura Pitcher."

Luce sipped her tea.

"The one you killed yesterday," she said.

"Yes."

"The one with the little boy."

Moses looked up. "Er. Yes."

Luce smiled. "Tell me," she said, placing her cup on the table then pulling the band from her ponytail so that her hair fell in scruffy waves.

Moses tapped his finger over the picture.

"This one," he said squinting. "Laura Pitcher, fifteen, all sweetness and light, smiling, happy, eyes uncomplicated by life and stuff.

"She was one of those girls, looked about twenty, eighteen at least. It was easy enough to find her, her new shadow was weeping and calling out.

"It was getting on for eleven thirty and I'd had a few beers by then so I didn't feel the cold. I sat at one of the tables outside..." he paused, pushed his finger into the newspaper photo again, then continued, "that same bar. Just there. It used to amaze me that people would come back to somewhere so quickly I mean, a week before, she'd been there, in that crowd. She must have seen and heard such terrible things. Death and stuff. It must be like revisiting the scene of a fatal car crash where you inexplicably escaped but your family died in a huge fireball of twisted metal and..."

"Moses," Luce said.

"Shit. Sorry. Yes. Sorry, Luce. Crap. She had gone into the bar with two friends. I'm guessing they were the same age as her, but the way they were all dressed. *She* was wearing a really thin white, flower-print dress that was quite short, I say quite, I mean not as daring as her friends, but short anyway.

"All I kept thinking, after a few pints of course, was how there was no way she was only fifteen. How maybe the paper had it wrong when they interviewed her. The way her breasts pushed out the lilac flowers on the dress and the way her ass and hips filled it out at the back. The light from the bar doorway shone through the gap between her thighs."

Moses stopped and looked up at Luce. Her blank expression said enough. He gathered his thoughts and continued.

"Okay. Okay," he said, leaning his head back and scratching the underside of his chin, "I knew, I thought I knew right away that her shadow was a young girl. It was crying. Like I said. I was so sure, Luce. So very sure.

"She came out the bar later with her friends and stumbled right past my table, leaning on it a bit. She smelled of fruit and alcohol, and she smiled right at me as I picked up my pint so that she wouldn't knock it over. I smiled back, obviously, then looked away and carried on drinking. If her friends weren't there I might have asked her to sit down a while with me. But they were, so I didn't.

"Anyway, yes, long story short. The three girls walked over to the river and onto the bridge. They called a taxi and her two friends got in, waved, squealed somewhat, blew kisses, shouted 'morning' and 'hammered' and 'same' and were gone.

"It was ideal, Luce. My old magic was still right with me and Laura was just standing there leaning against the stone wall smoking and waiting for another taxi to come past. No one else was around, Luce. I mean no one. Only one car drove past as I walked over, then it was gone in an echo of exhaust and over revving engine."

Luce made a noise. She hummed then sighed. Her eyes were closed, her head tilted back. She made tiny circles with her middle finger on her chest.

Moses continued. "Like I said, it was cold, Luce. I mean, really cold and for a second I thought about just brushing her over the short wall and into the river. But I figured she might not die right away, or that she would just float off, and I was not in a mood for chasing her dead body.

"As I walked up to her, she smiled at me again,

she actually smiled in such a friendly way I thought I might doff my hat to her. I punched her straight in the mouth, felt her lips split and felt the familiar grind and crack of her teeth breaking on each other. I reached behind her head, grabbed her hair and pulled her, quite easily I might add, down under the bridge. Her eyes were struggling the most. The rest of her tried, arms flailing, legs kicking about. But she was *so* weak, Luce. I smacked her down hard on her back into the concrete embankment and her body echoed."

Moses had his hand out in front of him and was twisting it slowly through degrees, a puzzled look on his face.

"Carry on," Luce said. "Tell me the end."

"It's weird, Luce. I tried to break her neck. I pushed the heel of one hand into her face and slid my other hand under her head and twisted. I usually find it easy. Hmm. Anyway, her neck didn't break. Her jaw did. It popped right out to the side. I had a devil of a time keeping her quiet then. I really had to concentrate to cover her mouth with just one hand."

"So she wasn't dead yet?"

"God no. She was just a whimpering mess of dislocated jaw and mad rolling eyes. I figured she wasn't going to bite, so I stuck my fingers in her mouth and pulled down hard. I think I was expecting another crack or something. Stupid really. There was just a ripping, tearing noise and her jaw almost came completely off in my hand. It just swung there. Luckily, for me I mean, she'd passed out by now. I guess having your lower jaw pulled off does that.

"I grabbed hold of her ankles and pulled her

across the concrete and then, oh, Luce this was great, she was so light, Luce. I swung her sideways and up by her ankles like she was a rag doll. Her head followed the arc of the underside of the bridge perfectly as I flung her through the air. Then her face slammed into the banked concrete. God, the noise it made, Luce. It actually made me jump, it was so loud. Like splitting a coconut with a lump hammer. Except... Echoier.

"Pretty decent amount of blood as well. Most of it ran down the concrete and was soaked up in her pretty dress. I knew she was dead when I turned her over. Should've seen her face, Luce. When I pulled her across into the river, it painted a pretty red line across the ground."

Luce leant back on two legs of the chair, her hands stretched out, grasping the edge of the table. She was smiling.

"Sounds like you had all the fun," she said.

"Oh yes," Moses said. "I was a bit pissed I couldn't break her neck. Bit worried about that one." He lifted his hands up and started to re-enact his movements again. He shrugged. "Ah well. Worked out for the best as it happens."

Luce pulled her shirt off, stood up and slid her jogging bottoms down. "Come here," she said, smiling.

Moses was there in an instant standing right in front of her wearing her robes.

"Now pretend you didn't have to kill her," she said. "What would you have done to her?"

She lifted his hand, slid his fingers into her mouth

and sighed.

Chapter Eight

The day after the warehouse, Jake stood staring out the window at the damp clumps of brown and yellow leaves that had gathered on the pavement.

He watched the woman across the street leave her house at 8:30 as she always did. She was wearing a smart blue business suit with a tan blouse that billowed out at the top as it always did. She opened the door of her charcoal grey VW Golf and stepped in, showing a creamy flash of her inner thigh as she always did. He stared at the side of her face and at her red hair that picked out the light of the morning sun. She adjusted her sunglasses, pulled down the sun visor and pulled out of her drive.

He watched Mr. Simmons come out of his front door wearing his black dressing gown, his fat knees and narrow shins hanging beneath it like stolen flamingo legs that wore stolen black socks and stolen, dusky blue slippers. Jake could see the direction of the sun reflecting on his bald head as he bent down to pick up his single bottle of milk. He stood up and examined the bottle, running his finger around the foil top. He looked up and down the street, turned, and went back inside. Jake was sure that Mr. Simmons was the only person left in the world that still had milk delivered in glass bottles. Maybe that's why he checked each one so thoughtfully.

Two children ran past Jake's driveway, skipping and tumbling as they fought with each other and their heavy bags that banged into their knees. He heard the familiar, worn-out squeals of the mother.

"Sam," she shouted. "Chrissy. Stop. Will you please just stop?"

Messing. Fighting. Arguing. Arsing around. The same sentence every day. Just a different, desperate ending.

She must shout that all the way to school, Jake thought. She came into view, leaning on the back of a three-wheeled buggy, its front wheel spinning just above the surface of the pavement. Out of the front of the buggy, a pair of pink leggings and pink shoes shot up and down. The mother was young, smartly dressed and her hair and face always looked like she'd taken some time to pamper herself before her school run. But her eyes were deep and dark and tired in their sockets.

A people carrier, dull and green like faded plastic garden furniture, pipped its horn as it passed and the woman raised her hand and waved enthusiastically. Jake could only guess that she was smiling as she was past his house by now.

The cars, the hair, the leaves, the milk bottle, the kids, the sun, the street. It all seemed so normal. So everyday.

Emma sat on the edge of the bath resting her cheeks on the palms of her hands and opening and closing her mouth to stretch it. She pulled faces like a fish gasping for air then stood up and looked at herself in the mirror. She imagined that she looked better than she felt and continued to pull faces, this time wiggling her jaw left to right so that she resembled a camel eating a tennis ball.

"Hey, you. Down here, at your feet."

Emma stopped moving her jaw and stared straight into her own eyes. "Oh, thank God for that," she said.

"What?"

"Nothing," she said, then ran into the living room. "Jake! It worked. It worked."

"Hey. Who's Jake?"

Jake looked around.

"Okay you can be quiet for a bit."

"Hey. What? No. I..."

"Isn't it wonderful. I'm gonna be okay. I'm gonna be fine."

"That's great. That's wonderful."

"Hey, woah. What's going on? I need to know."

"Oh for God's sake will you please be quiet please?"

Emma was barely able to keep up. The new shadow kept on talking, but it was hard to distinguish between its and Jake's voice. Her head couldn't split the two. She decided that the only thing she could do was watch Jake carefully. Watch his lips move. Watch the expression on his face. Her new shadow just wouldn't shut up. It was like the deep drone of ears full of water, gurgling and bubbling.

"Do you think I should talk to it?" she asked Jake.

A flicker of surprise crossed his face. "I think maybe you should. You'll just go mad otherwise."

Jake and Emma sat near the window staring out at the sun behind thin clouds.

"Wow, this one talks a lot," the little girl said.

"You can hear him?"

"Yes. When our shadows cross. Like now, on the floor here. When we touch we're like one."

"Wow. That's great."

"Is it? Is it really? He won't shut up. He keeps asking questions."

Jake laughed. Laughed hard.

"What is it, Jake?" Emma said.

"My shadow reckons your shadow never shuts up. I think that's hilarious."

"They're talking?"

"I don't think so. I think yours is just babbling."

"Well if he is, I can't hear him now. Which is good."

Jake stepped away from the window, and Emma's shadow began talking the moment Jake and the girl were gone.

"That little girl is ignorant," the shadow said.

"I don't know. I don't think she is. I'm not sure."

"Oh, so now you're talking to me, huh?"

"Look. Of course I'll talk to you. But right now I feel a bit shitty. Tired."

"Ha! You and me both, sister!"

"Sister? Did you just call me *sister?* You sound like a right dork!"

"What? Dork. Jesus, get over yourself. How the hell do you want me to talk? You're not the only one feeling a bit *shitty* you know. I'm having a pretty fucking rough time myself."

"I'm sorry."

"Good."

Silence.

Emma's head was quiet.

When her shadow next spoke it was in a clear voice, the soft voice of a young man. "I'm sorry too," it said, and Emma felt the genuine regret in its tone. "I tell you what. I'll try to be quiet for a bit eh? Just one thing..."

"Yes?"

"Who's the girl?"

Silence.

Emma was quiet.

"You killed him," the girl said.

"I know," Jake said, staring at his cereal, balancing his spoon so that it floated, then sipping strong black coffee.

"You killed that man, and then you shared your bed with *her*."

"I know. I was there."

"Why?"

"You wouldn't understand. You're just a little girl."

"Oh, I've seen things that make me more than just a little girl. I might not understand why you did the things you did, Jake. But I'm not stupid."

"Look. It's just something we do. Sometimes. It's like something that just happens between two people. When things are bad, or good. Sometimes."

"But you don't love her, do you, Jake?"
"No. It just happened."
"I don't think I'll ever understand."
"Maybe you will, one day. Later."
"Maybe."
"It's over now. Finished, I think. I think things will be back to normal now."
"Doesn't it bother you that you killed that man?"
"No."
"Why not?"
"It's just something that I think had to happen. Eventually. I always knew it would happen."
"And now you feel complete? Is that it?"
"No. It's more than that. I think. I think maybe it's just that I have no anxiety left now."
"None?"
"Right now? No. I don't think so."
"And her? Emma?"
"Like I said. It's just something we do. Did. It's over now like before. Things will go back to normal again."
"Oh. I see."
"I mean, normal for me and you."
"Do you think me and you are normal?"
"Yes. Yes I do."
"So there's a chance that we could go back to being normal, like before you and me?"
"What? No. I don't think so. I don't think that could happen."
"Good. That's good then. Jake?"
"Yes?"
"Eat your cereal before it goes soggy."

Chapter Nine

Normality crept up on Jake.

He'd been back at work answering other people's questions about computer problems that he hated. Winter was threatening to close Britain down but so far, at the beginning of the week, there had been only twelve snowflakes that Jake could count.

Emma had become distant, but as Jake saw her everyday at work he figured she wasn't so preoccupied by her new shadow that she'd taken up watching daytime TV in the same way he had. She was pleasant enough, but cold and hard, as if she and Jake had had a one-night stand and that was the end of it. Transaction complete. Their dirty little secret.

Jake's shadow had settled into her old routine of asking awkward questions and answering nothing really, truly important. She never mentioned Emma, or the incident at the warehouse, and for Jake the whole thing seemed to have slipped to the back of his mind like it had all been a dream.

Jake sat on a cold, metal bench, his fleece unzipped at the top so that warm air from his body lifted around his neck and face as he breathed. The arboretum was a welcome distraction from the greys and blues of the office. The trees whispered as their leaves fell green and orange and red in the fresh, crisp air. The fountain in the centre of the pond never quite sprayed vertically in the breeze.

He watched his shadow crawl to the edge of the pond where she reached out her hands to the ducks that sat huddled, beaks in backs. Sometimes as she touched them, they would stand up, startled, and waddle away into water, looking back, quacking.

"They can feel you?" he said.

"I think they can. I think they must know I'm here. Look." She reached out again and as her hand crossed the back of a green-blue mallard, it jumped up and into the water, only to be replaced on the bank by another duck that the girl would torment later.

"I think it's funny," she said.

"Don't you think they'll be annoyed?" Jake said. "They're trying to keep warm."

"Ha. No. I think it's funny. Look."

Another duck was dislodged.

"Hmm," Jake said, spooning tuna pasta from a plastic tub then chewing. "That would annoy me."

"Ah. You eat your pasta. I'll play with the ducks."

Someone to the side of him spoke.

"Can I get some of that pasta?"

Whilst Jake had been watching, amused at the duck swap game that his shadow was playing, someone had sat down on the bench beside him. Jake didn't turn towards the voice.

"No," he said, staring out at the fountain as it shifted direction again, its splashes creating a new pattern on the surface of the pond.

"Ah, come on," the man said. "There's surely not much left there. I'll give you back your tub."

With his spoon still to his mouth, Jake turned toward the voice and looked at the man who was looking out over the water. He was wearing a smart blue pinstriped suit and dull black shoes. The side of his face that Jake could see was clean-shaven, but his hair was a matt of long greasy clumps. Jake turned away again.

"Do I know you?" he said, pretty sure that he didn't.

"Ah well," the man said. "A few spoonfuls of that fish pasta and you'll know me then."

In front of them, all the ducks were huddled again.

"Look, mate," Jake said. "I only get an hour for lunch and this is my lunch and I'm going to eat it."

"Ah. That's a shame." Jake knew that the man had turned towards him, but he stared out at the water. He didn't want to see the man's face. He had a feeling it might put him off the rest of his lunch.

There was a rattling noise as if the man was opening a wrapper. Jake could hear him biting and crunching, and it was beginning to annoy him.

Then silence.

The man spoke. "You're just not the giving type are you?"

Jake breathed out hard.

"Take, take, take," the man said quietly.

Jake put the lid on his unfinished pasta, shoved the box into the bottom of a carrier bag and zipped up his fleece.

"Or have I got you wrong there?" the man continued. "Am I getting you confused with someone else?"

"Ah, for fuck's sake," Jake said. "I'm going now and I'm taking the rest of this pasta with me. So just fuck off."

The man laughed. A friendly, joking laugh and Jake turned towards him.

He recognised the man. He knew the face, the hair, the nose the mouth, the teeth, the ears, everything about the man, but he couldn't quite place him. He stared at every single strand of the man's hair and at the pockmarks on his forehead then at the suit and the tie.

The man smiled and slicked back his hair with a grimy hand. He seemed to see the exact moment that Jake recognised him and he spoke. "Hello, Jake."

Jake looked at the man's sweet-wrapper blue eyes.

"It's you. From town," he said. "From when we were sat out at the tables. That night."

The man waved his hands in the air. "Ta da," he said, then laughed. "I guess I do have one of those faces that you never forget huh?"

"No," Jake said flatly. "It was the suit is all." He grabbed his carrier bag and stood up. "Anyway. That just means I recognise you. I don't know you. In fact, yeah," Jake clutched the lunch box in the bag and stared into the man's eyes, "I'd still like you to just fuck off."

The man's face didn't change as he stood up and plunged his hands into his trouser pockets.

"Ah, Jake, this is little more complicated than just recognition now."

"What?" Jake said. "You're talking nonsense," he

pointed his carrier bag wrapped lunch box at the man, "And how come you know my name? Yeah. Don't think I didn't spot that you fucking weirdo tramp."

The man laughed and this time his trousers flapped up and down with the effort. "That's funny," he said. "Why so angry Jake? Why are you *so* defensive? What are you hiding Jake? Jake? Jake?"

Jake wondered what the man would look like face down in the pond with a carrier bag over his head, but before he could really visualize it the man spoke again.

"Okay, look," he said, turning towards the pond again, "I'm not going to piss about. Much as I was enjoying you doing a good cop, bad cop, all by yourself. No. I want you to come with me."

"Ah, just leave me alone," Jake said, shooing the man away.

"No. I'm serious. You have to come with me."

"Where to? A dark alley. Underpass? Get fucking real. I don't have any cash and I really don't fancy losing my ass virginity to a tramp."

The man coughed. "I was thinking somewhere a little more familiar. More, recognisable, if you like."

Jake walked away, fully aware that if the man jumped him from behind, or even if he held a knife to his ribs, that he would quite easily put the bag over the man's head, and the man face down in the pond whether he'd visualised it fully or not.

Jake stopped moving and his head fell forward as the man spoke again.

"The ironworks, Jake."

"Oh for fuck's sake," Jake said under his breath. In his head he saw himself in a million tiny frames from a million different movies: undercover detectives. Wronged loved ones. Rival gangs recruiting. Revenge attacks. Now he saw himself face down with a carrier bag over his head, lying on the damp, bare concrete of a warehouse floor.

"I really need to talk to you, Jake."

Jake turned around, his face red with anger and confusion and fear. More than anything he just wanted an answer.

"Go on," Jake said. "But remember. I only get an hour for lunch."

"Ah, that's too bad. I kinda figured this would take a little longer than that. When I say talk, I mean, well, tell I suppose. I want to tell you a story. But I need you to come to the ironworks with me."

"No fucking way," Jake said. "Get real."

The man looked at his watch. "There's a bus in fifteen minutes, Jake. We really should get going. I've got so much to tell you."

"I'm not interested."

"I need to tell you about that girl of yours."

Jake's stomach cramped, his head filled with dizziness and he clenched his fists. He felt violated and sick and weak and lost and he was floating in the clouds again. But as the man continued he came back with a bump of relief.

"Emma," he said. "She's been a bit of a stupid bitch of late." The man raised his hands in a defensive gesture. "If you don't mind me saying, of course." He smiled and raised his eyebrows.

"What about Emma?" Jake said.

"Ah. Lots. Lots about Emma. And the guy you killed. And, then there's the whole shadows thing of course. God that could take a while. So much to tell you about on that one, Jake. Woo." His eyes were wide, his cheeks filled with smile.

"I don't know anything about any dead man at the ironworks," Jake said. He didn't even convince himself that he came across as convincing.

"Come on, Jake. Twelve minutes. Don't worry about the guy you killed."

"Stop saying that."

"Okay. Okay. Just don't worry about *that* right now. I see. Okay. That's not important." He looked at his watch again. "Jake? These buses can be quite unreliable. Sometimes they're late, sometimes they're even early, Jake. I mean, like, five minutes early, when you don't want them to be."

Jake expected to hear the little girl telling him to go, or not go, or hide, or run, or be careful. There was only the sound of water splashing and Jake knew he had to decide for himself. He thought back to his two weeks of daytime TV. He thought about the ironworks. He thought about the man tumbling over the railings onto the metal and plants below. He thought about Emma and her new shadow and how, essentially, he'd been used and broken and discarded by her again. He thought back to his two weeks of daytime TV then looked the man right in the eyes and spoke. "You got drink out there?"

The man laughed then turned away. He gestured with an outstretched hand that Jake should follow.

"I wouldn't be going there if I didn't have drink, Jake. Ah well. You'll see, Jake. I have so much to tell you."

Jake took his lunch box out of the bag, handed it to the man, and they walked out of the park leaving the ducks huddled peacefully on the bank.

Despite being clean-shaven, despite wearing a suit and speaking in a soft, friendly voice and despite paying for Jake's bus fare, the man was, Jake knew, a tramp.

He offered Jake the window seat, saying that he'd seen the view enough, then sat beside him. He smelled of stale tea and pond water. He pressed his nose against the window to get anything like fresh air from the cold glass.

The tramp talked. For forty minutes, as the bus stopped and started and emptied and filled, he talked. And talked. And talked. Jake half listened to the soothing storyteller drone and felt comatose and child like.

The tramp talked about razors and how it was so hard to stay clean-shaven.

"The hardest thing to do, it is. Of everything, like eating and sleeping and shitting and fucking, the hardest thing I have to contend with is shaving. Most stolen thing in any shop anywhere, razors. Yeah. I know. Weird huh? They put 'em near the checkouts so that people can keep an eye on 'em. Security tag them up. It's just so damned hard to get hold of safety razors. A nice suit, now that's easy. Any charity shop will have old business suits, old wedding suits and these shops are usually run by volunteers with all sorts of problems, and they don't even know you've not paid when you walk straight out the door wearing a nice old Brown Brothers dinner jacket. Shoes are the same, you just pick a pair up, try 'em on and walk right on out. Yeah, clothes are easy. But safety razors, forget it. You know how I get mine, how I keep so clean-shaven? I hang around in the shops looking for people who buy 'em, and I watch 'em throw these things into carrier bags and I follow these people around for a bit, wait for 'em to sit down somewhere. Ah. Sometimes I just see a pack of razors through the side of a bag and that's it. I'm all over 'em. Who'd have thought, eh? Of all the crimes in the world, stalking people who have safety razors. I'd laugh if it weren't so serious. So yeah, I wait for 'em to sit down, on a bench, or a bus and I sit myself down there next to 'em and I take out my razor blade and just slit the bag along the bottom, or the side, sometimes the side, and bingo. Nice fresh pack of safety razors. Yeah. It's an art I guess. Now, I know what you're thinking, and rightly so. How do you get your razor blades? Right? Yeah. Ah. That's a whole other story. Anyway. Not like I haven't got *any* money. I have a bit. You know. But it mostly goes on bus fares. Yeah, I like buses now. Never used to. Too many judgemental women, with their perfume that I swear can kill insects in a confined space and just *has* to be flammable, and they're all just going out shopping for stuff they already have. Yeah. Ah. I used to catch the train for a while, but I just got so sick of being told what not to do. No running. No photography. No leaving bags unattended. Twenty-four-hour CCTV operation for *my* safety. Ah. Sent me quite mad. I kind of got banned from trains, you know. Ah. Yeah. I did a shit on a ticket barrier 'cause it kept refusing to take my ticket. They caught it all on the twenty-four-hour CCTV and, well. Guess it works after all. Anyway, you don't get that with buses. Shampoo. Ah, well, yeah. I could tell you about shampoo. God the trouble I have with..."

"Jake?" the tramp said, nudging him in the shoulder with his own lunch box. "This is us."

They stepped off the bus and everything was quiet and green and fresh, and above all quiet.

Chapter Ten

The tramp clapped his hands across his face. "Woohoo. It's cold out when you're clean shaved like me."

Jake stared blankly at him. His clean-shaven rants were becoming tiresome.

"This way, Jakey baby."

"Jakey baby?"

The tramp laughed and started to walk. Jake followed. They walked for a while in silence, through gates and over fields, before the ironworks rolled into view as they had before when Jake was there last. He couldn't decide if he felt sick, or tired, or both. If there was ever a physical feeling for confusion, the void filled with worms in his stomach was it.

They approached the ironworks from a different angle, down a steep slope of rough grass, and Jake could clearly see the yellow warehouse where he'd been last time.

As if the tramp had read his thoughts he stopped, turned to Jake and spoke. "Pretty sure I don't need to say anything right about now," he said, and stared intently into Jake's eyes, looking for a reaction.

"Hmm," Jake said.

The tramp walked on and spoke, waving his hands around. "I'm thinkin' that you're thinkin' 'Oh, the last time I was here was when I killed that guy' is what you're thinkin'. Right?"

Jake was silent for a bit longer than a single footstep, then the tramp started talking again.

"Or maybe you're wonderin' if I'm gonna kill you down there. The way you killed that guy."

Now Jake spoke. "I'm just thinkin'," he said, flat, stoic, calm, "That's all. Just thinkin'."

"Good man."

Jake wondered just how the hell this man knew so much about him and about Emma. He could understand how maybe he knew about the shadows. Maybe even about the tramp he killed in the warehouse. Maybe word got around about stuff like that. Then he realised.

"You shit," he said.

"Woo hoo," the tramp said, bounding down the slope faster. He looked like a child who was playing some stupid game, legs too fast, arms up in the air. Jake ran after him until they reached the chain-link fence.

"Careful now, Jake," the tramp said, pointing at one of the faded security signs. "Dogs and CCTV."

"It was you," Jake said, panting.

"Yup."

"In the doorway in the warehouse."

"Yup."

"But," Jake said. Paused. Spoke again. "How do you know about Emma?"

The tramp pushed through a triangular gap in the fence, "There are no cameras," he said.

"Yeah, I know. But Emma?"

"Blah de Emma blah. Come on."

Jake got the feeling that this man was both sides of a coin, and that he'd landed on his edge. He seemed crazy but sane, kind, but very dangerous. Jake was willing to play the game, but figured this wasn't actually a game. He followed, his feet crunching and clicking on the stones and pieces of metal.

The warehouse where he'd killed the man was quite a way off to their right, but Jake stared at it hard as they walked, as if it was staring back.

"Clever girl really," the tramp said as they approached another warehouse, this one dull grey and streaked and spotted with rust. "She figured she'd get herself a new shadow down here and no one would ever know eh? Fuckin' tramps disappear all the time. No one misses them. Another empty shop doorway in town just gets filled up again a couple of nights later. No one would ever know."

The tramp yanked on a huge metal door and it slid open. "Did you know?" he said.

"Know?"

"About your girl, Emma. About what she was doing getting hold of a new shadow?"

Jake pushed his fingers into the bridge of his nose and closed his eyes.

"I kinda figured, yes." He opened his eyes and looked at the tramp. "I knew she was after another shadow. I think I even knew she'd done it before. I kinda guessed why she came down here for one."

"Yeah, not the first time either."

"Yeah. If there was a first time for everything I

sometimes think she skipped it."

"What?"

"Nothing."

The pleasant smell of burning wood and paraffin and soap came through the door and Jake felt nothing but calm being in this place with this man right now.

The tramp gestured Jake inside and said, "I've got quite a bit of shit I need to tell you, Jakey Baby."

"Why the Jakey Baby thing all of a sudden?" Jake said.

"It's pally," the tramp said, smiling, "Pally and, well, I feel more comfortable about you now, and well, you're in my world now, so," his face changed ever so slightly, as if the light had been pulled low under his chin so that his eye sockets and lips and nose all cast deep shadows, "you're my guest. And guests are pleasant and polite and do as they're told and." He tugged at the ends of his sleeves so that they covered his bony wrists then continued. "Well, yes. There. There you have it."

Jake screwed his face into a ball.

"Look, just come on in and meet the family," the tramp said. "And be polite for fuck's sake, and, just come on in. I've got quite a bit of shit to tell you, so we need to sit down and maybe have a drink and..." His face became serious. "Well, Jakey baby, I think things are going to get quite a bit crazy, quite quickly."

Jake followed the tramp into the warehouse, and the tramp closed the door behind them.

Inside was similar to the other warehouse except

that there was no machinery, no tanks, no pipes or valves, nothing on the floor except bare, dry concrete. Around the edges, pinned to the walkways, large sheets of plastic or cloth, or metal or sack, created what looked like makeshift rooms. Rooms that twisted and fluttered. Rooms that flickered and shimmied in the light of fires or lamps inside them. The whole place looked somewhere between a shantytown and a Christmas grotto. White bed-sheet rooms next to plastic blue and metal grey and pinstripe cloth. Jake marvelled at how one room was clear polythene, but painted like a stained-glass window with a crude Jesus holding his fluttering hands out. Some of the sheets had bright Christmas lights running along their top edge, or ribbons hanging down in bunches, and dried flowers and fresh flowers and pieces of mirror or metal or tin cans and beads and bright glass bottles. Lying on the floor, just outside each room, was a tea-light candle, illuminating the steel upright posts, making them flicker and appear soft.

The smell of wood fires and paraffin and baking concrete and pollen, all on the edge of winter, made Jake feel comfortable and childlike and in his head he is camping again in a field with his friends, cooking peas he's stolen from a field over a wood fire and telling ghost stories. Then he remembered the moment his friends left him there on his own.

"Wow," Jake said. "This place is awesome."

"I think so," the tramp said. "Wait 'til you meet the family," he said. He laughed and shook his head.

He led Jake to the middle of the left hand wall

where a white silken sheet flickered with a pale peach light from behind, making it the colour of morning.

"Hey. Freesia," he shouted.

From behind the sheet came a mumbled, incoherent reply.

"You decent?" he said, pulling back the sheet a tiny amount.

Another reply, still muffled, but this time at least coherent. "Are you trying to be funny, Bob?"

Jake took his eyes off the sheet and stared at the side of Bob's face.

"Bob," he said.

Bob turned towards him. His face screwed up on one side. He shrugged.

Jake pointed at Bob. "Bob," he said again. "It only just occurred to me that for the last, God knows how long, I didn't bother to ask you your name."

"Yeah, well," Bob started to say, but Jake interrupted.

"I thought maybe you'd tell me in your own time."

"It's not *that* important," Bob said, turning back to the sheet and calling out again.

"Bob," Jake said. He felt cheated, disappointed almost, that this man, who incited so many feelings from calm to fear, excitement to annoyance, was called Bob. It just didn't seem right.

Bob pulled the sheet back and stepped inside.

Jake followed.

The room was warm. It smelled of camping gas and flowers and cigarette smoke and alcohol and perfume, all hanging inside, trapped by the sheet. Straight away, Jake felt light headed. In a good way.

On the floor, taking up half of the room, was a large double mattress, covered in bright pink, well made, bed clothes and two slightly less than pink, pink pillows that were well fluffed. Next to the pillows was a pink Hello Kitty bag. Fairy lights hung from a rafter; a tightly knotted ball of green wire dotted with shining blues and reds and yellows. The outer breezeblock wall had been covered with a sheet of wood, which, in turn had also been covered.

Every last inch had something pinned there. Dull black and white photos like the ones that come free with a cheap picture frame, a man and woman smiling, a young boy with a fat face, his thumbs up, massive smile, missing front teeth. There were magazine and newspaper clippings of brown and white horses in green fields or on white, snow topped hills. A photo of a young girl on a carousel ride was crying into a mane of gold painted wood. Twelve Polaroid photos of a cathedral clock face, each one showing exactly a quarter past the hour, each with a different colour of sky behind it from pink through blue to black. Newspaper clippings, headlines and photos. 'Boy raised like bird by mother', a black face smiling. 'Huge cat spotted near accident black-spot' and the blurred outline of something in some trees. 'Man killed in supermarket toilets was paedophile' a tiny photo of a row of shopping trolleys. There were wind chimes made of wood and metal. Dream-catchers made from fur and feathers and cotton and leather that swung slowly, suspended on plastic map pins. Ribbons and rosettes. Dried flower heads. Live flower heads. A small animal skull held up inside a circle of dress making pins, their tops alternating red and dark blue.

"Quite a lot of shit, eh, Jake?" Bob said.

"Mmm," Jake said, looking away from the board and down at the woman on the floor.

Freesia was sitting on a child's plastic chair. She was facing the wall, her black and green stockinged legs spread out in a V with dull red Doc Martens pointing up, swaying left to right.

She was looking into a mirror propped against the board, and Jake could see her looking at him through the one eye that was not covered by her thick black wavy hair. That one dark eye was smiling at Jake.

"Hey," Jake said, raising his hand.

"Hi," she said. Her voice was soft, almost childish and she mumbled like she was maybe applying lipstick, or chewing something.

"It'sh not sshit," she said, her eye rolling over in Bob's reflected direction.

Bob reached out and ran his hand across a row of pictures so that they fluttered and swung. "Sixty six shiny souvenirs," he said. He laughed.

Freesia raised a middle finger. "Fuck you, Bob," she said.

She pushed her hair out of her eye and raised her drawn on eyebrows, shaking her head, looking at Jake. Bob put his hand on her shoulder but she pushed it away and he laughed again.

"Say hello to Jake," he said.

"I already did."

"No. I mean, say hello properly."

Freesia sighed. She put her hands on her knees, pulled her feet in, stood up, leaned forward, brushed dust from her knees and shins, moved the mirror closer to the wall, raised her hands to her hair, pulled it back then let it fall. She pulled at the bottom of her green sweater so that the outline of her shoulder blades showed through, then she turned around.

"Jesus," Jake said, raising his hands to his mouth.

Bob laughed.

"She?" Freesia said, palms upwards toward Bob. "Happy now?"

Bob shrugged.

Freesia looked at Jake. Jake looked at Freesia. He tried not to look at her mouth. He stared into her eyes again, dark brown, smiling. He looked at her tiny nose and at the array of freckles that danced away from the top. He looked at one of her tiny ears that poked out from a loop of hair. He looked at her mouth again.

Her lips and the sides of her mouth were torn and ripped and scarred and broken. Pink and red lines ran up as high as her cheekbones. Behind what should have been her lips, Jake could see that her tongue was split as well. As she spoke, the loose flaps of torn, then healed skin rasped and rattled and spit dripped from her jaw.

"Fucking mesh eh?" she said, and all the slits and flaps opened out like a pumpkin smile carved in flesh.

"I... Well," Jake said.

"In here, we call her Starmouth," Bob said. "In

fact, outside of here, they call her Starmouth as well."

Freesia rolled her split tongue around her split mouth.

"What the hell happened?" Jake said.

"It was her husband," Bob said.

"Exsh hushband," Freesia corrected him, rolling her eyes.

Bob continued. "Hubby comes home one day to find Freesia sucking off a kid from her home economics class. A bit of out of hours education. The kid got out without so much as the loss of his trousers and blazer. Starmouth, well Freesia then, she wasn't quite so lucky." He paused. "You wanna carry on?" he said to her.

"Nah," she said. "It'sh okay." She smiled her pumpkin smile.

"Well," Bob said, "I told you how much trouble I have getting razorblades."

Jake pulled a face.

"Turns out, that Carl," Bob said.

"Colin," Freesia said.

"Colin. Turns out that Colin had shit loads of the damn things."

"'Bout eight."

"So, Car...Colin, he gets those eight razorblades and ties them all to a piece of chain."

"From a shink plug."

"A sink plug chain," Bob said. He paused as if imagining the process of threading eight razorblades onto a chrome bauble chain. He continued. "He holds pretty little Freesia down, and shoves the bundle into her mouth chanting something."

"It wass 'fucking bitch, fucking bitch'."

"Chanting, 'fucking bitch, fucking bitch', then he holds her mouth shut under her chin. He's not stupid this Colin. He wraps the end of the chain around his middle finger."

"Hish ring finger."

"Round his ring finger, and..."

Jake realised that he'd been pressing his fingers hard onto his lips all this time and he looked at them like he might see blood, or slithers of flesh, or shards of tooth. "Fucking hell," he said.

"Nope," said Freesia. "Fucking Jamesh. Fourteen. An a pluss shtudent." Her bright eyes flickered in recollection.

Jake imagined how beautiful she must have been before. He imagined himself as a fourteen-year-old boy as Freesia slowly pushed him into her mouth. He felt her cold lips and cold teeth become her warm tongue and hot throat.

"Turns out," Bob said, "that Colin actually created a monster."

"A good monshter," Freesia said, mocking a curtsey.

"A fucking great monster. He actually created one of the most divine experiences that man..."

"Or boy."

"...or boy, would ever likely experience."

Freesia moved closer to Jake. "Imagine thish mouth," she said. "Then imagine every other mouth that ever wrapped around your cock. Imagine them all one after the other after the other." She paused and ran her fingers down Jake's face. She blinked. "Now imagine thish mouth again."

"Honestly Jake?" Bob said. "You can't begin to imagine. It's like a warm, wet sea creature sliding up and down. Then you get these sharp cold rasps of air between the gaps. Oh man. And when she does the fluttering thing. Ah man. Just imagine."

"I think he's imagining," Freesia said looking down at Jake's trousers.

"Ah shit," he said, pulling out his shirt and letting it down over his crotch.

Bob laughed. "Don't worry Jakey baby. She gets that reaction a lot. She's a pleasure to have on board, so to speak. Makes a ton of cash as well out in the town."

"Shtudents," she said.

"Let's get going, Jake," Bob said. "I've got a lot of shit to get through." He looked as if he'd suddenly realised that he was wasting time. His face was serious, contemplative, his brow screwed up. He ran his hands over his cheeks. "Come on, man," he said. "I'm getting some stubble."

He turned, pushed back the silk sheet and left.

"How rude," Freesia said.

Jake looked at Freesia, at her eyes, at her nose, at her mouth. He smiled. "See you later, Freesia," he said.

"Hope sho," she said. Then, "And you *can* call me Starmouth. If you like."

Jake laughed, shook his head and left the room.

Back in the warehouse, it was cold and smelled of metal and concrete and damp.

"Yeah," Bob said, as they walked along the centre of the floor, gesturing to all the other brightly coloured sheets, "there's quite a few of us down here."

"I guessed there'd be a few of you down here," Jake said. He paused. "I thought maybe you'd all be a bit more..." He paused again. "Well…"

"Trampy?"

"Yeah. Trampy. I guess. I mean, I thought it'd all be dirty mattresses and needles and meth bottles and shit, real human shit everywhere and stuff."

"Yeah. We do all right. The guys that are here are kinda the core that is left. We all have our uses. We all contribute. We do our bit. It's more like we're here because, well, we just don't want to be out there, in the city among all those damned people. You know? All the glass and metal and cars and expensive watches and jewellery and sofas and shoes and God.

"All that shit that those people believe is a definition of themselves. Makes me sick and mad and sad. People discussing how great they are because they just bought something that is better than something they already had before. It's just plain weird."

"I can relate to that," Jake said, nodding.

"Good man."

"So, you're like the leader down here?"

"Since you mention it, yes. If you wanna use the word leader."

"You seem to have it all worked out."

"Yes."

"Hmm."

"Hmm what, Jake?" Bob stopped walking, swung around and looked Jake right in the face. He had taken on that huge concrete, immovable object look. Jake was more intrigued than intimidated.

"I mean, hmm. I was just thinking out loud. Bob."

Bob rubbed his cheeks again then pointed at Jake as if he was about to say something, turned away, turned back, his finger right at Jake's nose. He shouted, sounding like he was trying not to shout and spit flicked from his lips. "That fucking prick," he pointed away, outside, "Teach. That fucking prick, Teach?" He was glaring at Jake, his eyes huge, and Jake, for the first time at this place felt a cold wave splash over his body. He felt tiny and brittle in front of this man, a dried stalk of grass at the edge of a forest fire.

The girl whispered, she too sounded timid and scared. "Teach?"

"Teach?" Jake said, trying to keep Bob on his fear inducing rant without pushing him over the edge.

"As much as you've brought a massive fucking shit storm down on me," Bob said, waving his hands at the sheets while figures danced along the creases, listening, "and them, Jake. As much as I should fucking hang you from these rafters and peel the skin from your chest for doing what you did?" He suddenly became calm, his hands slumped to his sides. "I'd have probably killed the cunt myself before much longer. So the result would have been the same I guess." He paused. He looked at Jake again and all the anger was gone from his features.

He sighed. "The result would have been the same for him. For us. It would have been the end either way, I think." He smiled. "But for you, Jakey Babey, well, you're kind of our piggy in the middle now. Ah shit. Come *on* man. Let's stop pissing about. Come *on*."

Jake pressed on with the conversation, hoping Bob would stay calm. "Teach was the guy I killed?"

"Yeah. He wasn't with us. He was here for a whole nother reason." He spat onto the floor.

Anger. "Fucker."

Calm. "That's why he was out in the moss shed. He had us all clawing at each other's throats, the slimy fuck. Cat. Pigeons. Mess."

"So you're not mad I killed him?"

"I was. But I'm not now. Not me."

"Not you. Then who?"

Suddenly there was a shout from high up. "Below!"

"Ah shit," Bob said, checking his plastic strapped, digital watch, "Eight thirty."

Jake looked up to a walkway. Hanging over the edge of a rust orange railing was a huge pink arse.

"Below!"

Then shit. Big long logs of thick brown shit fell from the fat pink moon of an arse and thudded into the concrete not far from where they were standing.

"Ah, man," Jake said, holding his nose.

"That there fat pink ass belongs to Punxsutawney Phil," Bob said.

Jake watched the arse disappear back over the railing. He saw a man pulling up his trousers. Saw him pour something from a bottle onto one hand then the other, then watched him rub his hands together.

"Punxatawney Phil," Jake said to himself, distracted by the something in his memory by the fact that he'd just watched someone take a shit from twenty feet above.

"Groundhog," Bob said.

Jake clicked his fingers. "That's it. One of the ground hogs that those guys over in America pull out on the second of Feb. Yeah. That's it. If he sees his own shadow, they get more winter. And if he doesn't..." he paused, thinking. "If he doesn't, then spring is on its way." He paused again and pressed his fingers into the bridge of his nose. "What the hell is it with shadows? Damn."

Bob laughed. "No man," he said. "Well, yes. But no. Think Bill Murray."

"Groundhog Day. The film?"

"Yep."

"And?"

"Well, Phil, and his name really is Phil, he does the same shit every day. No pun intended. For Phil, every day is exactly the same."

"Is he crazy? Like properly crazy?"

"Not at all. He's pretty damned smart as it goes. Used to be a professor, or a tutor, or something, of mathematical science and its role in the natural environment. Or something. Don't even get him started on Fibonacci and all that golden number nonsense. Man. Just don't."

"Fibonacci?"

"Yeah. Look. Point is he does the same thing every day. Eight thirty, takes his shit. And well, look, now," he checked his watch. "Eight thirty six, he cleans it up and bags it."

Phil had come down from the walkway. Bob waved. Phil waved back, a dark smudge of weight swung in a clear carrier bag from his wrist.

"Hey, Bobby," Phil shouted.

"Phil," Bob shouted back, "say hello to Jake."

"Hey, Jake," Phil shouted, waving, the bag swinging more.

Jake waved a lazy wave back.

"I guess it's more OCD than GHD," Bob said. "But it's damn useful for us. Six a.m. we get fresh bread and cheese, veg and salads and boxes of cakes and stuff from the supermarket skips. All thrown out 'cause they're past their sell by date, all staying fresher in the cool metal skips than they would inside a supermarket open fronted fridge.

"Seven a.m. he sweeps the whole of this floor." Bob rubbed his shoe into the clean concrete. "Just past seven thirty, he disappears for a bit behind his blue tarpaulin and jerks off to BMX magazines. Don't ask.

"Eight o'clock dead, he collects any rubbish lying around and moves it out back, sorts it, splits it, composts some, buries some, piles some. He even made a rain chime from glass bottles, makes a really nice tune in a downpour.

"Nine a.m. he sits down to watch a DVD."

"A DVD?" Jake said.

"Yeah. He's got this little portable DVD player that runs off a car battery that he charges out in the sun. He has a kinda mini cinema going." Bob reached into his pocket and pulled out a pink Post-it note. "See? Ridiculous." He handed Jake the pink square and Jake looked at it.

Phil's Mattinee. It said in neatly sign-written felt tip, then beneath that, **GHOST**.

Bob rolled his eyes. "He even stops the film halfway through and walks around with a cardboard box strapped over his shoulder with string and sells popcorn or bread rolls, or peanuts and Smarties and M&Ms and stuff. Not so much the M&Ms and Smarties and peanuts anymore though since people started throwing them at the screen. OCD or not, he's not stupid.

"Point is, Jake, we know, every day, exactly what to expect. When to expect our daily bread, a film, the evening paper, all the candles replaced, a Spanish lesson, pedicure, manicure, facials and optional massage, half front, back or full body. And, more importantly, when the filthy git is going to take a shit off the walkway." He raised his hand into the air. "We digress," he said.

At the opposite end of the warehouse to which they'd come in, Bob slid another heavy door sideways and stepped out into a sliver of bright daylight.

Jake stepped out.

Jake is fishing with his dad, his fishing line sitting in shallow water, the static, pink float, poking straight up through shining black water that smells old and thick in the back of his nose.

"Don't worry, Jake," his dad says, off to his left.

"It's a waiting game."

Jake is rubbing his nose with the hand that he didn't use to squeeze a maggot onto the hook. He's rubbing his eyes so that he can see the float. He's willing the float to move.

His dad grunts then says, "Here we go, son. Got one."

"A fish?"

"Yeah. Help me reel him in."

Jake drops his rod and moves into the side of his dad. He cups his hands into the gaps between his dad's arms and feels the weight of the rod, feels the vibrations in his wrists. His tongue is poking from the side of his mouth. His eyes are narrow. He turns the reel. The wrong way. The right way. He pulls the rod into the air like his dad would, then lets it fall again, lets it rise and fall and he reels in and feels the weight of the fish pulling this way and that so close to the surface now. He's shouting "Dad the net, Dad the net," but he is gone somewhere behind him and as Jake pulls the rod one more time there is a silver shimmer on the surface of the black water that picks out the sun and reflects it into his eyes like diamonds exploding.

Then nothing.

Jake is sitting in cold mud, the rod in the air. And there is nothing. No fish. No net. And he's still shouting, screaming now, about the net and Dad how he needs the net.

There is warmth on his shoulder. His dad's hand.

"It's gone, Jake," he says into the back of Jake's hair, the smell of cigar smoke and beer clouding around him.

"The net, Dad. The net."

Jake looks at his white fingers and thinks how stupid he was to reel the wrong way. He wonders if that was the moment that, had he not done it, would have meant him catching the fish.

His dad speaks, his voice broken. "It's gone, Jake. That's what they do, Jake. It's just a dumb fish, Jake. They do that."

There's warmth on the back of his neck, and across his other shoulder and his dad's arms fold around the front of his chest. Jake is staring at where the diamonds were, and he drops the rod. He turns his head and looks at his dad, looks at his hair all slicked back and at the crow's feet around his eyes and the way his thin cracked lips are tight together. He looks at the moisture on the surface of his dad's eyes and wonders if they're wetter than they were before.

"Dad?" he says.

And his dad holds Jake's face in his hands and says, "There won't always be a net, Jake."

And Jake looks into his dad's face and he looks older than he did when he threw bait out earlier.

"Dad?"

And his dad is running his thumb and forefinger through Jake's hair, catching the lugs and pulling at his scalp, hurting him, and he says, "Just saying, Jake."

"Sorry, Dad," Jake says, looking at the mud, "I'm sorry I lost your fish."

And his dad takes his hands away from Jake's

head and laughs.

"That was your fish, Jake. I saw your float go a couple of times before he took mine." He flicks Jake hard on the ear. "You can only reel one way or the other. You keep reeling all day and you'll catch something."

There is silence.

His dad says, "I'm not always gonna be here with a net, Jake." He lights a half burned cigar and Jake hears it crackle, sees the end glow orange and the smoke struggle into the air. "You just keep reeling Jake. You'll get there one day."

Jake only saw his Dad every first weekend of the month after that. They never did go fishing again.

"Jake."

That smell.

"Jakey baby. Open your eyes, man."

It was the exact same smell.

"And stop wiping your damn nose."

Jake opened his eyes, and for a moment, Bob was the same black silhouette as he had been in the doorway.

"It's not that bad, Jake."

"Hmm?"

"The smell. You get used to it."

"Yeah. It's not that bad," Jake said, checking his hands for snot. "Just reminded me of something. That's all."

"Damn," Bob said, his features back in plain view, a confused look on his face. "You are weird. It smells like shit to me."

"Yeah. Shit."

Jake blew his nose into the gap between his thumb and forefinger, then wiped it down the side of his leg.

Bob shook his head. "Come on, man. This is where *I* live."

A few feet away, lying almost on its side in what looked like thick black mud, was a boat.

"A boat?" Jake said. "You live on a boat?"

"It's a barge, Jake."

"In no water."

"I never get the need to go anywhere in it."

Jake shrugged. Bob made sense.

The barge was huge, probably sixty feet in length and lying at an angle so that its tall wheelhouse poked out over the edge of the bank. The top half may have once been white, but was now dull beige and pocked with teardrop rust making it look like a giraffe. Where the bottom poked out of the mud and water, Jake could see that it was a gaudy crimson, stitched to the beige top with a thick line of rust that seeped down the sides. At the front were four large round windows. At the back, behind the wheelhouse, two large rounded but rectangular ones. One had pale creamy glass, the other had a blue fertilizer bag taped on with silver duct tape. The tall square wheelhouse was framed with rotting wood and Jake could see flat, shiny brown mushrooms growing along it like leathery ears. A mast lay broken across the deck. A TV antenna that looked like a whirligig washing line sat vertically up despite the angle that it should have been. There was a faded plastic owl. A bicycle that looked rusted solid to the deck.

"It used to be a real canal once," Bob said. "Carried coal down from Shipley. You can still follow it all the way back there. If you want. But yeah, when it closed, this bit was bought by the ironworks so they could keep the water or something. Can you believe they used to make bombs here Jake? I mean, shells and casings, that kind of thing. For the war and stuff. Apparently they even tried to make concrete torpedo shells or something as well. All interesting stuff, eh? But yeah this is pretty much all that's left of the canal, and it's no use to anyone now. Except me of course."

Jake realised he was pulling a face.

"Don't ask man," Bob said. "I don't know how this barge came to be here. Pretty sure it wasn't used for coal or bombs. Come on man. It's neat."

"But it's got mushrooms and plants growing out of it," Jake said.

"Yeah I know. You can eat 'em."

Bob ducked down, crawled into the wheelhouse and was gone.

Jake muttered to himself. "That might explain a few things."

He crawled into the wheelhouse, careful not to touch the rotten wood, or slimy mushrooms. The barge made no noise and didn't move at all as he dropped onto the sloping floor.

He stepped through another door.

Inside, the barge was huge and spacious. The wooden clad walls were covered in ivy and other creeping plants. The ceiling was adorned with mosses that spread out from light fittings and air vents where the sun crept in. The carpet was thick with mud along its middle and more plants grew along each edge, leaning up and into the walls. Small flowers, bushes, a blueberry plant?

"Table's clean," Bob said, wandering along the room with ease, despite the strange angle it was at. "And the seats."

There was a corner seat of bright polished wood with beige and blue scatter cushions on each side, and in front of the seat, held up by two shining metal legs was a table made of the same polished clean wood.

"It's only really the plants that make it look a bit grim. Unless you like plants of course. They get everywhere. They have a way of creeping in, clinging on when everything else has just given up and died. Eh, Jake?"

Jake saw more than a little resemblance to the warehouse where the green tide had crept over the metal structures and cylinders.

"Can you believe I actually mist them?" Bob said.

"Missed them. What?" Jake said, as he struggled to walk over to the table. His hand hovered over a wood-burning stove and he felt warm air brush the hairs on his wrist.

"Mist. Water." Bob reached into a high cupboard on the wall and pulled out a plastic bottle which he sprayed into the air. "Mist. Psst psst."

"Mist. Sure. This is weird," Jake said.

Jake's feet dug into the thick carpet. He shuffled his way across to the table and slid onto the seats.

Two cushions slid out the other end.

Bob moved through another door closed it and shouted back. "Galley's back here. And my bedroom's through here too. But you don't need to know that. Drink?"

Jake was silent, staring at his hands on the table as he pressed them down to prevent them slipping forward.

"Jake," Bob shouted. Glasses clinked. A door slammed. Another opened. "Drink." This last word sounded more like an instruction than a question.

Bob came back in holding two wine glasses upside down by the stems. In his other hand was a large bottle of what must have been whiskey. There was no label. He pulled the door shut behind him. There was a thud against it, then a faint grumble. Jake watched the door shifting in and out at its base as something behind started to scratch and scrape. Another grumble. There was another thud and the embedded round brass loop handle shot up then settled again.

"What the hell is that?" Jake said.

"Ah, that's Zeek."

"Zeek?"

"Zeek. My dog."

"Shit," Jake said, as he tried to sit more upright. "I really hate dogs."

Jake felt the little girl shudder, felt her squeeze into the gap behind him on the seat. He expected her to say something, but, as she had been since entering the warehouse, she was quiet.

"Ha, I'm sure he'd be pleased to see you too. He's

not been fed all day. At least he hasn't shit on my bed. Shove up," he said. "You can take the stove end if you like." He smiled. Jake thought there was a certain refrain to it, like it was forced.

He sat down next to Jake and handed him the glasses. "Hold these," he said. He bent down to the side of the seat and lifted up a board with a cushion attached to it, which he pushed onto the table, squirming it down with his free hand so that the top was level. He placed the bottle on it and watched for a while, making sure it would stay. He watched the liquid slosh then settle.

"Not bad. Not bad. These granny tables are awesome, don't you think?" he said, then without waiting for an answer, "Glasses."

Jake put the glasses on the board and noticed that on its surface was a picture of two fluffy yellow ducklings. He arranged the glasses so that each one was on a duckling's head.

"Okay," Bob said. "Now who's got OCD? Weird." He filled the glasses, and Jake got the whiff of strong whiskey that overpowered the earthy, musty smell of the plants.

"He used to have a brother," Bob said, looking at the door. "Seth. But Seth, er, well, he passed away. Ironic really."

Jake stared at the door. "What kind of dog is it?" he asked, pretty sure the answer would be a big one.

"He's a bulldog. British Bulldog. He's getting on a bit now and has this problem with his lower spine so he walks kinda funny. Nothing wrong with his front legs though. Or his mouth."

"Yeah, I can see that."

"He'll be quiet in a bit. He's just sniffing you out, Jake, is all. Like I said, he's not been fed all day." Bob smiled. "He's my guardian angel." He stared at the full glasses on the table. "Like your little girl. Kind of." He sighed. "Let's take this one straight down." He bowed his head towards the glass and his hair fell forward. He sighed again. "You know I don't have a shadow right?"

"I had noticed. Yeah."

"And you also know I'm not dead right?"

Bob swallowed his drink. Jake did the same and felt the old familiar sting. Bob filled the glasses back up.

"Kinda figured you were *between* them," Jake said, sounding harsher than he'd expected.

"No. Not at all. I've not had any kind of shadow for nearly two years now."

"What? How?" Jake said. He felt a sudden loss that everything he'd done for Emma had been a waste of time. "Two years. I mean. *How*? I've seen people dead, Bob. Seen them just lying dead the moment they have no shadow."

"They give up too easy. It's like packing up drinking, Jake." Bob lifted his glass. "People are weak. You think you could just give up the drink in one day and not touch it again? Takes a brave man, Jake."

"And you're a brave man right?"

"Nah. I was just lucky I think."

"Lucky."

"Yeah, listen," he said and moved in closer to

Jake as if he was scared someone else might hear him. "Turns out, if you don't have a shadow for a while you just become a goddamn beacon for any old Tom Dick or Harry shadow that's out there wandering around. And if you get the wrong one, or the wrong one gets you, they just fuck you up. You think it's only us humans that have a thirst for running around collecting shadows like we collect football stickers or porcelain cats or IKEA furniture? No."

Jake sniffed at his drink. Something about 'giving up the drink' was sticking in his head, making him think twice, making him test himself that he didn't have to drink this glass right away. "So they're just as goddamn materialistic as we are," Jake said. "Do they run commercials on shadow TV suggesting the next big thing in mobile shadow communication?" He downed the drink.

Bob laughed and Jake got the feeling he had seen the whole 'shall I shan't I drink' thing going on in his head. "And they don't like dogs, Jake. Bet you didn't know that."

"I can understand that."

"Those things won't come anywhere near me when Zeek or Seth are around. Well, when Zeek's around now. I don't know why. I don't know what would happen if Zeek got hold of a shadow. Hell not even sure he could. But there you go. No shadow for...God it's peaceful without them." He waved an arm. "You don't need to know all that shit. Probably never will. All that shit about the Reapers and the dogs and Luce and…and..."

"Reapers?" Jake said, raising an eyebrow.

"Reapers. Not sure that's really what they are, but. They're the ones you saw at the party. The ones that don't need a host, or ones that can detach somehow and move away. They're the ones that'll get to you." He shuddered. "But, not while Zeek's still around. Nope. They hate dogs, Jake. Did I tell you that?"

Silence.

Bob lifted his full glass into the air and examined it. "Right we'll get down to business," he said.

"To business," Jake said. This was it. This was what he was here for, he'd known it since stepping off the bus, but hearing it said out loud felt like he'd stepped into a cold waterfall. He lifted his glass.

"It's not a toast," Bob said. "But, okay. To business." He wasn't smiling. He was looking at Jake. Jake was looking back.

During the next few emptied then refilled glassed of whiskey they talked.

"That stupid little girlfriend of yours, she thought she was being clever. Smart. In a way she was. She thought she could waltz in here and get herself another shadow. No one would know. No one would miss another homeless person, especially from out of town, right? Well, she might have been right, except someone did miss this one.

"Edward Teach. I already said, he was a prize pain in the ass and when you guys killed him it was no big deal to me. Three days later though? It became a big deal. Moses turned up."

"Moses?" Jake said, taking another mouthful of drink.

Bob leaned back. "Yeah. Everyone who's anyone who ever had more than one shadow knows Moses. Except of course those that have no need to know him. Have no need to keep out of his way so to speak. You never heard of Moses and Luce?"

"No."

"Well, that was probably a good thing."

"Was? But now I have heard of him right?"

"Yeah. Like I say, anyone who ever hears the names Moses and Luce should probably be pretty pissed off. You pissed off, Jake?"

"No."

"Well, you should be. Or rather you will be. Have some more drink." Bob leaned over and filled Jake's glass. He finished his own and filled that.

"Moses and Luce live over the other side of town. Luce pretty much stays put, kinda quiet and out the way. But Moses, when he comes all the way over here for a *chat*... Well, If you can imagine alarm bells the size of fucking church bells ringing, that's what I heard. And felt. That motherfucker comes breezing over here and starts asking everyone politely if anyone has seen Teach. Scared most of the guys out there to death without even laying a finger on 'em.

"Anyway. I come back from town with a bag full, and I mean *full* of nice new razors, expecting to spend a while just shaving and chilling out, and Starmouth and Phil and Bent Jerry and Little Sis, they're all crowding me and tugging on my arms like they've just seen a ghost wander through. And they tell me Moses is here. And now I'm shitting myself and I pretty much lost my desire to have a shave, which I *never* do, Jake. Ever. And I come in here and there he is. Sat at this table, his arms out, his hands clenched, his knuckles pressed together and he asks me to sit down next to him."

"Just like we're sitting."

"Just like we're sitting. Yeah. This guy, Moses. He's huge. I mean big every way you look at him. He's like a concrete water tower that's always boiling. Massive square shoulders, big coat, stupid hat. And I'm sitting next to him and I just think, this is it, this is the end man and Zeek's nowhere to be found. Game over. And do you know what he says?"

Jake sighed. "Let's get down to business?" he said, drinking, waiting for Bob's exciting, scary gem of a bombshell to drop.

"No. He didn't even say that, the canny fuck. Didn't even waste time with that cute one liner. He just said, 'Tell me who killed Teach,' then he spread his hands out and clenched his fingers in and out a few times like he was counting the number of people he'd killed with them. So I told him straight. Told him I didn't know. And he just shook his head really, really slowly then pulled off his hat and put it on the table. And I swear to God, Jake, I felt my insides, from my throat down, just drop like a bag of shit into my anus. And Moses leaned back pushing his shoulders into the boat and I swear I hear the whole hull creak and squeal under the pressure. And I'm just wondering if I can make it out the door, through the wheelhouse and off across a field, when he starts snoring. Big fat rumbles deep in his throat. I dare to look over at him for the first time and he's fast asleep. Gone."

"And you did nothing," Jake said.

"Right. I did nothing. I sat next to him for twenty minutes watching my plants grow. All those thoughts about running away, or killing him, or squirming my way out, or shouting for help were all just jumbled into this tiny point of noise inside my brain that kept yelling 'you're fucked'.

"I've been scared before, Jake. I've been in so many impossible situations you wouldn't believe. And don't even think about saying 'try me'. You're not a stupid man. I think you get the picture."

"I'm not scared of Moses," Jake said. And he meant it.

Bob swallowed a near full drink then topped it up. Jake did the same.

"I used to tell myself the same thing, Jake. Until he sat down here and fell to sleep. Did you ever believe in God?"

"No. Never."

"That's good. So imagine one day, God comes and sits next to *you*."

Jake thought about the eventuality, about how he would feel, and what he might say to God.

"I'd probably ask him where he'd been all my life," he said, watching a stray drop of whiskey run down his finger and across the back of his palm. "Ask him why he'd spent so long fucking everything up for me and only just thought of sitting down with me."

"Good. And?"

"Ask him why, if he's so fucking big and clever he didn't visit more often so that I could ask who's fault everything was."

"And?"

"And what he was thinking when he made giraffes."

"Cool. But then imagine all of a sudden, you realise that this God sitting next to you, this guy with all this power that can just break everything you ever did into nothing, imagine he was sent by someone else."

Jake stared at a dull amber porthole, half covered in ivy, and he suddenly saw an image of Luce in his head that was the biggest thing he'd ever seen.

"You getting it now? The biggest, scariest, most confusing, most powerful thing in the world was told to sit down next to you by someone else."

Jake was angry. All this talk of gods and bigger gods and the mythical Luce, that for all he knew was made up, was distracting from the one big question. He slammed his glass onto the duck print wood and turned to Bob, who just looked right back.

"What the fuck has this got to do with me?" he said. "Seriously. Get to the fucking bit where you tell me how I'm all fucked again." The drink was making him slur, but in his head, his voice sounded solid and threatening. He felt he could take this Bob, this Moses, this Luce, the same way he'd taken Edward Teach.

"Hey. Don't get mad at me, Jakey. Not yet."

"So, how about I just get up and walk off this lopsided boat, sorry barge, and take my chances?"

Bob shook his head. "You can't just ask me to get to the good bit then threaten to walk out. You fucking idiot." Now it was Bob that was angry, and that anger came out as tiny balls of spit that splashed onto the bottle, onto the glasses, and onto Jake's arm. "Okay listen. In a bit, I'm going to take out a knife, Jakey. Big. Sharp."

Jake turned fast and his hands were around Bob's throat.

"I'm sick of this shit," he shouted into a blank face. "Fuck you. Fuck all of you."

"Let go, Jake. Now." Bob said.

Jake let go and shouted. "Arghh."

"I am going to take out this knife and I'm gonna stand up and I'm gonna go stand over there near those pretty purple flowers, and after I tell you what I need to tell you, *then,* I'm going to watch you just walk away, Jake. You get it? That's how this is going to go."

Silence.

"Good," Bob said. "Good."

He continued his story as if nothing had happened. "Moses is a collector. He goes out and about and he harvests shadows. For Luce."

Jake was drinking faster, he wanted the story to finish whilst he was in no fit state to hear it. So that he could wake up in the morning and worry about it then. Like some filthy one night stand.

Bob continued. "He's been doing it for ages now. Everyone knows. And Luce? She actually collects the shadows. Not like your dumb little girlfriend. Not like one at a time. No. She collects them and she keeps them and then, well, God knows what she does with them, but that's the story. I mean, Jake. Jake?"

Jake pulled his head up from a slump.

"So," Bob said, "she sends Moses out here to get all frosty, 'cause it tuns out, Teach, he was kinda trying to collect shadows for her as well. Or at least trying to find them. He was out here, scouting the place for shadows when all of a sudden you killed him. Luce got mad. Real mad apparently, that she'd lost this valuable resource and, all of another sudden, Moses turns up and falls asleep."

Jake groaned and pushed his fingers into his eyes.

Bob stood up and took a kitchen knife from his pocket. "And when he woke up. I spilled the beans."

Through half closed eyes, Jake watched him walk across the room and lean against the wall near the pretty purple flowers and look out the dull amber porthole.

Bob sighed. "I told him about you. And I told him about your stupid girlfriend. And Moses, he puts his hat back on and stands up and just stares down at me with eyes that, I swear, are full of every emotion there ever was, and I carry on talking. I tell him how Emma must have got Teach's shadow, and Moses, he actually looks like he's softening, like maybe I'm getting the answers right now. And then..." He turned to face Jake and held the knife low across his stomach in a clenched fist, "...as he looks at me some more with those eyes, I tell him about your little girl. About your shadow."

Jake understood now why the physical aspects of the conversation had gone this way, why he'd been sat down the same way Bob and Moses had. Why Bob had led him up to this point with a background story almost excruciatingly long, and why now, Bob stood the way he did with the knife the way it was.

Jake clutched the glass, saw himself hurl it towards Bob, saw himself slide around the table and crash into the tramp, crushing his ribs, wrestling away the knife and hacking away at his throat the way they don't do it in movies.

Instead, he finished his drink and picked up the bottle.

"What did you tell him about my little girl?" he said.

"Just what I saw, Jakey Baby. You, Emma, Teach, his shadow and your shadow. A little girl, maybe seven, eight, or nine. Clinging on to you like she'd always been there."

"You stupid, ignorant, selfish, stinking..." Jake swigged from the bottle.

"You should've seen Moses man. His eyes. They just lit up and he smiled. And me. All my insides came back to where they should be."

Jake stared for a long time, imagining what Bob's face would look like without skin, with the eyes gouged and hanging loose across glistening white cheekbones. He stood up.

"I'm tired," he said, swaying in the lopsided boat. "Sick of all this shit. If they come anywhere near me, Moses or Luce or anyone I don't know, I will kill them. Properly." He waved the bottle at Bob, and for the first time noticed how much more drunk he was than the clever bastard who stood opposite with his firm stance and shiny knife. "And if I see you again I erl." He tried to spit, but nothing came out.

"Hmm," Bob said. "Now you're really gonna be mad at me."

"Ah, fuck," Jake said, leaning on the table, his head hanging like a dead weight. "Here we go."

"I kinda told Moses where Emma lived."

Jake exhaled and his lips rasped. "Fuck that bitch," he shouted. "Fuck her."

"They probably will. They might even ask her where you live. Ask *her* all about your little girl. About you. About what makes you tick, Jake. I say might. I think I mean *will*. Just so's you know."

Jake slumped to the floor, his legs sliding down the boat, the bottle tumbling from his hands and rolling to where Bob picked it up and swigged from it. Bob opened the door, and Zeek came plodding out. He was a huge white bulldog with a patch of brown down his left side. His head was massive and square, his eyes pink and partly closed, his nose big and wet and his tongue fat and swaying. Jake watched the massive white beast become larger in his vision. He watched the ripples and creases of muscle as each shoulder lifted and fell, closer, lifted and fell, larger.

Zeek's face was so close that only one half of it was visible. Jake grumbled. Zeek grumbled back, a deep guttural sigh. He moved one large brown eye right up close to Jake and exhaled like a tired old man then lay down, his paws sideways, his chin on the ground so that his jowls spread.

The little girl shuddered. Zeek lifted a fat, saggy

eye. His ears picked up.

"To business, Jake," Bob said, and swigged from the bottle.

Jake closed his eyes and the angel was gone.

Chapter Eleven

In the dark of the cellar, bright white light picked out the smooth edges of stone as Luce twisted the square spot-lamp left to right. She lifted her fingers to her nose and inhaled the stench of her woollen gloves that had been toasted by the heat of the halogen work light. She shifted the lamp some more.

Standing with his back against the wall, Moses swayed from one foot to the other, his hands outstretched, palms forward to stop the glare.

"Moses," Luce said, standing up straight and rubbing her hands down her hips. "Stay still."

In the glare, Moses could see Luce as nothing more than a shape, a swarm of black and grey bees shimmering.

She walked around the tripod that held the lamp. She was wearing a long, red dress that shimmered on the side lit by the lamp. The other side still looked pure black. As she approached Moses, she rubbed at two white crescents of dust across the top of her breasts. The white faded into pink and motes of it picked up into the air and fell as slivers of silver around her. She rubbed her fingers together and more dust fell. The dress stopped just above her ankles, just above white socks and black church shoes with silver straps. Her bare forearms stopped just above black winter gloves that were white at the fingertips. On her head was a dome hat made of feathers laid in concentric circles; grey at the top fading through pink then to blue around her forehead and ears. The feathers fluttered as she bent down to a table and picked up a large piece of pure white chalk.

Moses stared past the feathers, past the hat, past the straightness of her nose and into her cleavage. He shuffled his feet again and pulled at the front of his trousers.

"Moses," Luce said, pointing the bevelled end of that pure white chalk at his face.

"Okay," he said, pulling his trousers again then pressing his back against the damp wall.

"It's time to take this one off you," she said, smiling on one side of her face.

Moses grunted like a waking pig. Luce raised an eyebrow and jabbed him in the shoulder with the chalk.

"Hey," he said, batting away her hand then looking down at his brown shirt and rubbing at the chalk dust mark. "This was clean on." He rubbed some more, spreading the mark into a faint blotch.

"Then get your head," she pointed at his trousers with the chalk, "both your filthy heads, out of the gutter and into the cellar or I'll chalk up your whole damn wardrobe."

Moses stopped rubbing and flattened himself as much as he could against the wall, palms flat on the cold stone.

"You wouldn't waste the chalk," he said.

"Then I'll burn your clothes." She meant it. "With you in them." And she meant that as well.

She ran her tongue along the length of the chalk then flicked it across the end, closing her eyes and moaning.

"Motherfucker," Moses said, moving his stare to the brown-black ripples of the floorboard ceiling.

Luce laughed. She stepped back and raised her hand to her chin, examining the scene before her like it was a painting on a gallery wall. She stepped forward, crouched and rubbed at the faint white marks to one side of Moses. She examined her gloves. Rubbed the wall some more. Stepped back. Examined some more.

"Okay, now half a step forward," she said.

Moses, staying perfectly straight and upright, shifted forward like a slow motion cardboard cut out in a ghost train.

Luce stepped back, stood up and waved her hand in front of the spotlight casting her shadow across Moses and the wall. She closed her eyes, sighed, then opened them again.

"Half a step more," she said.

Moses, his eyes closed against the glare of the light, barely moved.

"He's crying," he said.

"I know," Luce said. She crouched, resting her backside on her heels. "Good," she said. "Now don't you move. Either of you."

She took a step towards the wall and with her arm stretched out to one side so as not to block the light, she drew the outline of the crying boy in chalk.

Silence.

The hum of white-blue light.

A shuffle of church shoes.

A voice like that of a mother talking to a child with grazed knees. "Okay, Moses. Step away."

Moses took a long step away from the wall. There was a bright flash in his head and pain like lightning striking him in the teeth. He fell hard onto his knees and threw up, vomit filling the gaps between his outstretched fingers then splashing onto the floor and back up into his face. He shook his head and wiped sinuous strings of spit and sick away from his lips, watching it slop to the floor.

"You okay?" Luce said from behind him.

Moses rubbed the mess from his hand into the floor. "Yeah. Okay." Sick ran down the bone of his wrists. "But how many times, Luce? A bucket. A towel. A glass of water?"

Luce didn't answer. She stood staring at the thick white outline on the wall. Inside that outline was pure black that even the spotlight couldn't pick out.

"Another little party boy for the pot," she said, placing the chalk back on the table.

As she walked up the steps out of the cellar, she turned to see Moses, his face, hands, and hair slick with bile. He stared at her with empty, soulless eyes.

"Turn out the light when you come up," she said.

Upstairs, Luce sat at the end of the table, her red dress still dusted on her breasts, shoulders, and hips with fine chalk. She had taken off the feather hat, and her silver hair stood up in wisps like a growing thundercloud. The stereo played a Tibetan Singing Bowl mediation CD. She was arranging Mahjong tiles into a pile, face down in the middle, face up around the edges.

Moses sat at the corner of the table next to her.

"That shirt was clean on," he said, pulling at the one he wore now. He pulled it up at the shoulders where it was tight. He pulled it out at the front, looking down at his breasts.

"It needed washing," Luce said, placing the last two tiles, face up on the centre of the shallow pyramid she had built.

"It did not," Moses said, grunting as he pulled the too short sleeves down over his wrists. Everywhere he pulled, another part of the shirt tightened. "It was clean on," he said, examining the way the shiny white buttons on the cuffs strained not to break.

Luce took a tile from the edge of the pyramid, a single, large circle imprinted with a flower pattern, then another matching tile from the other side.

"It had chalk on it," she said.

Moses reached over. The button on his left sleeve popped off and hung from its thread. He turned over the two tiles that Luce had uncovered so that their patterns showed.

"East wind," he said looking at the picture on one of them, "And a two bamboo." He pulled the other button off and rolled the sleeves up to just below his elbows. They wouldn't roll up any further.

For the next few tiles there was only the low resonant sound of Tibetan Singing Bowls and the clicking of tiles being turned.

"Another wind. South," Moses said. Luce took them from the pile.

"I can play this game forever," she said, running her fingers over the tiles, feeling the bumps and indentations of the patterns.

Moses sat back, unbuttoned the top of his shirt and twisted his head around like he'd been freed from a noose.

The pile on the table was getting smaller.

"Forever?" he said.

Luce looked at him, "Forever is only until the end, Moses."

"Why do you play with these tiles?"

"It's relaxing, Moses. You?"

"I just want to know if we can finish it. This bloody game is too much like every day for it to be relaxing for me."

"How many times have we matched *all* the tiles?"

"Two. Three times maybe."

"Two times. We turn over hundreds of tiles, together. We match them and we feel tiny moments of hope. Tiny bits, when we uncover another tile that we know will match and we can uncover more."

"Still too much like everyday for me to relax."

She looked at him with genuine sadness. "You never always thought that. Did you?"

"I don't remember now," he said, his voice flat and quiet.

"It's strange you think that way. Like you just want to win all the time. Every time. To get to the end. To finish."

Moses was quiet. He reached across to the pile, his forehead creased up above his eyebrows, and matched winter and summer. Luce turned over two fresh tiles.

"Fuck it," Moses shouted. He stood up, waved his hands in the air, pulled his shirt out of his trousers and left the room, still tugging at his elbows and shoulders.

Luce looked at the tiles and smiled. She pushed them all into a dark cloth bag and pulled the string around its top.

As the tiles clattered, Abe spoke. "He's just a brute now," he said, matter of factly.

"He's worn out, Abe. He just wants to see an end to everything. To win all the time."

"I think he just wants the end."

"No. Abe. You're not to touch him. Okay?"

"Just saying."

"And after that? What then, Abe? You'll go out and do his job for me?"

"You know I can't do that."

"Then shut up."

"But what's the use? He used to set the tiles up and play with you for hours. Remember he used to insist that you play Chopin or Philip Glass or..."

"Steve Reich," Luce interrupted.

"Steve Reich. The piano ones. You'd match as many of the tiles as you could and when you finally realised there were no more to match, he'd set up the whole thing again while you...while you did stuff to him. Now, he just walks off when he can't get his own way. He wants the end. But he's scared to admit it. A brute."

Luce heard Moses up in the bedroom. Heard the wardrobe doors slam. She placed the bag of tiles on the table. She heard Moses walk down the bare boards of the stairs. She leaned forward and rested her forehead on the soft bag. She heard the front door click shut. *I wish*, she thought as the sound of singing bowls became louder, *that all the tiles just matched this time. We were so close.*

"I know you do," Abe whispered. Then he said, "Luce?"

"Mmm?" she said, fingering the tiles through the cloth and listening to them click.

"He's not taken his hat."

"Looks like he's gone out to set his own game up then."

"Yes," Abe said. "One that he can win."

Chapter Twelve

Jake opened his eyes. There was pain in his temples. His neck was stiff. His back hurt.

"Where am I?" he said, staring at a scratchy circular pattern of amber light reflected in plastic.

"Nearly home, my friend," said an unfamiliar voice. "Good night?"

There was a jolt, and Jake fell back into a comfy seat.

"A taxi?"

"Yeah man, big yellow taxi. Nearly home now. Man you look messed up. Good night?"

"No," Jake said abruptly, rubbing at the back of his neck. "Not a good night."

"Ah, like that, eh?" the taxi driver said.

Jake looked around at the parked cars flashing past, all tinged with the orange of the streetlights.

"Where am I going?" he said. Panic was setting in. He didn't recognise the roads slithering past. He couldn't turn his head to focus on street signs as they rolled behind into nothing.

"Hey, don't worry, my friend," the taxi driver said. "Rowan Grove. Right? Rowan Grove."

"My street. Yeah." Jake couldn't decide if he was surprised or not. Why was he in this taxi? Why was he going home?

The driver laughed. "Good. Your house, my

friend. Let's hope you've got some food in eh?"

Jake grunted.

The taxi driver laughed. "Maybe stop off on the way back. You'll have change from the twenty I'm sure."

"Change? No. No food. Thanks. Twenty?"

"Yeah man. Man. You are messed up. Just don't go being... Anyway. Yeah. Home soon, James."

"James?"

"Not James? Ah. Well. Okay."

"Who told you James?"

"Your friend. He bundled you in, tells me eighteen Rowan Grove and hands me a twenty. Nice chap. Clean-shaven, daft hair. Drunk as you, I think. But nice. Bit stinky mind, but hey, you out all night partying and dancing and drinking and such and well. Let's just say I get used to the smell." He tapped his knuckles on the plastic that separated him from the back seats. "Not just for the dick heads you know. Keeps out the smell as well." He laughed.

"Did my friend say anything else?"

"Nope. Just to take good care of you. And I am. Home soon." He flicked on the indicators, and Jake heard the familiar, friendly 'click clack—this is your taxi home'.

"The girl smelled real nice though. Like alcoholic fruit. She been drinking Bacardi Breezers? Melon?"

"The girl?"

"Yeah. The girl with the eyes. Hey man. Pretty, pretty eyes. Smelled nicer than you."

Jake shook his head and smiled at the thought of Freesia.

"Where'd you pick me up from?" he said.

"The old ironworks," the driver said. "I can't tell you I was happy to take that job. It's a bit spooky out there at night. Nice quiet country lanes and all though. But yeah. What were you all doing tonight? Some kind of illegal rave?"

"No. Not a..." Jake paused and pressed his fingers into his eyes. He really didn't want to go through this now. "Yeah kind of I guess. Just a rave. Not illegal though. More like just a gathering." He stared at the tiny camera on the taxi's dashboard and only then noticed all the tickets and plaques that said this was a real taxi with a real driver with real fares and real fines for being sick and real surveillance for your comfort and that of the real driver.

"Ha. No worries my friend."

Jake pushed himself back into the seat in an attempt to stop his spine aching.

"Rowan Grove. Which one?" the driver said.

Jake rested his forehead against the cold glass and felt his teeth chatter with the vibration of the taxi. "Yeah. Just down here on the left. Brown Mondeo."

"Brown Mondeo it is."

The taxi stopped.

"Fourteen eighty," the driver said. "Told you there'd be change. Could have got yourself a pizza or a kebab after all. Still not too late for ordering a takeout, my friend."

"I'll be fine," Jake said, pulling at the cold silver handle in its plastic goldfish bowl guard. The handle didn't budge.

"Hang on there," the driver said. "Okay, try it

again."

Jake pulled the lever up and stepped out. "Keep the change," he said.

"You sure, my friend? I mean it's nearly five pounds."

"Yeah I'm sure, my friend. It's not my five pounds anyway."

He slammed the door shut and dug around in his pocket for his house keys. He dug in his other pocket and lifted them out. The taxi drove away. Jake examined his keys. There were only two but he was having trouble focusing on them so he ran his finger across them feeling for the one with the more severe, sharper ridges in it. He squeezed it hard between his thumb and forefinger and holding it out, trudged up the drive, leaning along the length of his car for support. He burped, and acid came up into his throat. He opened the door on the first attempt and stepped inside. He found the light switch on the first attempt.

"Emma?" he said. There was no answer. "Emma. You here?" He stumbled over to the chair and leaned on its back. There was still no answer. It was her smell that made him think she was in the house. He looked around. Sniffed hard. It was her perfume, her smell.

He reached into the fridge, pulled out a plastic bottle of milk and drank, clutching his head as the cold hit. He drank the rest of the bottle and put it back, empty, into the fridge door. He stared at an open packet of sausage rolls, at an opened packet of mini scotch eggs, at an opened tub of cheese spread with its edges stale the colour of ear wax. He reached into the fridge and curled his fingers around an unopened tub of apricot yoghurt which he tilted towards him. As the rippled, glossy, foil numbers came into view, they told him that the low fat apricot yoghurt was almost a month out of date. He let go of the yoghurt and watched as it rocked back into place then he closed the door.

He shuffled over to the kitchen sink and drank straight from the tap, ignoring the ice-cold water that ran down his cheek, his chin, his neck, and into his armpit, his back, his legs.

He stood staring out the window at the black and orange-lit street but there was nothing, no cars, no people, no animals.

"Jake?" the girl said, her voice warm inside his frozen head.

"Not now."

"But I need to tell you something."

"Can't it wait?"

"No."

"Until my head's better?"

"No, Jake. I need to tell you this. While there's time."

Jake continued to stare out the window, willing leaves to blow past, for a fox to poke its head out from behind a wall, for something, anything, to happen.

"There's no one out there, Jake. Not now. Not yet," the girl said.

Jake sighed. "I'm done now," he said. "For real."

"Done?"

"Yeah. Done." He turned around and slumped

down, sitting on the floor. "Those fucking tramps. Bob. Those freaks. Moses. That woman witch, thing, Luce. I'm done. I'm just going to keep my head down and let them get on with it. They're welcome to each other."

"And *her?* Emma?"

"Whatever," he said, rubbing his temples then pinching the top of his nose and making a clucking noise through his nostrils. "If she's smart, she'll keep her head down as well."

"But I don't think they'll stop, Jake."

"Hmm?"

"Not now. Not any of them."

"No. I'll just ignore all of this. It'll be fine." He could feel himself drifting off to sleep, and he honestly felt happy with his plan. He felt like it should work.

"Yeah," he slurred. "Just keep my head down."

The girl laughed.

"I wish I could laugh," he said, exhaling a faint grunt. "But my head hurts, and my ass is now wet."

The girl sounded angry but full of pity at the same time. "It's not about you, Jake. Remember your dream about the storm? You made it rain just so that people would recognise you. So that you could feel important and feel loved and wanted and noticed. Remember?"

"Of course I remember."

"But it was never about you, Jake."

"You?"

Silence.

"This is all about you?" Jake said, blinking to

keep his dry, stinging eyes open against sleep.

"I think so. Yes. Emma only came round after I was here."

"I was ill."

"You were never poorly before?"

"Well of course I was."

"And she came to see you all the times you were poorly before? Did she help you then and buy you medicine and..." she paused as if thinking about whether or not to continue. "Did she go to sleep in the same bed as you all those times as well when you were poorly?"

Jake shook his head.

The girl continued. "And that stinky, smelly man, Bob. He knew me, Jake. I could feel it. When we were on his boat. All the time he was thinking about me and trying to work me out, I could almost feel him asking questions in his head about me. And the dog knew me, Jake. The dog came right up and just laid his head next to me. Like he was my very own pet. And I wasn't scared of him then."

"He lay next to me as well. In case you'd forgotten. He slobbered on my face. Not yours."

The girl sniggered. "I know. That was funny."

"No. Not funny," Jake said, rubbing his face, glad that the tap water had cleared his cheek of sticky, foul smelling dog slobber.

He felt the girl shudder. "And Moses and Luce. I have heard of them before," she said.

"You've heard of them. And you never told me?"

"Until you heard of them, why would I? They know me as well, Jake. I think. The tramp and the dog and Moses and that witch Luce. I think they all know me. I think it's all about me. I think you know that as well don't you, Jake?"

"I think I always did," he said sighing. "I knew something like this would happen."

"I'm scared, Jake. I don't think they'll stop. Never ever. And I think you are just in their way now. But they won't stop."

Jake's eyes had been closed for a while. His head was hanging forward, swaying gently on the edge of sleep. But he could still hear his breath as a deep rumble in the back of his throat, and above that, quiet and soft, the girl was still speaking.

"I want to show you something, Jake," she said, her voice drifting left to right in the emptiness of his skull.

"Show me?"

"Yes. I want to show you where the shadows came from. The ones at that party when they came and I helped you get away. When I helped you hide from them under the big telly screen. Remember?"

"Hmm. But why now?" Jake whispered.

"Because I don't want you to give up on me, Jake. Not now. I'm scared, and you're the only thing that makes me not scared. And I need you, Jake. I love you."

"You just want me between them and you, don't you?"

"Yes. But for us, Jake. I need you to look after me so that we can be together. That's all. Isn't that why people love each other?"

Jake jumped. He'd been wakened from his near

sleep. He opened his eyes and began to stand up. "I guess you'd better show me then," he said.

"No. Sit down. Sit."

"Hey," he said, slouching back down, "I'm not a dog. Is this going to make my headache go away?"

"Ha. I don't think so. Close your eyes and I'll hold your hand and you just follow me." Her voice sounded light, excited.

"But I can't feel your hand," Jake said, looking at his own hands resting on his outstretched legs.

"Oh. Well. Okay."

There was a pause.

"Okay," she said. "Listen to the clock. That might help. Don't think about my hand holding yours. Just listen to the..."

...faint tick...

"...quiet tick of the clock that's..."

...faint tick...

A small cold hand in his.

"...ticking ever so slowly. The broken ticking..."

...faint tick... fainter...

"...in the background. A long way away..."

Cold fingers gripping the side of his palm.

...faint click...a high ping of a piano note...tick...

Jake felt his arm lifting and then his whole body tilted forward and he was in the air for a fraction of a second being pulled by his arm and teased and stretched and his fingers and arm and shoulders were all being gently teased through a tiny hole something like a funnel, and then his head and shoulders and chest were all compressed and moulded and thinned out to a fine stream of existence in a cold breeze that smelled of freshly washed clothes and wet soil and his senses stretched and whistled into the air like ripped cloth strands as he was drawn into precisely nothing then further nothing then he felt all teased back out into something the way he'd come with the breeze as the smells became stronger and his body seemed to find substance as the rips were all stitched back together. He felt the air shifting around him and her tiny hand in his and there was cold at his back and...

"Don't move, Jake."

"Hmm."

"Don't lean forward and don't let go of my hand."

Her grip was firm. And warm.

Jake stood with his back firmly pressed against smooth, cold rock.

"Jesus Christ," he said, looking down. His feet were on a narrow ledge of moss-green rock, his heels against the wall behind him and his toes almost poking out over a sheer drop. His right hand clutched a smooth brown, pitted iron railing that ran around the ledge behind him at waist height. His shoulders, calf muscles, and buttocks ached with the effort of holding on. A few small shrubs grew out of the sheer rock face just below him, and past those, hundreds of feet down, he could see a swirl of black and grey like smoke crawling along a ceiling.

"Where the hell are we?" he said, his voice shaking.

"Just don't let go. Please."

"I'm not letting go. Believe me. Where are we?"

"This is the Giddy Edge."

"Giddy Edge?"

"It used to be a place of fun, Jake. A place of fantasy. The Victorians used to walk along here just because it was frightening and beautiful. That's what they did. I like that story. Can you imagine those people in their big dresses or their top hats and suits, pulling themselves around this ledge using the railing, maybe holding umbrellas, and talking about how great it was and how beautiful and frightening it all was? And, well, it must have been just *grand*."

"Grand. Yeah. I can imagine." Jake stared out across into nothing. No grand views. No grand ravines or grand rivers. No grand people. "Why have you brought me here?"

"Because things change. People do things that are wrong or bad or stupid and everything changes and it can never go back to how it was."

"Is that why you brought me here. To tell me that things can never go back to how they were? Don't you think I already know that? I've spent my whole life knowing that."

"But do you know what else they called this place?" She squeezed his hand harder and Jake thought he could smell fresh flowers, or perfume.

"It was Lover's Leap. Men and women who were in love would come here. They were scared of the future. They were so deeply in love that they wanted to be together forever and never let the future get in their way. So even when they loved each other so very much, they would come up here and hold hands. And they would say, 'I love you', and maybe kiss, and say how they would love each other forever. Then they would just step off the edge, Jake. Still holding hands. They would be dead together forever."

She was crying and Jake could hear her close to him as her breath caught in her chest between sobs. He felt a lump in his throat. "Hey," he said, squeezing her hand, "that was a long time ago, sweetie. A long, long time ago."

"I know," she said through her sobs. "But it's just such a beautiful thing for them to do. Don't you think?"

"I don't know. I can't imagine being *so* close to someone that I could ever do that." He looked down. "Hey, hang on."

The girl laughed and it was the loudest, most real, warm laugh that Jake had ever heard from her.

"Don't be silly. We're not going over there. Not now." She laughed again and there was the fresh smell of wash powder, or cherries. Bubblegum or soap.

"Good. You had me worried there for a bit. You holding my hand so tight like that." He squeezed her hand again in his.

"Don't you see that this place changed after that?" she said, "All the beauty had gone away. The people that were so in love were dead at the bottom of this cliff. And no one else could ever come up here without knowing that. Not ever again."

Jake understood what he was seeing at the bottom of the cliff. "And their shadows had nowhere to go," he said, knowing that what was below them was a mass of writhing shadows, darting and weaving like a flock of starlings hemmed in on all sides by a predator. "They're all the shadows of people who died here. Aren't they?"

"No. It started that way. I think. But over time, lots of years, well, they're all the shadows of anyone who ever loved or felt loved. Ever. Or shadows that were sad and lost and needed to feel loved just once for real."

Jake heard the girl breathing. He felt her tiny thumb drawing circles in his palm.

"They are the real Lost Dark, Jake."

He stared again at the shadows. "Wow. That's awful."

"They have no future. They just stopped being."

"Gone apart from being," he mumbled.

"Jake?"

"Hmm?"

"Look at me, Jake."

Jake was trying to pick out individual forms in the mass below, trying to recognise the faces of men, or women, or children. He stared at the moss beneath his feet. He turned his head.

And she was there.

He looked into her small round face, at her large amber eyes that were wet and glassy with tears. He let go of her hand and she smiled, her tiny pink lips lifting freckles up on her cheeks. Jake felt his legs go weak, felt his heart stop, then start, then flutter. He placed his left hand on top of her long, straight blonde hair, and the smell hit him again.

"Shampoo," he shouted.

The little girl wrinkled her nose and laughed.

"Shampoo."

He ran his thumb across her head feeling the individual strands of hair. "Cherry shampoo," he said.

The girl laughed. "Yes, Jake. Cherry shampoo. I always use it when I wear this dress." She reached down and pulled at her long shiny red dress so that it spread out and floated down. Then she fiddled with a large red bow around her waist and teased it out into a ribbon. She held it out over the ledge and dropped it so that it fluttered down.

"Oh, sweetie," Jake said.

He wanted to bend down, to pick her up, to hold her and to inhale the smell of cherry shampoo into his nostrils and to rub his cheek into her hair and wipe the tears from her face and he let go of the iron railing to reach around so that he could hold her in both hands.

He saw her eyes widen. Her mouth opened. Her eyebrows flickered up. He heard her tiny voice scream and watched her recede into the distance as he fell back past the ledge, past the green shrubs, past the grey rocks. She became a tiny red light that dimmed as he fell away further and into the shadows.

Chapter Thirteen

Jake opened his eyes and groaned. He was sitting with his back against the kitchen cupboards. He pushed his hands down his thighs and rubbed his knees. His whole body was hot and stiff.

He stood up stretching his feet, his calves, his thighs, his arms, and his shoulders. It felt good to be so stiff and aching but to stretch it out.

He brought his hands to his face and inhaled fresh cherry shampoo.

"Out there on the edge," he said to the girl. "You were real."

"I am real, Jake," she said.

"I know. I mean, you were real. Solid. I could touch you."

"You were where we are. That's all."

"I could smell you. I could feel the warmth from you."

"I can't take you there again."

"But you were real."

The little girl sounded cross. "I *am* real."

"I want to go back," he said, clenching his fingers in and out to stretch more pain out of his forearms. "I want to go back there now."

"No. It's not...natural."

Jake laughed. "Natural?"

"Then it's too dangerous."

"Dangerous?"

She spoke in such a way that Jake imagined her stamping her feet.

"Then there's no time. That's all," she said.

Jake looked out the window. "Figures," he said.

The air felt thick and heavy. He looked up at the clouds.

"He's coming, Jake."

"I know."

"He's close. And I'm scared."

"I know," Jake said again. He watched a young girl with blonde bobbed hair, pink coat, blue jeans, and black trainers, as she dropped her BMX onto the pavement. She walked up the path of Mr. Simmon's house and posted a newspaper. She walked back down the path, closed the gate behind her, picked up her bike then cycled on.

"Wait," he said.

The little girl sounded anxious. "What? What is it? What do you see? Is it him?"

"I've just realised that I don't even know what day it is."

The little girl sounded relieved. "Really?"

"Yeah, really. The last time I remember, it was Tuesday. I think."

"It's Tuesday today, silly" she said, a hint of a laugh in her voice.

"Really?"

"Yes, really."

"Crap," he said, peeling off his shirt and throwing it in front of the washing machine that stood out from the counter at an angle.

Any other day, he would have been self-conscious, standing in his window shirtless, while a young girl delivered papers, and an old man in his black dressing gown stared at him whilst adjusting the belt around his middle. But right now, he didn't care.

"I need a shower," he said. "Badly."

"You can't," the girl said, fear back in her tiny voice. "Not now."

"Why not? I stink. I feel slimy. I feel like shit."

"But he's so close. Moses is so close. I can feel his emptiness."

"Well," he said, walking into the bathroom. "Maybe I feel like being clean when he arrives. Maybe even naked."

"Jake. What do you mean?"

"Maybe it will put him off. Maybe the sight of my naked body will actually scare him."

"I don't think I understand you sometimes."

"Good," he said, looking at his teeth in the mirror, at the way his gums looked yellow and grey and pulled back around his teeth. "I'll stick you on my list of people who don't understand me."

After the shower, Jake brushed his teeth for a long time, concentrating on his gums. When he switched off his electric toothbrush, he could hear the TV in the other room, an advert for cruise holidays. He imagined it all. A dark blue expanse of calm ocean. A huge, pure white cruise-liner cuts across the screen. The camera swings up and over the ship, then down onto the deck. There's a woman in a yellow bikini. Slim. Tanned. Huge, bug-eyed sunglasses. She's sipping an impossibly pink cocktail. There's a man. Tanned. Broad shoulders. Huge white smile with perfect teeth and perfect gums. He's sipping whiskey and ice from a square tumbler.

Jake pushed his hair back and clenched his teeth. He pushed his shoulders back and his chest out.

"When this is done," he said, licking at the smoothness of his teeth, "I'm gonna go on a cruise."

The girl sounded surprised. "On a ship. On the sea?"

"On the sea," he said.

"But," she paused as if wondering whether to carry on. She carried on. "You're afraid of the sea aren't you?"

"Only a little, but...hey, how did you know that?"

"I don't know," she said.

Jake opened the bathroom door and the steam billowed out around him. He felt cold, fresh air across his damp chest and shoulders.

In Jake's chair, a large man in a perfectly pressed, off-white shirt, sat staring at the TV. He pointed the remote, and with each click, jabbed it towards the TV.

"Moses," Jake said.

He'd never seen the man before, but his presence was, as he'd been led to believe, impressive.

"Hello, Jake," Moses said, still flicking through the channels. "You actually watch this shit?" His voice was deep and rough, like a man who'd spent his life shouting at people but now knew how to control it. He leaned forward, his elbows sinking deep into the fabric of the chair.

"Sometimes," Jake said, walking over to the fridge and opening it. "Can you stop flicking channels?"

He reached into the fridge, pulled out a carton of apple juice and flipped open the plastic lid, surprised to see it was a fresh, sealed box. "It's really annoying. There are only five channels." He picked at the foil seal under the white plastic cap, the edge pricking under his fingernail, before he managed to pull the tab off. He threw the foil tab back into the fridge then turned around, the cold from the open fridge on his back.

Moses switched off the TV and placed the remote on the arm of the chair.

"Helps when you're drunk," Jake said.

"Helps?" Moses said, sounding genuinely intrigued.

"When you're drunk, it seems like there's more channels than just the five."

"I guess that makes sense," Moses said, rubbing his broad chest with one hand.

Jake noticed that his knuckles were leathery, brown and cracked, split across the middles with white-pink scar tissue.

"Drink?" Jake said.

"You do know why I'm here?" Moses said, and for the first time he turned to look at Jake.

Jake understood then why everyone was so scared of the man. He had never seen a grizzly bear before, but he had heard that their eyes are deep and black and intelligent and timeless. Moses had those eyes.

Eyes that didn't seem to have enough time in the world to tell the stories that they could tell. Jake felt smothered and tiny, swallowed in a dark blanket.

"Are you scared, Jake?" Moses said.

Jake felt his face pull its usual look of puzzlement and realised that Moses must have seen it too.

He smiled. "Shit no. I always pull this face when I drink cold apple juice. It's the cold and the acid all at once. Couldn't tell you why. It's just my apple juice face." He drank some more juice and pulled another face. "See?" he said.

Moses stood up, rising like a mountain in an earthquake, slow, solid, immeasurable. But Jake thought that something about his hair made him look softer than he should have been, it seemed to smudge out his harshness.

"You know, Jake," Moses said, pointing a lazy, bent finger, "I'm not sure if I'm pissed at you being such a wise ass, or if I'm maybe just from a different generation and I just don't get you."

Jake shrugged but he was scared. Right down to the cold apple juice in his stomach, he felt scared and trapped. He knew that if Moses were to close the gap between them now, that he'd be crushed into a ball against the inside of the open fridge.

"Scotch," Moses said. "If you have some. I'll take a scotch."

"There's a half a bottle of CO-OP stuff over on the kitchen worktop. Help yourself."

"Very kind. Very...reasonable."

"Hey, Moses, listen. I can be reasonable."

Moses walked to the worktop, picked up the

bottle and, staring out the window, took a large swig. "Some people, woo that's harsh whiskey, some people do try to reasonable, Jake. But, to tell you the truth it's usually too late. I don't usually do reasonable."

"But you drink my whiskey anyway?"

"Jake, this is not great whiskey. I'm doing you a favour."

"Moses, you're my guest, in my house, and you're telling me that my whiskey is unreasonable?"

Moses reached up and looked as if he was adjusting a hat that wasn't there. He smoothed his hair.

"I'm not your guest," he said, staring at Jake, "I let myself in." Moisture bubbled up along the side of his lips. "You fuck."

"I left the door open, Moses."

Moses shook his head. "I've not got time for your bravado. You have something I want and I'm here to take it. Invited or not invited."

He moved towards Jake, slow deliberate, powerful steps. As he picked up speed, he was on Jake in three or four steps, hunched forward to ram him.

Jake reached into the fridge and it was more luck than skill that, as Moses got close he slipped on apple juice that Jake had let dribble into the floor from his tilted carton. Jake swung his arm and Moses's head connected with a heavy ceramic oven dish. He fell forward and Jake managed to dodge the crashing, grasping man. The oven dish was snapped in half and lay on the floor in a pile of wasted pasta sheets and ratatouille. As Moses tried to scramble to his feet, Jake kicked at his face with his bare foot. Moses caught Jake across his shin with his forearm. Jake tried to stamp on Moses with his other foot, but Moses brought his hand up and shoved Jake back. Now it was Jake who was on the floor, and Moses was pushing himself up from a kneeling position.

Jake was on his back and tried to push himself upright, but his arms wouldn't bend far enough. There was an almighty white flash and he screamed. Moses had kicked him hard in the groin. The blow hadn't hit Jake's balls but had connected between them and his ass cracking hard into the bone. Moses placed one knee on his chest, crushing the wind out of him and exerting so much pressure that he thought his breastbone might snap down the centre.

"Well," Moses said, his breath heavy and laboured, "that doesn't happen to me so much."

He brought his fist down into Jake's face, just below his left eye. Another white flash. But no pain. Jake scrabbled around the floor for something to fight back with. The oven dish had been pure luck. Now he'd run out of luck.

Moses grabbed the front of Jake's hair and lifted him up so hard that his back cracked between his shoulder blades. His head smacked into the floor, and he closed his eyes tight, waiting for another blow. He heard the little girl screaming. He managed to squirm around and push himself back against the bookcase where he lifted himself up a little, opening the one eye that still worked.

"You see, Jake," Moses said, standing over him

and holding something large and black in his hand, "all that talk. That bravado. That cocky, younger generation shit. It all meant nothing. Just a convenient breather for you."

Jake reached up to the shelf above him, feeling around for something, anything. Moses stepped over him and brought the long black object down hard on his hand. There were multiple sounds, bones cracking, sinew separating, cartilage popping, wood splitting, a thump on the carpet beside him. This time the pain was remarkable and Jake held his hand in front of him. It looked like a soggy, weather-beaten baseball. Two tiny off-white crescents of middle knuckle showed through a split in the skin. His forefinger was bent underneath his middle finger. The tip of his ring finger was a soggy, bloody mess. He couldn't work out, through the panic and the hot pain in that finger, if the white-blue point at the end was a ripped off fingernail, or his bone jutting out. His thumb and little finger seemed relatively unscathed.

He took a deep breath and screamed until his lungs were empty. As he was just about to black out, he placed his good hand on the floor to steady himself and felt the thing that had fallen from the shelf. He took another deep breath, and curled his fingers tight around the handle.

Moses smiled a smug defiant winner's smile.

Jake smiled back on one side of his face as the other swelled.

"It's such a shame I can't actually kill you, Jake," Moses said stepping in even closer so that his right foot was between Jakes legs. "But I will. Once Luce has the little girl. I'll kill you then. Might even practice my strangulation." He laughed. Then he tilted his head and looked confused as Jake spoke.

"Don't worry, sweetie," Jake said. "I won't let him." He thrust the screwdriver straight into Moses's shin. The long, flat blade scraped off the bone inside, but Jake felt it punch through muscle and pop out the back of the leg. He rolled onto his side, and the blade pulled sideways then scraped back over the bone before sliding out at the front again.

Jake was on his feet, shaking the blood out of his eye and holding his bad hand outwards so that it didn't bang into his side. Moses was still standing, a look of mild surprise on his face, but something less mild in his eyes. He looked shocked.

He spat as he spoke.

"First the oven dish. Now a fucking screwdriver?"

By the time Moses had finished his sentence, Jake had barged into him, reeling him around, and as Moses stumbled, his leg gave up and he fell backwards over the arm of Jake's chair, knocking the remote to the floor, and skidding the chair around as his weight, combined with Jake's, pushed him down. Moses swung violently and the cosh caught Jake under the ear towards the back of his head. He jumped up and stepped back, trying to nurse his latest injury with his broken hand. He realised that he'd lost his screwdriver, but when Moses heaved himself up again, he saw that it was buried up to the handle in his shoulder. Moses swapped the cosh into his other hand and lifted it high in the air to bring it down onto Jake's face. Jake raised his forearm, wondering what the sound of two large bones snapping beneath flesh would sound like.

There was a loud bang, a shout, Jake felt cold air, heard the chair move across the floor, heard Moses cry out, felt himself pushed sideways. He landed on his broken hand and even through his own screams he heard something thump onto the floor then a sound like cloth ripping. Moses let out a muffled yell. There was the smell of perfume. Another thud.

Silence.

Heavy breathing.

A murmur.

As he crawled onto all fours, Jake looked up. He could see Moses's feet at the base of the chair, one off to the side, the other straight down. He could see a large dark, weeping red patch on Moses's trousers where he'd shoved the screwdriver into his shin. He looked up to the large body, arms hanging useless over the outside of the chair. Moses's shirt had been ripped open from the armpit to just below his chest. His neck was fat and swollen red. His face was slack and spit hung from his bottom lip. His eyes were closed. One had a large cut above it. Blood ran down his face.

Jake looked up past Moses. Standing behind the chair, hunched over and leaning on it, was Bob.

"Wow," Bob said, waving the slick, dark cosh, his breathing laboured, "These things work better than I'd imagined."

Jake stood up. "Get the fuck out of my house," he shouted. "Get out, you freak. I swear to God I'll fucking kill you."

Bob looked surprised and pointed the cosh at Moses. "Jakey, baby. I just saved you. Why are you so angry at *me*?"

Jake's mouth opened but no words came out for a while. Then, "What...the? Are you? You drugged me. You dragged me out to your shitty freak show warehouse boat and drugged me."

"Jake."

"No, shut up. You're the reason Moses is here in the first place you..." Jake struggled to find a word for double-crossing. "...cunt!" was the best he could do. "You grassed me up. You grassed Emma up. You told them where we lived after stalking us like some sick, dog shit eating, child molesting clown."

"Jesus Christ, Jake. Steady on. Let me..."

"No. Fuck you, Bob." He reached forward and pulled the screwdriver out of Moses's limp body.

He pointed the red blade at Bob's throat. "'Just business', I think you said. No. 'To business', I think it was." He started to move around the chair with every intention of ramming the screwdriver into Bob's neck.

"Jake. Wait."

For a split second, Jake thought it was the girl who had spoken. Then, as if it had always been there, but her voice had made it more real, he smelled her.

"Freesia?" he said.

Freesia had been standing near the door all the time, but Jake had been so angry and focused on Bob, that his tunnel vision, his red mist, hadn't let him see her. He felt calm and happy, and all the bits of him that were hurting stopped hurting. For about two seconds.

"Jesus Christ," he said. "You brought the whole fucking family?" He threw the screwdriver down and waved his arms in the air, screaming at the pain in his broken hand.

"No, Jake. Jusht me," Freesia said, smiling a genuine smile as only she could smile.

"I give up," Jake said. Then he shouted. "Again." Then, quiet again, "I give up giving up. There. Fuck. You two can't just turn up here having put me in this position in the first place, kill Moses after I was almost going to kill the fat fuck myself, then act all pally and like you're here to help. You're nuts. Both of you. Off your trolleys."

"We knew he'd be here, Jake," Freesia said, closing the door so that the room suddenly became that bit darker.

"So all that shit about 'it's just business' was just about setting me up as bait? Classic. Absolute classic."

"No, Jake, it wasn't like that." Freesia said. Her eyes were large and dark, and wet.

"I'll be honest, Jake," Bob said, "I meant every word of it."

Jake grimaced like a viscous monkey, his lips curling up, his freshly brushed teeth showing.

"Bob," Freesia said.

Bob glanced at her, then looked back at Jake and continued. "Just being honest, babe."

"Babe?" Jake said.

"Her, not you," Bob said. "At the time I meant it. It was a way out for me, for the family."

"The easy route," Jake said.

"Yeah, the easy route. Why not? I never gave a fuck about you, Jake."

"Bob," Freesia squealed.

"I really didn't," he said. "You were a means to an end."

Jake shook his head, pressing his good fingers into his eyes. He walked over to the kitchen and from a drawer, pulled out a tiny green first aid kit with a large yellow 99p sticker on the front. He slammed it onto the worktop.

"Then just why are you here? Now. What's the point in that?" Jake held the kit down with one elbow and tried to unzip it with its stupid small zip. He picked it up and banged it a couple of times on the worktop. Freesia walked over to him and picked up the kit. She unzipped it, opened it out and placed it back on the counter.

"Phil'sh dead," she said quietly.

Jake said, "Phil. How?" He pulled out two plasters, a pair of scissors and a small bandage.

"Guess," Bob said, poking the back of Moses's head with the cosh.

Freesia took the plasters, scissors and bandage off Jake and put them back in the kit. "There'sh nothing small enough thoshe thingss will cover," she said, her eyes flicking from Jake's head to his eyes, to his face, to his hand, to his thighs.

"I'll tell you on the way back to the warehouse, Jake," Bob said.

"What?" Jake said. "I need a doctor. The hospital. I'm not going back there. With you two."

"It'll be fine, Jake," Bob said. "We can patch you up there. I've got loads of cool stuff. Some great drugs too. I'll personally see to it that you get your hand back to normal. It's probably just a dislocated finger and some rupturing of the blood vessels around the metacarpal tissue. Some bruising to the bones as well."

"What? No. No way. I don't like you, remember?"

"Jake?" Freesia said. "Go on. You'll be fine."

"But the hospital is the usual place you know," Jake said.

"Not today," Bob said. "You may end up with rather a lot of explaining to do."

Jake knew that they were right. He looked down at his bent, busted hand. He nodded, feeling how stiff his neck was just below his skull.

"Here," Freesia said, looking down at Jake's thighs again. She handed him his towel. "Put thiss back on and go get dreshed."

"Ah crap," Jake said. "Why didn't you tell me I was proper stark naked?"

Freesia took the towel back after watching Jake struggle with it. She stepped in close, pushing her body against him, opened the towel out, then leaned around to tie it at the back. "I wass enjoying it," she said into his ear.

Jake walked off into his bedroom and pulled on a large T-shirt, jogging bottoms, and a pair of trainers. In the bathroom, he wiped his face the best he could, staring at how shiny and white the lump on his cheek was. God, I hope that's not bone, he thought as he brushed his fingers across it, even though he knew it would hurt.

Back in the living room, Bob was swigging from the bottle, Freesia was staring out the window and Moses was still sitting slumped in the chair.

"What about him?" Jake said. "Is he dead?"

"No, he's not dead, Jake," Bob said. "Woah. You look like a mental patient that fell out his chair and down a flight of concrete steps."

"Bob!" Freesia said.

"But he does. It's okay for you, I gotta catch the bus with him." He gestured for Jake to follow then walked out the front door.

"What about you and him?" Jake said to Freesia as he headed for the door.

Freesia lifted up a bright pink Hello Kitty bag to just under her nose and unzipped it. "Oh, I have to shtay here," she said. She pulled out a thin chain and on the end was a bunch of rusty brown razor blades that swung like a horrific medieval wind chime. "I've got shomething I jusht *have* to do."

Jake felt ill at the thought of those blades in his own mouth, at the damage they would do. Then he looked at Moses and felt better at the thought of those blades in his mouth and the damage they could do.

"Okay," he said. "I'll see you round then I guess."

"Hope sho."

"Oh," he said as he was stepping through the doorway, "there's a toolbox under the sink next to some drain cleaner and bleach and WD40 and stuff.

You know. In case you get bored and maybe need a hammer and some nails. Hell. Stick a couple in for me eh?"

Jake had never seen a grizzly bear before.

He'd never heard the sound of razorblades being drawn through someone's mouth either. But he knew, as he closed the door behind him, that that was what he had just heard.

Chapter Fourteen

On the bus, apart from Bob telling the driver that Jake had fallen down some concrete steps at the care centre, very little was said. Bob sat looking into a small, palm sized book filled with pictures of plants, bright flowers and berries.

"Eat for free," Bob said. "Plants and stuff." Then he just sat and read the book, licking his fingers to turn the glossy pages and occasionally scratching at what he thought must have been stubble on his cheeks.

Jake was at a window seat again, but instead of being a cooling distraction, the faint breeze from the glass dug into his swollen face making him close both eyes whilst opening his mouth to prevent everything becoming too balled up and cramped. He nestled his broken hand in his good arm and clutched it close to his chest. He found that digging his fingers into the wrist of his bad hand soothed the pain. A little.

By concentrating on the pain and not passing out, the bus ride seemed quicker than it had before. *Maybe I have passed out a few times*, he thought. *Maybe it's because I've been here before. Maybe I just don't know time the way I used to.*

It was the little girl who spoke the most. Quiet and angry and sad and friendly as only a small girl could be. She kept telling Jake it would be okay. That he was going to be okay, and that he'd get better. That his hand would be okay, and that if he were a poorly cat, she'd pick him up and squeeze him better.

During an agonising walk though the fields, Jake tried to stop his fingers banging on his hips, and fought the pain of the cold wind in his face.

They dropped down to the edge of the chain-link fence and the familiar fairground smell of mud and grease filled Jake's head.

"Didn't think I'd be back here any time shoon," he said, as they ducked into the ironworks and wandered across the old tracks.

"Me neither," Bob said. He was still quiet. Too quiet. "We'll go round the back, to the barge. Not through the warehouse. Not today," he said.

"Mmm," Jake said, not particularly interested in which way they went or why.

"I have some good stuff on the barge, Jake. Some good first aid bits and some good painkillers. Codeine and Percodan and some, er, yeah, some Fentanyl. But Fentanyl is in a lollipop form and your face might not be up to that. Strong though. And then there's some oxymorphone. Now that's good stuff painkiller. But I think I only have suppositories of that and well, you having a bad arm and being so beat up and all, I guess the last thing you want is to have something shoved up your ass." Bob was quiet again. As if he'd run out of comforting things to say.

Sunlight glinted off the dull paint of the barge and off its open windows. *There is no smell of stale pond water this time*, Jake thought. He decided it was due to his bunged up nose. All he could smell for the past couple of hours was a slightly old butcher's shop display, sickly sweet, congealed blood.

"It looksh good today," Jake said, nodding towards the boat. And he meant it.

"Yeah, it's the sun. Picks out the shiny bits. Hey, you sound like Freesia."

"Nnnng. Probably look like her too." As Jake said that, a wave of cold passed through his whole body. "Sshit, I didn't mean that. Like that. Sshit."

Bob laughed a quiet laugh. "Don't worry. I know what you mean. I can only imagine how beautiful she was before."

"Nnng. Yeah."

"You got a thing for her, Jake? I mean besides the sexual curiosity?"

"Nnng. Yeah. Itsh her eyesh. Sshe looks at me like..."

"Like she knows you inside."

"Yeah," Jake said. Bob was right. "Like sshe knowsh me."

"She does have nice tits as well, you noticed."

Jake felt a flush of heat in his face and neck. "Can I pleashe jusht get shome derugs?" he said.

Inside the barge, Jake sat at the same table as before. Bob brought out a bottle of drink, the same bottle as before, and Jake took a swig that stung cuts inside his mouth that he didn't know he had.

"Should I really be drinking thish sshit again?" he said, eyeing the bottle. "If I'm going to be taking tabletsh and shtuff, I mean."

"Yeah," Bob said, dropping a dull blue canvas bag on the table. "All that drinking and tablets stuff? It's all bullshit. Imagine the money pharmaceuticals would lose if you could take cough medicine and gin, or codeine and brandy, and all your pain just went away. They'd be selling prescription drugs in your local off license. They'd lose a mint."

Jake swigged again. Bob opened the bag and pulled out a silver packet of pills. He held them up.

"Put your hand on the table, Jake."

Jake put his hand on the table. The cold bit into it. Bob placed the crinkling silver packet back and pulled out another. Put it back. Pulled out another.

"A couple of these Tamazepam and some oxymorphone should do. Drop 'em with a mouthful of that whiskey." He looked at Jake's hand, moving his head side to side, examining the way the fingers bent, the way the skin was split, the way that clear liquid oozed from beneath congealed blood. "Give it half an hour or so," he said.

"Half an hour for what?" Jake said, swallowing the tablets.

"For the pain to go away."

"How will I know? If I'm all drugged up?"

Bob lifted Jake's hand and gently twisted it side to side. "Well, if you don't scream when I reduce the dislocation of the metacarpal?"

"Nnng," Jake said.

The whiskey, on top of the night before, and the lack of food and the fight and the emotional trauma and the tilting of the boat, had all blended into a surreal, pointless moment that made Jake think that the squidgy baseball of broken fingers wasn't his own.

"Why is it always the hands?" he said.

"Yeah. Happened to your stupid...to your girlfriend. To that Emma." Bob said, then sighed. "Remember being a kid and getting into fights at school? It was always the hands. Always spiteful grabbing at fingers. Bending, twisting, and snapping. It's the easiest way to hurt someone, Jake. Some people never grow up. Or maybe they just remember that it's the easiest way to hurt someone."

Bob rested Jake's hand back down on a white towel.

Jake didn't feel anything. It was like his hand wasn't his any more.

Bob sat down next to Jake and swigged from the bottle. "He killed Phil," he said.

Jake said nothing.

Bob continued. "Moses came into the warehouse all filled up with anger like a wild, wounded animal. Apparently he was blundering around knocking the shit out of everything. Pulling down sheets. Kicking over bins. Most of the family, they all just hid right back into corners. Hid into nothing, like they're so used to."

Bob leaned forward and pushed Jake's hand flat onto the towel.

"Can you raise your fingers? One at a time?"

Jake lifted his thumb, then his little finger. His index finger twitched a little.

"Good," Bob said, swigging. "That's quite good, Jake. Moses, he got to the end of the warehouse, and

Phil was sweeping a yard-square patch where people bring in tiny bits of oil and gravel on their feet. And, well, Phil, he wouldn't stop sweeping."

Jake could picture Phil sweeping in autonomous, robotic lines, Up. Down. Move over. Up. Down.

"Can you give me a thumbs up?" Bob said.

Jake rolled his hand over and watched as his thumb pointed upwards.

"Good. That's good, Jake. It looks like flexion and extension is good. Your deep and superficial flexor tendons seem okay. See if you can spread your fingers wide."

"Nnng."

"Good, Jake." Bob placed his own hand on Jake's and closed his eyes.

"Phil wouldn't get out the way. Had to finish his sweeping. Apparently, Jessie, a little girl here, she yelled at Phil to let Moses past. Yelled that the floor was fine. Clean. Finished. Feels like your radial and ulnar pulses are good. Nothing wrong there." He smiled into the table. "This feels good, Jake."

"My hand? It feels good? It's fucked."

"No, Jake. Your hand. It feels good." He smiled again. "But Phil, he's not listening. He's just doing his Phil thing. Sweeping. Doesn't even see Moses. Doesn't hear Jessie shouting herself dry. Moses pulls out this blade and clutches it so's it's pointing out between his fingers."

"I'm going to be shick," Jake said, his good hand going to his mouth.

Bob passed him the bottle, and he swigged.

"The blood flow's fine," Bob said, rubbing Jake's

hand. "You're fingers are all pinked up. This one is fucked up bad between the proximal and middle phalanges. But I can pop that sucker back in."

"Now? I think it still hurts," Jake said, staring at his hand, not sure if he could feel anything at all.

"In a minute or so, yeah. It'll be fine," Bob said. "Moses just starts plunging that tiny blade into the side of Phil's neck. Up his face, into his temple. And Phil, Jessie says he was lying on the floor flat, and he was rubbing at the concrete with one hand like he'd found some stubborn dirt that he hadn't cleaned."

There was a loud pop. Jake looked at his hand. All his fingers were pointing in the proper direction and he'd felt nothing. He swigged from the bottle.

"Turns out, Phil was rubbing at a line of his own blood that had splashed out over the square he'd been sweeping. Rubbing his own blood into the bumpy concrete because it was making such a mess."

Jake passed out.

When he woke up, Jake stared at a dimly lit sheet a few feet above his head. Strung out below it, criss-crossing on different coloured threads of wool and rope and cotton, were lines of bottle tops. Beer tops, mostly. He'd been sleeping without a pillow. He sat up and rubbed at the back of his neck but something scratched. Then he remembered everything that had happened back at his house, and he held his hand out in front of him. His middle two fingers were strapped neatly together with a thick bandage. Tape ran around them, back across his hand, and around his wrist.

"Neat," he said, twisting his hand, examining both sides. It was a professional looking job.

The bottle tops above him clinked in a subtle breeze as he shifted himself into a sitting position against the cold brick wall behind him. He looked around. The walls to his left and in front were covered in a soft cream drape, shadows bulging in it like vertical waves. To his left was a neat row of old blue milk crates, some had barely visible worn out names printed on them. Riggs Dairy. Mattius Milk. Baxters Deliveries. On top of them was a single sheet of wood and on top of that was a piece of carpet with what seemed to be a 1960's pattern on it in reds and golds and browns.

The whole carpet was littered with small trinkets. A row of plastic Star Wars figures arranged in height order from Ewok through to Darth Vadar. In front of these, a row of small plastic weapons. There was a huddle of curious Subbuteo players. Some had two heads. One, a goalkeeper, had six arms. Another had a toy soldier's green plastic head neatly grafted on. Three piles of red and green gemstones. A model made from matchsticks that appeared to be a Mayan temple with neat steps leading up to the entrance. All the matches still had their bright red heads.

At the end of the room, near his feet, on another blue milk crate was a small portable DVD player. Surrounding it was a cardboard box with its centre cut out and at each side of the opening, tied back, was a crimson and gold curtain complete with twisted cord pull string and tasselled ends.

"Phil," Jake said. He closed his eyes and

imagined Phil handing out tickets and collecting stubs as he invited people into this tiny auditorium. He imagined a pre-show speech, maybe about the film, the director, the genre, the narrative, year it was made, special effects techniques, film type - Cinemascope or Technicolour. He could see Phil stopping the DVD player with its tiny plastic silver stop button, then handing out paper cones of sticky toffee popcorn. Then he saw Phil lying in a pool of his own blood, scraping and rubbing at the concrete as he died.

"Jake?" the voice of a young girl said.

"Hello?" he said in a hushed voice.

"Can I come in?" the girl said.

Before he could answer, Jake's little girl spoke. "It's okay. She's my friend. She's Jessie."

"Your friend?" Jake said.

"What?" Jessie said from behind the sheet, her tiny pink fingers poking around the edge waiting to pull it back.

Jake''s little girl spoke again. "My friend. She's nice."

"Okay," Jake said.

The sheet pulled back a little.

"Just don't let her shadow near me," the little girl said.

"What? Why not?"

"What?" Jessie said.

"Nothing," Jake said.

"Her shadow, Jake. I don't like it."

"Should I let her in then?"

"Yes, let her in. She's my new friend."

"Can I come in? Or can't I come in?" Jessie said, and the sheet wavered with her indecisive hand. "I'd like to see you, Jake. If that's okay?"

"Er, yeah. Sure. Just, er, watch your shadow."

"Oh?"

"Yeah. Just stay that end of the room for a while, eh?"

"Oh. Yes. Of course. I will. I don't want to be any trouble, Jake."

Jessie walked in.

"Wow," Jake said. "Look at you."

The girl was about ten years old. She wore a long dark black dress that was covered in tiny white prints of randomly placed flowers. The sleeves came down to her elbows and ended in bright white fluffy trims. Past her skinny, peach elbows, she wore black fishnet gloves. The hem of the dress was thick white ruffles of silk. She wore short, white socks to just above her ankles and her shoes were shiny black with silver bows. On her head was a white bonnet that fell slightly to one side, too large for her head, tied under her chin with a red bow. Around her neck was a shimmering red bow, the ends falling over the front of her chest. Her huge blue eyes made the rest of her features look tiny. Tiny nose, tiny red mouth, tiny pointed chin. Her golden hair fell in ringlets.

"You *are* a picture," Jake said, surprised at himself for sounding so paternal.

"That is what they say," Jessie said, her voice soft, tinged with boredom. "Like a picture."

Jake thought he might have said something wrong. "Oh. I just mean, well," he struggled with his words. "I mean you look very pretty."

"Momma Jane dresses me. She has this painting of a child in her place. Oil painting, I think." Her tiny face scrunched up. "She dresses me like that picture. Most of the time."

"Oh. Is that bad?"

Jake's little girl spoke. "I think my friend looks beautiful."

"My little girl says you look beautiful."

Jessie's face brightened. "Tell her thank you," she said, and curtseyed ever so slightly.

Jake felt his little girl shudder while she giggled.

"Freesia says I look like a dork. But I never saw a dork for real, so I don't know."

Jake laughed. His forehead hurt. "That's just Freesia, I guess."

Jessie's face became vacant. Slack. She blinked and kept her eyes closed for a short while. When she opened them, they were wet and shiny.

"Phil always said I looked like a million dollars. Like a film star. Phil said I reminded him of Judy Garland. I liked Phil."

Jake said nothing. A lump welled up in his throat. He looked around the room and stared at a tall, neat pile of DVDs that he hadn't noticed before.

"You know? I think Phil was right," he said, and watched as the girl's eyes wandered to the side, remembering.

She started talking again as if nothing had happened. "Bob's coming over in a minute. He wants to see your hand. To see if you're okay. I think Bob likes you."

Jake snorted accidentally. "You should tell him not to drug me with cheap booze and throw me into a taxi then."

"Pardon?" Jessie said, shocked.

"Oh. Nothing. Sorry. Just an adult thing. That's all."

Jessie smiled, but she looked confused.

"I turned the mattress over for you before Bob brought you in here. It's quite clean. Always was."

"Yes," Jake said and slid his hand across the soft surface of the dimpled mattress. "It is clean. I think I slept well. I feel well." He rubbed his neck again.

Jessie laughed, and the ribbon around her neck moved up and down her throat. "I threw the pillow away. I did turn it. But then I threw it away. It smelled a bit...funny."

Jake felt wide-awake now. He had expected to be feeling the effect of his beating, of the drugs, of the booze. But he felt fresh.

"Want to watch a DVD?" he said. He was enjoying this new company.

"I don't think that's a good idea, Jake," Jessie said.

"Oh," Jake said, feeling foolish. "Okay."

"I have to go really. I came to see if you were comfy. And you are. And to tell you that Bob will come see you. And he will. So, I think I'll go."

"Oh. Okay."

"Watch *The Wizard of Oz* if you like."

"Er, okay. Yes. Maybe I will."

"It will cheer you up. I promise." Jessie smiled and blinked.

"Okay. In that case, I will."

Jessie pulled her gloves up, rubbed her hands down her dress and said, "If it helps. I don't blame you for what happened to Phil. And Bob doesn't. I don't care what the rest of them say. If that helps."

She left he room and pulled the sheet back closed.

All that calm. All those pain-free moments after he'd woken up in Phil's bed, they all went away and were replaced by a hollow feeling in the pit of his stomach and confusion in his head.

"Ah, crap," he said, as the realisation of what the family would think of him pulled at his insides and made him feel ill again. He shuffled forward. From a third of the way down the stack of DVDs he pulled out *The Wizard of Oz* and put it on.

"I think I remember this film," the little girl said.

"Really? That's great. You remember this film?"

"I think so. Yes. It makes me feel warm. Like I want to pull my blanket up round my ears and just watch it."

"You remember watching it? I mean, really seeing it on screen?"

"No. I just think I know it. And it makes me feel all fuzzy."

He couldn't be sure, but Jake thought this was the first time the girl had spoken about feeling something from her past. He peered hard at the screen.

"You remember the scarecrow?" he said.

"No."

"The lion? You've got to remember him."

"No."

"The tin man?"

"No."

"Steady on, Jake." It was Bob. He pulled the sheet back and stepped in, staring down at the tiny screen below him. "You trying to scare her? Or yourself?"

"What?" Jake said, staring up at Bob's dark face.

"Just go easy on questions with shadows. That's all. You poke them with a stick and, well."

Jake remembered lying on his living room floor watching the moth. "I know." He said. "I was just, well, I just felt comfortable with it. That's all."

Bob walked over. "This film does that to you. Damn. Even I get that cosy feeling watching this bloody film." He waved his arm. "Budge up."

Jake began to protest that he couldn't move any further but Bob had already sat next to him on the mattress.

"Jesus," Jake said. "Watch the hip."

"Oh. So your hip's bad as well?"

"Yeah. I think. Feels like I took a good whack on the bone in there."

"Here," Bob said, handing Jake a foil pack of tablets. "Swallow these."

"Aspirin?" Jake said, reading the packet.

"Aspirin and scotch," Bob said, handing him a bottle of nearly finished whiskey. "How's the hand?"

"It hurts a bit. More like a hot throbbing pain. Feels all fat."

"Good. That means it's healing up." Bob looked at the two pink finger ends that poked out of the bandage. He smiled. "Nice and hot."

"You bandaged my hand?"

Bob laughed. "You sound so surprised. Yeah, I

bandaged your hand, reduced the dislocation and reset the fingers. There's a splint in there from a wooden oral spatula. If it itches, just ignore it, otherwise you'll get splinters if you go poking around in there."

"Thank you."

"Woah. Check out the manners on Jakey baby."

Jake stared at Bob right in the eyes and screwed his mouth up.

"Guess it's the film making you go all soppy on me, eh?" Bob said.

"How do you know all that shit? About hands and metacarpals and names of finger bits?"

"I used to be a doctor," Bob said. "Paediatric mostly, towards the end."

Jake was suddenly aware of how itchy his fingers were inside the warm bandage.

Bob shook his head. "Some kid's mum said I'd acted inappropriately. Said I'd touched her daughter wrong. I swear, that's what the report said. Touched her wrong." He sighed. "I was checking her glands under her armpits at the time. Young girl. Thirteen."

"They tried to sue you?"

"Yeah. They, the mother, guess she wanted a new car or sofa or holiday in Mallorca. The low life scum sucking whore."

"Did you?"

"What?"

Jake handed Bob the bottle.

"Did you touch the girl wrong?" Jake said.

Bob rubbed his face, picked up a fresh bottle from out of nowhere, and drank some of that. "No. That's what I said in the statement. No. It was a yes or no answer. Hardly even multiple choice. So, no. I never. I felt under her chin. I cupped her face in my hands. I ran my fingers under her armpits. Checked her pulse. Felt her warm soft neck. I even ran my thumbs over the top of her chest." He swigged again. "But the answer, even today, if you asked me again? The answer will still be no."

"Is that why you gave up? Why you came out here?"

"God no. I mean, no. Maybe that was the start of it."

"Did you get done for it?"

"No. Turns out the mother had a history of filing malpractice suits against doctors, McDonald's workers, even lawyers. She was a freeloader."

"So nothing happened. You got off. You did nothing wrong."

"No, I did nothing wrong. But it was like, in my head, I think I might have."

At that moment Jake felt close to Bob. Like he'd turned a corner and understood what made the man tick. "But you *did* nothing wrong," he repeated.

"Six months later. Another young girl."

Jake felt his newly realised bond breaking.

Bob continued. "Another young girl, her name was Helen. She'd not long left school when I saw her, and she's sat on that crispy white paper on the bed and she has pain in her shoulders and her chest. And I ask her to lie down and I'm just staring at her breasts. I'm thinking how she's sixteen and that her breasts are small, but perfect. Apart from a dark brown patch that looks tight above her sheer pink bra top, above her left nipple. Thinking back, I'm thinking how if I go start touching that puckered, tight patch, how her mum or worse, her dad or brothers, how they might bawl about me trying to finger her in the ass. So I run my thumbs across her clavicle, that's shoulders, Jake, shoulders. And um and ah. And I say to her how maybe she's just a bit underdeveloped and it's her bones and muscle tissue growing out and not to throw balls so hard, and I'm thinking shit, throw balls so hard? Should I really say that?"

Bob went quiet. He licked his lips. Drank some more. Licked his lips again and scratched at his chest above his left nipple.

"She had cancer," Jake said.

"Bingo. Malignant melanoma on her breast. She was diagnosed three weeks later by a Well Women's clinic. Fucking Well Women's clinic. She should have gone there first. Fuck me. Later, I read her obituary, on the exact same day I got a letter of malpractice."

"Made you wonder why you bothered?"

"Shit. Kinda. No. All I kept thinking was how I felt so bad that I must have known she had cancer but that all I could think was how I didn't want some fat, jobless woman sitting on a beach in the Seychelles at my expense. I already knew she had died, but, reading it, in a newspaper like that, I just remember thinking how I couldn't think. I cried. I'll tell you that much."

"And you got struck off?"

"No. Three other areas had failed to spot the cancer. Me? I was third on the list. I was the fail-safe. She died for nothing."

Jake is trundling around the garden on his big plastic trike. He stops. There's a small bird on the path. Its head is all crushed, and red ooze is drying in the sun. He's looking down at this thing, wondering what happened, when his dad comes out and bellows in his ear, yanking his shirt. "What the fuck did you do to it?"

Jake blinked and stared at his empty hands.

Bob was still talking.

"...And this other girl, she's twenty and she's complaining of burning and pain in her vagina. I suggest the Well Women's clinic but she says how they just pull 'old people faces' and tell her it's maybe thrush and stick yoghurt up there and stop sleeping around. She tells me how she doesn't want to stop sleeping around.

"And I swear, as I'm staring into her face, pounding away on her on my desk, all my papers are flying away and my pens are on the floor and my computer is all black because the cable's came loose. She smiles and kisses me so hard on the lips. The whole room smells of antibacterial wipes and sex and she says, 'There's nothing wrong with me'. And she digs her heels into the small of my back and I come. And, and this is the weird part, she kisses me, looks right at me and says, 'now we're both cured, Doc.'"

"Shit. And you got another letter?"

"No. I set fire to my room and burned the whole fucking clinic down. I guess I might have a letter. Somewhere. But I was already here."

"And you chose to stay here?" Jake said, looking into the side of Bob's face and at the dark stubble poking through.

"Yup. Figured I might as well."

"How long you been here?"

"Ah, years now, I guess. A few years at least."

"Shit. Didn't anyone come looking for you? Your family?"

"No. Well, they might have been looking in the wrong places I guess."

"Don't you miss anyone?"

"No. Not now. Everyone is exactly the same, Jake, deep down. We're all losers. We just sometimes end up pretending we don't know that our friends and family are just as fucked up as we are. This lot here, *this* family, we all just accept it, we don't pretend we have to fit in any more. Do you know what I mean?"

Jake is twenty-something. His best mate, Carl, is showing him his new car.

"Whaddya think? Cool ain't it?"

"Yeah. Pretty cool, man." Jake is staring at a bright yellow hatchback with tinted back windows.

"Cost me eleven grand," Carl says, smiling.

"Wow. Eleven grand."

Jake stares at a fat grey pigeon that's flapping furiously as it tries to land in a dark green conifer nearby.

"Yeah. Check out the alloys. Good alloys them."

Jake is thinking that they're just wheels.

"Yeah. I did look at another car, but," Carl opens the driver's door and waves his hand at the interior, "well, the dashboard on this one is just so much better. Heated seats as well, Jake."

Jake is wondering who in God's name gives a shit what the dashboard is like.

"Remember Sam?" Carl says, stepping into the car and grinding himself down into the seat.

"Yeah, I remember Sam. Of course I remember Sam, we saw him like, last week."

"Yeah. Well, Sam, he bought a car a few weeks back but it's at least three years older than this and it's the previous model."

"Oh. And?"

"Jake. That model doesn't have the cup holders in the dash." Carl prods at the dashboard, and two arms fold out to produce cup holders.

Jake is thinking, *I knew it would come to this. I knew he wouldn't be able to show me his new car without telling me how much better it was than someone else's. Didn't have to be Sam's. Anyone's would do as long as his was better than someone else's.*

"I knew a guy called Carl," Jake said. "He was a prick. Always made himself feel better by pointing out how shit everyone else was."

"Yep. They're the sort," Bob said. "The world's full of 'em."

"Thing is, he never actually did anything himself.

I could never understand how buying a car, or a large TV, or an antique chest of drawers made him better than anyone else."

"Bet you never told him that. Did you Jake?"

"No. And it made me angry all the time. I wish I'd just said shit like, 'But Carl, they're just wheels. Carl, your TV is exactly the same as my TV from the same shop, just bigger. Carl, you are a prick.'"

"So you just got yourself more and more wound up by him, instead of sticking the boot in. Looks like he had the upper hand on everyone after all, eh?"

"Not exactly." Jake smiled and rubbed his face with the back of his broken hand. "His wife was having an affair with a guy we used to know. He had a car without cup holders, but he owned his own indoor parachute business."

Bob laughed. "Yeah," he said, standing up. "You're gonna like it here."

"What? No. I've got to get home."

"Might want to give that a while, Jakey. Assuming the police *aren't* crawling all over the place picking pieces of Moses out of the carpet and from the chair, then the whole place is going to stink for weeks."

"What? You think Freesia actually killed him then? I mean dead?"

"Killed. Dead. Yeah, both. Knowing Freesia she probably did some nasty stuff to the big man. She's pretty handy with her Global cleaver and filleting knife. Reckons they're the only two she needs."

Jake felt nauseous.

"Shit," he said. "I mean, I know she, you know,

maybe cut his mouth up. I know that. But, killed him?"

"You've seen her eyes, Jake. I think you know what she's capable of when she's pissed. And believe me, when she found out what Moses had done to Phil, and when she sat up all night holding little Jessie and singing nursery rhymes to her, she was," Bob paused, "apocalyptically pissed."

Jake felt a certain amount of pride at that moment.

"Is she here? Have you seen her since?" he said.

"No. She's not back yet. She's probably waiting for the right time to take the bigger pieces of Moses out the house in bin bags. She's smart like that."

Jake wondered if she might have posted back his latest DVD for him.

"Get your head down, Jakey," Bob said. "That hand won't heal all by itself. It needs rest and gentle exercise."

Jake lay down.

"Gentle exercise?" he said.

"Yup," Bob said, turning off the TV. "Tomorrow you go skip jumping."

"Skip jumping?"

"Skip jumping."

"With one hand?"

"With one hand."

Jake smiled then closed his eyes.

Wake up, Jake.

Jake swatted at something with his hand.

Wake up. Come on.

"Emma?" he said, opening his eyes, seeing the

bottle tops spinning above him.

"Get lost," Bob said.

"Shit. Sorry," Jake said, stretching his mouth and blinking so that the bottle tops looked like tiny stars all smudged out. "Must've been dreaming. Those drugs I guess."

"Yeah. Blame the drugs," Bob was whispering. "Whatever, fruit boy. Get up."

"In a minute."

"Now," Bob said, poking Jake's broken hand.

A sharp stabbing pain shot up Jake's arm and into his armpit. "Jesus," he said, somehow managing to stay quiet. "You idiot."

"Come on, we gotta go get food."

"Food? Now? What time is it?" Jake looked at his watch, but it wasn't there. "Where's my watch?"

"I didn't know you wore a watch, Jakey. Was it expensive?" Bob laughed and pushed Jake in his ribs. "Come *on.*"

Jake stared at his bare wrist. "Shit," he said. "I don't know if I did have a watch now. Shit."

"You're going mad, Jakey baby. Welcome to the family."

Jake, still fully dressed, stood up and stretched, trying to avoid straining parts of his body that he hadn't realised were hurting. "Okay. I'm up."

"Put this on," Bob said, handing Jake a tan corduroy jacket with a grey fur collar. "It was Phil's."

Jake shuffled his broken hand down one sleeve, then pulled the coat on. *Great*, Jake thought, *I sleep in a dead man's bed, watch a dead man's DVDs and now I'm wearing a dead man's coat.* Bob handed him a large blue, threadbare backpack.

"Is this Phil's too?" Jake said, examining the way the backpack was barely held together and smelled like sweet, rotting fruit.

"No. It's yours now."

Jake held the backpack out in front of him and pulled a face.

Outside the warehouse doors, a bitter cold wind whipped over the fields bringing a fresh, cool, empty smell.

"No. Really," Jake said, peering out into blackness across the ironworks to tiny orange lights of the snaking motorway in the distance. "What time is it?"

"It's skip o'clock, Jake. Three fifteen." Bob said. "Don't worry. It'll be more like four by the time we get to the supermarket. No buses at this time of day. Even the moon stayed in bed." He started to walk away, his feet lifting the smell of earth and oil into the empty air.

They walked over dark, uneven fields, Jake's hand throbbing and hot. Bob whistled, badly, then seemed to realise he was whistling and stopped himself with a strange snorting noise.

As they reached the edge of the motorway, the ground took on a ghostly green-blue hue, and Jake thought that this is what it must be like to wear night-vision goggles. Through a wet, concrete tunnel beneath the thunder of traffic still flowing, Jake thought he could see the bright figure of someone at the exit.

"Shh," he said, his hiss echoing like white noise.

"What?" Bob said, stopping and staring out at the exit.

The figure was gone.

"I thought I saw someone. A figure. A person."

"Ah crap, that's all I need. You getting all jittery and hallucinating. Think you might need some more drugs." He pulled another packet from his trouser pocket and handed it to Jake. "Here. Take these."

"What are they?" Jake said, twirling the packet round in front of him.

"No idea. It's too dark to read 'em. Could be painkillers. Could be laxatives. Just take them." Jake pushed two oval pills out into his palm and shoved them into his mouth.

Bob walked on, his head thrust out and moving left to right like he was an owl.

"Got any water?" Jake mumbled.

"No."

Jake crunched the pills and felt them tickle in his dry throat. He let out a sharp cough that echoed.

"Jesus," Bob said. "Shut up will you? Now you got me on edge."

Once outside the tunnel, they looked around in the soft glow from the motorway lights above. Nothing. Bob shrugged. Jake thought maybe it *was* the drugs. They walked into the darkness.

"Not far now, Jake. See that thin ribbon of water over there?" He pointed. "That's the canal. Just over there. Supermarket's on the other side."

"Bob."

"Yeah?"

"Why did you come to my house? I mean. Why did you rescue me?"

"Starmouth. Freesia."

"It was her idea to come help me?" Jake felt his mood lift.

"No. It was her idea to go get Moses. It was a lucky guess on my part that he was at your house. That's all."

"Oh." Jake felt his mood sink.

"Yeah. I told you. Should've seen her eyes, Jake. You've seen her eyes, but not like the way they were.

"That little girl, Jessie, after she saw what she saw, first person she bumped into was Freesia. And Freesia held her right in close to her face for something like hours. And all that time, Jessie was just crying and sobbing, and she said she didn't want to blink ever again, 'cause of what she'd seen. Said that when she blinked she saw Phil all red. And you know what Freesia said? Said she'd do all her blinking for her. Turns out, as Jessie lay sobbing and not blinking and her tears were cooling into Freesia's lap, turns out, Freesia is blinking as much as she can, and that every time she blinks, she can see Phil all red."

"Jesus. That's bad."

"Yeah. Bad. After Momma Jane found Jessie and tidied up her face and hair and brushed her dress straight and they'd gone, Freesia reckons she blinked hard a few more times. And she saw Moses, all red." Bob stopped walking, and wagged a finger in the air. "No. In fact, what she said was that she saw *pieces* of Moses, all red. And when she was telling me this,

I swear to God, Jake, I really could see the red in her eyes. So that's why we came to *rescue* you, Jake."

Bob walked on.

"So why you being so nice to me now, Bob?" Jake said to his back.

"It's not about you, Jake."

Jake fell into a dumb silence.

Over the canal, they stopped next to a breezeblock wall with some graffiti on it. There was a dripping phone number and a message, *For a good time ring this and ask for my mum.*

"I like that," Bob said, pointing at the graffiti. "Makes me smile. I rang the number once, but it turns out the *mum* had died of colonic cancer. So not such a good time huh?" He laughed. "Right. We go over here."

Bob held his hands out and boosted Jake up onto the wall, where he hooked his one good arm over it and swung his legs back. Bob jumped up, grabbed the wall and was sitting next to Jake in a second, smiling.

"Like free running," he said.

As they dropped over the wall into the yard behind, four huge floodlights lit up.

"Shit, security lights," Jake said, staring into them, blinding himself.

"Don't worry. No one checks. Not always. This is just the bin yard. Look."

Bob walked over to a red plastic skip, pulled open the lid and shoved it up hard so that it banged on the wall behind. Jake winced at the noise and looked at the huge double gate in the wall opposite.

"Relax, Jake. Shit. Open that skip over there and grab some stuff."

Jake found lifting the lid difficult with one arm and had to follow the edge of the skip and lever the lid up that way near its hinge.

"Woah," he said, staring into the skip.

"Good?"

"Bob? This looks just like a friggin shop display."

"Cool, what you got?"

Jake stared inside. The bright security lights reflected off cellophane packets of colour. Cartons of tomatoes, sticks of celery, packs of three-coloured peppers that looked like discarded traffic lights. The whole skip was a multitude of bright vibrant colours. The smell that rose up was not what Jake expected. It wasn't shit and decay from a bin left out in the sun.

"It even smells like a grocer's shop," he said, reaching in and shifting packets to the side so that he could see beneath them. "It's all fresh."

"Freecycling, Jakey baby. Most of the stuff isn't even out of date yet. Check it out."

Bob was right. A packet of tomatoes, their vines still attached, had a display until date of yesterday and a sell by of only two days away.

"This is ridiculous," Jake said. "Most of it's, well, I'd actually buy this in the shop."

"Well, that's a whole other argument," Bob said, pushing something into his backpack. "These crazy freecyclers, they live off supermarket bins like these. It's a *lifestyle choice* apparently. Reckon they can afford the food but why should they? Dickhead hippies. But other people reckon that if they actually went in the fucking shop in the first place and bought the food as it was about to be go out of date, that it wouldn't end up in these skips in the first place and so it's actually *their* fault that it gets thrown out. You see?"

Jake picked up a twelve pack of white rolls and poked them with his strapped up fingers. "Dickhead hippies," he said. He decided he hated freecyclers.

"Jake," Bob said, "Stop playing with your food and fill your bag. Get veg and bread."

"Yeah, okay." Jake put the rolls in his backpack.

"Jake," Bob hissed.

Jake was startled. "What. What is it?" He looked around at the gates again.

Bob jabbed a finger in his direction. "You put the hard stuff in the bottom of the bag. Potatoes and carrots and stuff. Then tomatoes and salad bits. *Then* the bread. Jesus." He shook his head as Jake plunged into the skip and pulled out a bag of new potatoes and smiled.

Jake couldn't stop smiling as he shifted bag after bag of seemingly fresh produce into his backpack on the floor. "What you getting?" he said to Bob.

Bob lifted out a bumpy pink bag. "Chicken," he said.

"Chicken? Are you crazy? Surely a thrown out chicken *has* to be bad."

"Nope. It's only out of date, ooh, four hours ago. It's cold like a fridge in here anyway. And if it don't smell bad, then it's not bad."

"I don't know about chicken," Jake said, realising that whatever they picked up now, he would probably be eating that afternoon.

"We spray the bag over with disinfectant," Bob said. "We take the chicken out, give it a light spray as well, wash it loads, then cook the hell out of it. Usually stewed."

Jake pulled a face, more at the thought of a disinfectant tasting chicken than at bacteria.

"Anyway, I've got four of the buggers now, and some bacon, and a few tins of chickpeas and a whole massive bag of brown rice. The sort of brown rice you'd take into school for underprivileged Ethiopians 'round harvest time to make you feel better after you'd been taught to feel bad."

"Well, if I get sick later, I'm coming to get some pills from..."

There was a screech of tyres. Two car doors slammed. Jake's heart pounded, and his vision narrowed. He was aware that he was saying shit over and over, but couldn't hear himself. He picked up the bag and slung it over his shoulder.

Bob was already on the wall, even with a heavy bag of meat and tins, and he reached down to pull Jake up. Jake winced as his chest and ribs grazed against the bare breezeblock. Behind him, he heard the padlock and chain being dropped to the floor. He heard the heavy gates being dragged back, whistling and screeching. He heard two deep voices shout, "stop" and "oi" and "you" then he was running down the canal tow-path, tiny flecks of light flashed past him on the water, "you" and "oi" and "stop" bellowing behind him as he reached a gap in the wall and skidded through it, bouncing off the edge to point himself in the direction he wanted to go, then down an alley behind some houses, a dog barked and he heard a woman on her mobile phone in her garden laughing and then another turn around the walls of the houses and across a children's playground and through a hedge and into a playing field and then he was sitting behind another skip next to a large hut staring out through a gap at a cricket pitch in the gloom.

He tried to hold his breath as he heard footsteps stomp past him on the grass, but he couldn't because his lungs were burning and he was wheezing and could still feel the tickle of the tablets in his throat, and his chest hurt and...

"You!" someone shouted into his face.

Jake couldn't see anything except a tiny black dot in the centre of a blazing torchlight, and he felt himself being pulled up off the ground, backpack and all.

"You thieving gypsy scum," the man's voice shouted.

Jake pushed the man hard and the light went away. He heard the man hit the grass and heard a wheeze of air. Jake kicked at the smudgy figure on the ground but didn't feel like he'd made any real contact, his foot skidded off an arm or shoulder.

"Jake," someone shouted, harsh and wispy behind him.

"For Christ's sake," the man on the floor shouted. "Fuck off. Get him off me."

Jake kicked again, this time he felt his toe connect with something, and the man made a noise like a dog yelping.

"Jake. Stop," Bob shouted.

A hand grabbed him by the shoulder and he skipped and shuffled backwards, off balance.

"You idiot," Bob said.

Jake breathed deep and slow, his lungs burning. He leaned himself onto his thighs.

"Bob, you tit," the man on the floor said. "Where'd you get this arsehole?"

"You," Jake wheezed, wiping his dry mouth, "know him?"

The man stood up tapping his torch on his hand as it flickered on and off. He wore a smart but crumpled suit with a bright yellow security logo on one arm in the shape of a semicircle.

Bob was at the man's side.

"Yeah, I know him," he said. "This is Dennis."

"Den," Den said.

Bob continued. "And this, Den, is Jake. Looks like you two guys are getting on pretty well."

"Practically engaged," Den said. "I thought it was Phil until he rounded on me. And the way he ran, damn. Explains a lot. Phil were never that fast. Or that random."

Den twisted his elbow up and examined a brown-green smudge with his torch.

Jake stood upright. "You *know* this guy?" he said again to Bob.

"Yeah," Bob said. "It's Den."

"Why the hell," Jake said, pinching the bridge of his nose whilst looking at Den, "did you chase me then?"

Den shone the torch into Jake's face so that all he could see was that bright white light with a dark blob hovering in the centre.

"It's my job," Den said, sounding like he was addressing a child. "And I take my job very seriously." He waved his torch at his dirty elbow again. "And I take my suit very seriously too. I have to pay out my own pocket to get this dry cleaned."

"Blah blah blah," Bob said. "Kept you on your toes didn't we?"

When the torch wasn't shining directly into Jake's eyes, he could see the men quite clearly in the gloom. He had a small round face with ears that seemed too low down. His eyes were thin and squashed in at the centre by a deep furrowed brow. He had no eyebrows. His nose was tilted up so that Jake could see right into it. His mouth was tiny and thin and, even in such a small face, it seemed lost. But it smiled a tight smile.

"Was a good run," Den said. "Boss'll have no worries believing I at least *tried* to catch you. All that commotion in the back alley and stuff. Scared up some wildlife."

"Is someone else with you?" Bob said, looking around the field.

"Eh? No. Why?"

"I thought I heard someone else get out the car. Had me worried it might not be you."

"Oh shit yeah," Den said, excited. "It's my new thing. I get out the car. Close the door. Open the door then slam it again. Makes it sound like there are two of me." He looked confused at his own statement.

"Worked a treat," Bob said.

"Cool. That's great." Den's tiny mouth made a tiny smile.

Jake said, "How the hell do you keep your job if you let everyone go?"

"Ha. Not everyone." Den levelled his torch at Jake's chest. "Just you, and Bob, and Phil and, well, any of the family who are out here at stupid o'clock."

"The family?" Jake said, a sudden realization waking up in his brain.

"Yeah. But the freecyclers? I'll call in backup and book them in a heartbeat. Bloody hippies."

Jake was still angry but not sure at who. At Den? At himself for being caught? At Bob for finding it all so amusing?

"Freecyclers you *book*?" he said. "Great. So you *catch* old men and hippy women and kids. Good job, Den. Great. Must be a real effort. No wonder your boss is proud."

Den shone the torch in Jake's eyes again. It was beginning to piss him off, and he felt heat rising from his chest and out around his chin.

"You have no idea," Den said. "These guys are so far up their own arses, so moralistically correct *all the time*, that I actually wish they would run more often. Mostly they just stand there and lecture me. *They* lecture *me*." The round torchlight shone under Den's round face emphasising the 'me' bit of his speech. "Last week, this old guy, with a face like a turtle taking a shit, nice white teeth and a grey pony tail, I caught him with two huge bags. Not shopping bags, I mean the big ones that you put shopping bags *in* to put in your car boot. And they're both *full* of food. Mostly expensive stuff, like he'd actually cherry picked the skips. So I stop him. Tell him what he's doing is illegal and that I'm gonna book him, and he just stands there talking dead calm, giving *me* shit about third world starving kids and soup kitchens in the Bronx." He paused. "Yeah, the Bronx. But this smarmy old git, he's wearing this really nice leather jacket over a Ben Shermans shirt that even I can't afford, and his shoes are like golf shoes or something, with tassels. Yeah, and his face was just so full of despise for me, and that holier than thou beaming expression just really drilled into me.

"I punched him so hard in his nose. Broke it."

Bob laughed.

Jake raised an eyebrow.

"Yeah," Den continued, quieter, calmer. "Boss reckons I'll end up in court. Again. But hey," his voice became louder again, "Sunny Day Rainbow Night Time Securities keep renewing my contract, so I must be doing something right." He winked. "Where *is* Phil?" he said to Bob.

"He's gone," Bob said. "He broke from routine."

"Ah, shame," Den said. "I like Phil. Used to enjoy his crumby matinees and stuff on that shitty little DVD player of his. I blame him for my swearing thing as well. See No Evil, Hear No Evil. Last film I saw back there. Fuckin' A."

"Well you can come back and visit any time, Den. You know that. The family miss you."

"Really? They say that? I mean, after the sewage thing? They miss me?"

Bob snatched the torch and shone it into Den's face. "No," he said. "I was being polite. They still call you Dennis the Menace."

Den's tiny mouth half smiled. His eyes screwed up against the light. "Not *so* bad. I suppose. Considering."

Jake looked at the men in turn, a confused look on his face.

"Yeah," Bob said. "I was being polite again. Most of 'em say 'Ooh that cunt that fucked up my home with shit?'"

Den punched the air at the side of his hip and grunted.

"Well," Bob said to Jake, handing the torch back to Den. "Got your breath back?"

"Yes," Jake said. He just wanted to get back to the warehouse now. His hand throbbed, and Den was annoying him more and more.

"I'd say it was nice meeting you," Den said, clicking the torch off, then on. "But you kicked me in the ribs and elbow. Not very well, but the intent was there."

"Next time," Jake said.

Den laughed. Bob grabbed Jake's arm and steered him away back to the footpath.

"Be seein' you guys," Den called out as he criss-crossed his way through the cricket pitch, whistling the theme from *The Great Escape*.

"Fuckin' A," Jake said.

When they got back to the warehouse, Jake and Bob dropped their bags into a huge concrete room that Bob explained never seemed to get warm. Jake went back to Phil's room, took off Phil's coat and lay down. He closed his eyes. His whole body was warm and tingling from what had been the most exercise he'd done that he could remember since cross-country running at school.

"I think we'll be okay here," the little girl said as his mind became fuzzy and wandered close to sleep.

"Mmm," Jake mumbled. "We'll see. I'm still not..."

Bob poked his head around the sheet. "Get some rest, Jake. I'll get you up later for dinner. You did good, Jake."

Jake couldn't see Bob, he was still on the edge of drifting off to sleep.

"I like Bob," the little girl said.

"Me too," Jake mumbled as slobber dripped from his open mouth and down his chin.

"Hmm?" Bob said.

"Thank you," Jake said, his lips clapping together, as random orbs of light flicked behind his eyelids.

Jake didn't quite catch what Bob said as he left.

The little girl whispered, "Something about your shell cracking, Jake. He was smiling."

When Jake woke up, the bottle tops were clinking above him. He sat up. On the sheet wall beside him, a patch of sunlight painted itself as six slanted peach gold squares. He reached out and ran the back of his hand across the fabric, feeling the difference in heat where the patches were and were not.

He gulped down half a bottle of water from the table beside him then stood up, stretching. He noticed, on his pillow, a small pink pouch, tied at the top with purple string. He picked it up and opened it, emptying the contents into his dirty, bandaged hand.

"What the hell?"

In his palm were six tiny figures made from cloth and string. All brightly coloured. None larger than a postage stamp. Some had yellow ribbon jumpers and green string legs, black hair and tiny pink faces. Others had grey hair and pinprick cotton eyes, blue trousers made of twine, or purple skirts made of weaved cloth.

"They're worry dolls," the little girl said.

"What?"

"Worry dolls. You tell each of them a problem or worry that you have and, when you're asleep, they help you."

"Really? That's cool. I guess." He picked up each doll and examined it closely as if it might speak to him. "Hang on. How'd they get here? I don't think they were here last night. This morning rather."

"Jessie brought them. While you were asleep."

"Jessie? Wow. I didn't even hear her come in."

"She told you the story of how to use them, but I don't think you were listening."

"I was very tired."

"You were. Are you okay now?"

"I feel better, yes. You?"

"I feel better as well, Jake. Jessie is my friend and I like her shadow now."

"I know. It's good, I guess, to find new friends."
"Like you and Bob?"
"Hmm. Maybe."
"Don't be mean, Jake. Bob is very nice to you."
"Yeah. I know."
"And Jessie likes you. That's two new friends, Jake. In one day. Jessie kissed you while you were asleep."

Jake stared at the yellow-blue-pink face of a worry doll upside down in his palm. "She what?" he said.

"She kissed you."

Jake felt odd. His mouth turned down at each side.

"On the forehead," the girl said.

Jake smiled. "Oh. Good. Yes. Well *that's* okay. I guess. Did she stay long?"

"No. Someone came. A woman. And shouted at her. Called her some names that I didn't quite understand, but sounded quite bad."

"Ah, crap," Jake said, pushing the dolls back into their bag and pulling the string to close it.

"What's wrong? I don't think the lady was angry at you."

"We'll see. I guess it's a good job I've got these little fellas on my side eh?" He shook the bag and threw it back onto the pillow.

"If they work," the girl said. "Sounds like a pretty story. But a bit mumbo jumbo."

"Mumbo jumbo," Jake said, laughing. "Mumbo fucking jumbo."

"Jake," the girl squealed.

"Sorry."
"Good."

"Hey, Jakey baby." Bob poked his head around the sheet, his face shining, wet looking, his eyes shining, wet looking. "It's Sunday. Midday. Dinner?"

Jake looked at his dirty hands, and at how his wrists seemed thinner than he'd noticed before. At that exact moment, his stomach felt empty.

Bob's head disappeared, but his voice carried on. "You're guest of honour, Jake. It's all cooked up and ready."

Jake pulled at the sides of his trousers, rubbed his shirt flat onto his chest in an attempt to look what he thought might be considered smart. He couldn't decide if the feeling in his belly, and the twinge in his lower back, was hunger or trepidation.

He stepped out of his room.

In the exact centre of the warehouse was a long table held up on thin wooden legs with wire supports. It was covered in a set of different coloured, pristine clean tablecloths, and around it sat about twenty people. They all stared at him.

He saw Jessie, dressed as she was before, her face beaming a smile at him. He lowered his eyes but smiled at the same time. Bob was standing at the end of the long table and he pulled out a dark green, plastic garden chair, offering it to Jake. Jake looked directly at the chair and nothing else as he walked over and sat down. He didn't make eye contact with the people around the table.

Bob sat down next to him on a cream and brown

faded plastic garden chair.

Jake stared along the length of the table, and his mouth opened at the sight of the food there. It was a banquet. Pieces of brown, moist chicken were set on plates. Vegetables steamed into the air. There was a bowl of salad. Bottles of cider. Beer. Wine.

Jake is at a medieval banquet, sitting next to Elaine. She's asking if he's ever been to one of these banquets before, and Jake is shaking his head whilst staring at a serving woman's cleavage as she pours a pale yellow drink from a metal jug. He's thinking how nice it is to pick up a huge bronzed turkey leg and just rip at the flesh, and he's scared that, at any moment, he might be picked out to re-enact a sword fight with the massive square man dressed in a dull tunic and bottle blond, highlighted hair.

Elaine leans over, her face close to his, and she rubs at the side of his mouth and pulls away a tiny piece of grey meat that she holds in the air. She's smiling with her redder than red lipstick and her whiter than they should be teeth, and Jake squeezes his legs together as something inside him tickles. Elaine's face is so close that Jake can smell mead and cherry balm lipstick and face cream and she pushes that tiny grey piece of second hand meat into her mouth, closes her eyes and says, "You missed a bit."

Jake turns his face away and stares at the man with the stupid highlights from a bottle that they can't have possibly had in medieval times, and he can still feel Elaine's breath in his ear and the man is walking right to him, and Elaine is whispering so that the words tickle, "Come on, Jake. Let yourself go." and the guy with the hair, he's staring right at Jake, eyes on eyes, and he lifts a long broad sword out in front of him while Elaine is saying, "Just one night, Jake. Just one." and Jake is standing and looking for the toilets but he doesn't know where they are and the blond man's face screws up and he lowers the sword and just lets it hang there as he stops advancing and Elaine is still talking and she says, "Emma doesn't have to know." Jake is watching the man's eyes as they flick very quickly to one side, and then Jake is hobbling towards the toilet and he hears Elaine slam her fists into the table and he hears metal plates clatter and hears, as he shuffles past the man with the sword, a sigh that sounds like a sigh he's sighed a million times before.

In the toilets that smell like normal pub toilets, Jake stands in a cubicle, pushes one hand into the wall, stares into the lavatory bowl of yellow-brown stains, and waits for his erection to go down.

"That's Jerome Kid," Bob said.

The small, black man sitting a long way opposite, had a face that looked like it had been drawn in charcoal then rubbed out around his forehead and cheeks and jaw, a shiny black face outlined with grey-white stubble.

Jerome shouted across the table in a soft, almost feminine voice. "Jerome Kid. I'm black." He smiled and drew a circle with his finger around his face.

Jake smiled. "I noticed," he said.

"Jerome used to be a singer," Bob said.

"Singer *songwriter*," Jerome corrected him.

"Singer songwriter," Bob said. "He was even on Top of the Pops once."

"Yup," Jerome said. "I was on Top of the Pops. He raised his hand, palm down, as if to show the top of something. "Number three. Three. *Love's Lost on Nobody*." His smile seemed wider than his cheekbones, melting away into his grey stubble. "You ever hear it? Number three."

"No," Jake said. "Never really one for music."

"You got any cash?"

Bob interrupted. "Jerome. Not now, eh?"

"No, I haven't," Jake said.

"I'll sing for cash," Jerome said, rubbing a thumb and forefinger together next to his ear.

"Jerome. No. Come on," Bob said.

"I don't have any cash," Jake said.

Jerome placed one hand flat across his chest and inhaled. "Love's lost," he sang.

"Kid!" Bob shouted.

The rest of the table, especially Jessie, were laughing as Jerome continued to sing. Jake was astonished by the man's voice. He was pitch perfect, powerful and soft at the same time. Bob stood up, leaned forward and put his hands around a large glass bowl of something brown. He pulled it towards him, sat down and cradled it to his body.

"...on me. On you..." Jerome sang.

"Kid," Bob said.

Jerome stopped singing. He stared at Bob clutching the bowl. He rubbed his eyes and sat down.

The table applauded.

"Don't encourage him," Bob said, shaking his head, pushing the bowl back out onto the table. "Bomb is diffused," he said chuckling. "I cut the pudding wire."

Jake laughed.

A big, fat woman, her neck all pushed up around her jaw like she was pink toothpaste being squeezed from her tight toothpaste tube dress, banged her hands, equally fat, rings barely visible beneath folds of fingers, onto the table.

"Enough," she growled. "You all quit laughing and let's eat. I'm hungry."

"That's Jane," Bob said out of the side of his mouth. "She used to run a pizza shop in town."

"That's Momma Jane?" Jake said, looking at the woman who was sinking onto the table like a melting candle. He looked at Jessie, his mouth open, his eyes wide. Jessie smiled and shrugged so that her ringlets bobbed up and down on her ruffled shoulders.

Momma Jane glared at Jake from the pits between her forehead and her cheeks. She hissed so that flecks of froth escaped into the air.

Bob saw Momma Jane open her mouth to speak and he stood up. "So let's eat," he said. "We'll do more intros on full stomachs. First, I think you should all thank Jake."

Jake felt his stomach knot up.

Bob carried on. "Most of this food is what he got us last night. This morning."

Some of the table said a quiet thank you. Jerome nodded his head. Jessie waved. Momma Jane grunted. They all started to eat. They passed plates around, picking food off onto their own plates. They filled glasses with wine or water. Jerome grabbed a bottle of something and shuffled it to his side. Momma Jane glared at Jake. Every time his gaze met hers, he felt an uncomfortable flash of something close to guilt.

"Jane," Bob said.

The people continued to eat.

Momma Jane shifted her neck ever so slightly and spoke to Bob. "You will address me as Momma Jane or Momma. Or I'll be calling you Robert and ignoring you all at once."

Bob shook his head.

"And don't shake your head at me. It's him that should be shaking his head. Bowing it and hiding it and shaking it." She pointed a swollen finger at Jake.

"Momma Jane?" Bob said, his hands out, pleading. "Will you just eat?"

"Not hungry," she said, moulding herself back into her chair.

Jerome stopped chewing and looked into the side of Momma Jane's face, his mouth open, half chewed bread sitting in its corners.

"Shit, Momma," he said. "Did I just hear you right? Did I just hear you say you weren't..."

"Can it," she shouted. Her whole body shuddered.

Jerome canned it. Continued chewing. Slowly.

"I'm not eating anything that he," another glare, another pointed finger, "brought in here."

"Momma," Bob said.

"Fuck you," she said, her words coming out as a thick growl from her over stressed throat.

Jessie squealed.

Momma Jane continued. "It's all *his* fault that Phil's dead."

Everyone around the table stopped eating. Their eyes danced between Momma Jane and Jake and Bob. All eyes wide. All mouths dripping food.

Jake felt like he'd been hit in the chest by a hard thrown ball, a pain shot down his arms and made his hands cramp.

"Now you shut your mouth," Bob shouted, standing and leaning his weight on the table.

"No," Momma Jane croaked. "You shut yours."

There were gasps from around the table.

"We all know it," she went on. "I'm just the one that said it, is all. So no. I won't eat."

She swiped at the table, knocking food and plates to the floor. Jerome watched a chicken leg roll around, then he sighed as it fell.

"*I* wasn't thinkin' that," Jerome said. "You fat bitch."

Momma Jane swung her massive arm like a fleshy tree trunk, but Jerome moved out of the way, laughing.

"Jerome," Bob shouted. "Jesus. Don't you start."

Jerome shrugged then gestured to the food on the floor.

"Jane," Bob said in a low voice, his eyes fixed on her like he was a hawk on a telegraph pole staring at a field mouse. "Yeah, Jane. No Momma. No, Momma Jane. Until you apologise. And you can call me Robert all you like. See where that gets you."

Momma Jane stared at the roof and attempted to

fold her arms across her breasts, a gesture which failed, much to the delight of the rest of the table who sniggered. She buried her palms, one above the other, into her stomach below her breasts.

There was absolute silence.

Then Jessie spoke. "Momma? It wasn't his fault." She placed a tiny gloved hand on Momma Jane's shoulder. Momma Jane grunted.

"If it's anyone's fault," Bob said, "it's mine. Okay? Everyone? It's my fault that Moses came back here, and it's my fault that *I* wasn't here when he did. And, well, I'm dealing with it how I'm dealing with it. Okay? And Freesia? Well, she dealt with it how she deals with things. Shit, we're all just dealing with it okay? So all of you, just shut the fuck up and eat."

Everyone bowed their heads like a schoolroom of naughty children. Except Momma Jane who started again.

"That's very brave of you, Bob. So, we all blame you now that Phil is gone. Great. I can deal with that."

Bob placed his hands over the back of his head as he rested his forehead on the lilac tablecloth.

But Momma Jane wasn't finished.

"Are we all to suppose it's your fault that Jake is a pervert as well?" she said.

Bob didn't move. The rest of the table stared between Jake and Jessie, their faces screwed up between disgust and bewilderment.

Jake picked up a huge glass jug and hurled it at Momma Jane and it flew through the air in slow motion, catching the light from the windows flash on flash off flash on impact, glass breaking into tiny shards as it cleaved into Momma Jane's soft fat face and her cheeks and her lower jaw ripped apart and flew into the sunlight as dull pink pieces of flesh and red dots of spray and her left eye was closed but thick sinuous jelly and a disc of iris slid down her face onto her chin and she fell forward so that her massive head made a thick wet slap on the yellow tablecloth, her blood and flesh and fat and shit seethed out of her and ran along the edges of the cloth.

Jake shook his head violently. He clenched his hands into fists and stood up. He stared Momma Jane right in the face, wondering just how close he'd actually been to smashing that jug into it; wondered if his little daydream would have been so bad after all.

"Fuck this," he said. "I think Jerome was right. You are a fat bitch."

He picked up a chicken leg, shoved it in his mouth, picked up a handful of buttered potatoes and some green beans and walked away back towards his room.

Behind him, he heard Jerome singing, "Push my buttons, baby. Push them all." He heard Bob shout. Heard Jessie squeal. Then he was inside his den and watching Eddie Murphy push himself around on a wooden trolley in *Trading Places*.

Someone tapped on the steel upright and Jake jumped. For a horrifying moment, he thought it might be Momma Jane, come to throttle him for being a murdering, foul-mouthed, pervert.

"It's okay, Jake," his little girl said. "It's not that nasty woman."

"Can I come in?" Bob said.

"Sure," Jake said.

Bob walked in. He had brought Jake a glass of red wine and placed it on the side next to the six armed footballer. Then he stood next to Jake, looking down at him.

"It wasn't your fault," he said.

"See?" the little girl said. "It was him. Bob. He said so."

"I know," Jake said to both of them at once.

Jerome burst in, panting. His eyes all wide, his smile all wide and his face all sweat.

"Hey man," he said. "I just spent ages avoiding Momma. She's started throwing stuff now. Plates, food, jugs. Man, it's like a hurricane out there."

"Jerome," Bob said. "Give us a minute will you?"

Jerome looked over his shoulder at the sound of glass breaking. "Thought I might sing Jake a song. You know? Cheer him up," he said.

"Not now," Bob said, his voice flat and tired.

"I really don't have any money," Jake said.

"I know," Jerome said. "This'll be on the house."

"Kid. Not now," Bob said. "Just get back out there and stop that mad bitch from destroying everything. Sing *her* a song. A lullaby."

Jerome stood upright, his chest out, his head nodding. "Yeah. A lullaby. Yeah. Got it. I'll do that." He left humming the musical scale.

"What can I say?" Bob said. "He has a way with song. He could sing to an angry gorilla and have it eat out his hand. It's his gift. He brings in quite a bit of cash, from pubs and stuff. Just goes out there, sits down, sings, and people are all tripping over themselves to give him money."

"I'm not interested," Jake said. "I'm leaving."

"Now, come on, Jakey."

"No. I'm out of here."

"Look, man, I said. It wasn't your fault. Okay?"

"I know."

"You do?"

"Yes. It was yours."

"I know. I said as much didn't I?"

"Yeah you did. Did you think that by taking a bullet for your own guilt it would make you feel better? Paper over some cracks. Help you sleep at night?"

"Something like that, yeah." He sounded even wearier now. "Phil is dead because I lied to Moses. Okay? Shit, no one liked Phil anyway when he was alive. They all hated his stupid little routines, his childish matinees. The shitting off the walkway? Fucking hated him for it. Funny how they hated him so much until he was dead. Then they're all missing him and looking for someone to blame. They're all scared that our little family has been broken into. I think they wonder who's next."

Jake stood up. "Whatever," he said. "I'm leaving."

"You can't go," Bob said, his voice croaking. "Your hand's a mess and your house is probably crawling with police, or rats, or both."

"Bullshit. I don't think Moses was the kind of person the police would find even if he *was* dead.

And you said Freesia would clean him up."

"Yeah, I did. But still. Jake, come on. Be reasonable."

"This is me being reasonable," he said pushing past Bob. He lifted the sheet and started to duck under the corner.

"Arggh," Bob said. "This is ridiculous. Think about it will you?"

"Thought about it. Thanks for the hand. It actually feels pretty good." He wiggled his fingers at Bob as a mocking goodbye wave.

"I never told Moses where you lived okay? Even I didn't have it in me to do that. I took more than just a bullet for guilt, Jake."

"Then pick a colour for your medal, Bob. Purple's nice. Purple for bravery."

Bob followed him out into the warehouse where the group of people, including Momma Jane who was cradling Jessie under her huge wing, were sitting in a circle listening to Jerome singing his soft lullaby.

Bob placed his hand on Jake's shoulder and spun him gently round to face him.

"You don't quite get it do you?" he said.

Jake just stared, waiting for some clever, enlightening punchline, something that would keep him in the family and have him get up every morning to collect unwanted food for the unwanted hungry.

Bob scratched at the top of his forehead then spoke slowly, "I, never, told, Moses, where, you, lived."

"And?" Jake said, his forehead hurting from the effort in his scrunched brow.

Bob continued, his hand gripping Jake's shoulder hard. "And yet he turned up *at your house* and did a dance on your hand."

Jake was confused, enlightened, scared. But above all, he felt stupid. He swayed, unsteady on his feet.

"It was her," the little girl said in a slow matter-of-fact tone.

"Emma," Jake said.

"Most likely. Yes." Bob said.

"Do you think she'll be all right?" the little girl asked with a hint of mischief in her voice.

"You know what?" Jake said, angry again.

"Go on," Bob said, looking like he was trying too hard to smile and failing.

"It's a shame Phil *is* dead."

"Eh?"

"Well, so far, he's the only one that hasn't shit on me from a great height."

Bob suddenly looked very guilty, a look of genuine regret.

Jake walked back to his room, lay down on his bed, and listened to the soft lullaby from Jerome Kid whisper in through the sheet. He fell asleep.

For the next four days, Jake kept himself to himself. He collected food by himself, only bumping into Den once and then politely telling him to fuck right off or he'd mess his suit up again. Most of the family kept out of his way as well. An old man, Boris of

Borris, all pale and covered in brown blotches like wet seaweed on a dry beach, took to staring at Jake with dazzling silver eyes during the twice-daily gathering around the table. Momma Jane didn't make eye contact. The rest of the family went about doing what they did as if Jake was not there, like he was watching it all, and himself, on a reality TV show.

Bob would check his hand but said almost nothing, his mouth moving like he was chewing his own guilt behind his lips. Every time he checked and poked and massaged, Jake's hand was stronger. There was no more pain, and he spent most of the day scrunching a soft blue teddy bear he'd found behind the crates in his den. His fingers and palm felt good again.

Jessie acted as if nothing had happened at the dinner table, but whenever she sat down with Jake she would leave the sheet propped open across the back of a blue plastic picnic chair.

His little girl seemed to be going through a rather excitable stage. With Jessie coming and going and all the other family brushing close by, she was full of light-hearted conversation, the occasional dumb question about how much water weighed, and how she liked the way the sun filtered through the skylights and made her feel like a jigsaw puzzle sometimes.

Every day, Jake pulled back the sheet to Freesia's den and peered inside and everyday the room smelled more of damp concrete and wood, and less of her. Wondering if Freesia really had killed Moses and if Emma had indeed told Moses where he lived, was beginning to eat him up. He had never smoked before, but he did now. He found a pack of Richmond Menthol up on a beam, and stood out by Bob's boat smoking two, one after the other, listening to Zeek blunder around inside the metal hull like an out of control rubber ball.

Jake is at school in the headmaster's office. He's looking across a desk that smells odd, at a young smart man with oily black hair, a garish pink tie and a white shirt that's so thin his breasts show through.

"It's very serious," Ballbreaker Butler is saying. "We go to a lot of effort to ensure our pupils don't go down that path."

"But I don't smoke."

"Shut up!"

Butler is spinning a crumpled pack of cigarettes on the desk and tiny flecks of tobacco spin out like the rings of Saturn.

"So when we catch pupils smoking, I, we, have no choice but to be harsh."

"I didn't smoke them," Jake says. "They're not mine."

"But you were caught, behind the football boards, with this very pack." He holds the pack up and waves it.

"I found them."

"Of course you did, Jake. What? And you don't smoke?"

"No."

"Liar!"

The packet is slammed down hard onto the desk

so that the Newton's cradle clicks and shakes, and a wave of stale coffee breath hits Jake.

"You were found with the cigarettes," Butler shouts, holding up a dull grey cardigan. "And your cardigan reeks of stale tobacco."

"My dad smokes."

"Of course he does. What? And you don't wash your clothes?"

"But it's not dirty."

"But it reeks of tobacco smoke. You smoke. I'm having none of it. You hear? What? Your mum doesn't even do the laundry?"

Jake is furious. He can see the pages of a calendar flicker by. All the days he'll spend in detention.

"My mum is dead," he says.

"Liar," Butler shouts. "You see? A liar. What? Two weeks after school detention."

Jake's dad is shaking his head and pulling the various tiers from his fishing box, placing them on the dinner table.

"Jake," he says. "You are such a dick sometimes. Why'd you go tell him your mother was dead?"

"I was angry."

"Damn. Such a fool. I'll go speak to Mr. Butler and sort it out. I was hoping me and you could go fishing this week." He takes out a sealed plastic pack of luminous coloured floats and waves them. "This week and next."

Jake clenches his fists on the table and cries.

"I don't smoke, Dad."

"Hey," his dad says, pushing his finger and thumb into the bridge of his nose. "*I* know that. Shit. I know. Like I say. I'll have words with this Mr. Butler guy." He laughs. "Might even turn up all smelling like fish, and see if he accuses me of smoking kippers."

Jake laughs and rubs tears from his face and the table.

"Thanks, Dad." he says as he moves around the table to help pack the fishing kit back into the box.

Jake stubbed the cigarette out by the side of Bob's boat. "Three fucking weeks of detention for fuck all," he said, exhaling the last of the smoke. "Cheers, Dad. What a guy. Fucking Kippers."

"She's back," the little girl said, and Jake looked down to see his shadow wavering around his feet.

Jessie ran out from the doors of the warehouse and grabbed Jake's hand.

"Freesia's back," she said, looking up, beaming.

Jake felt his bowels drop then relax. He felt like he might throw up.

Jake is sitting in his car listening to Huey Lewis and the News and he's on his way to meet a girl that isn't Emma when it should be. As he parks the car at the bottom of her drive, he feels light-headed and weary, like he has the flu, and he looks in the rear view mirror. She's walking up the tree lined road behind him, black hair, short tartan skirt, fake fur jacket. She's swinging a small gold handbag and smoking a thin brown cigar between stark purple lips.

Carla walks up to the car window and Jake's insides knot up and he sees her breath on the glass and watches her thick lips open and close and sees her pink, studded tongue and he throws up into the foot-well of the car down his clean for once jeans and onto his polished for once shoes and Carla laughs then finishes her cigar and throws it down and Jake watches the way her shoulders and her ass make opposing up and down motions as she walks up the drive into her house and leaves the door open and he looks up to the top window and sees the curtains close.

Jake opened the sheet to Freesia's den and stepped inside. It smelled of sweat and perfume and incense. It smelled of her. And something else, something sweet he couldn't quite grasp.

Freesia was naked apart from pale lilac knickers. She had her back to Jake and was bending over a bowl near the mirror, splashing her face. Jake watched her shoulder blades move in and out, watched her ass and thighs as the muscles tightened and slacked. Though he'd imagined her to be athletic and fit, this was the first time he'd seen her naked.

"Freesia?" he said.

"Hello, Jake," she said, still splashing water on her face and spraying it back into the bowl with a fast exhalation of breath.

"Freesia."

"Yesh, Jake?"

"Are you okay?"

"I'm fine."

The conversation was monotone.

"Is he dead?"

Freesia stood up. She looked taller naked. She turned around.

"Yesh," she said, her face blank, her eyes dull. "Very dead."

Jake smiled and frowned at the same time.

"What happened?" he said.

"I told you," she said, patting her face and breasts with a dark grey, threadbare towel, "he'sh dead."

Jake was aware that he was staring at her breasts as they moved up and down with her breathing.

"Dry me?" she said, handing Jake the cold, damp towel.

Jake looked at the towel like it might bite him. "Sure," he said.

Freesia turned around and pulled her hair to one side. Jake balled the towel up and patted it onto her shoulder, near her neck. He felt mechanical, lifeless, like he was drying the roof of a car.

"So it's over. He's really gone?"

He felt the towel heave up and down sharply.

"I shaid sho, didn't I?" She breathed into the mirror, one eye looking back at Jake.

There was silence as he patted her other shoulder, then he let the towel unfurl and rubbed it up and down her spine, feeling the firmness of her back. His other hand was hanging by his side and he wondered why he wasn't reaching up and laying his mending fingers on her pale flesh. He just didn't want to.

"Passh me that shirt," she said, gesturing towards her bed.

Jake picked up a clean but crumpled shirt.

"This is my shirt," he said.

"Yesh."

"Well that's okay. I don't mind."

"I didn't think you would."

She took the shirt, put it on and fastened the buttons. She rolled the sleeves up in untidy rolls and rubbed her arms. She sighed, and a flicker of life flashed across her eyes.

Jake smiled and this time he didn't frown.

"Ish your hand okay?" she said, picking up an opened bottle of red wine.

"Ah, yes. It's fine. It's almost better already. I think."

"Good. Good. Bob ish quite the technissian when it comess to human flesh and bone."

She sat down and patted the bed beside her. Jake sat and felt the warmth from her body. She leaned back, her arms out behind her, and looked up at the ceiling to where three tiny black toy angels quivered on thin silver threads. She sighed.

Jake spoke. "You were gone for nearly a week, Freesia. What happened?"

"Have they been treating you okay? The family, I mean?"

Jake took the wine and swigged. It tasted old and flat and watery. "Compared to?" he said.

Freesia shrugged.

"It's not been great," he said. "They hate me for what happened to Phil."

"Yeah. I did too," she said. Her voice contained no emotion. "I sheem to have gotten that out my shyshtem now though."

Jake looked at the side of her face and for the first

time, he saw a glimmer of a smile in the gaps of her broken mouth, a faint quiver in the strands of tissue.

"I'll be honesht. If Mosses, washn't there when I got there," she paused, then turned to face Jake. "I wash going to kill *you*."

"Figures," Jake said.

She pushed her hand softly under his and grabbed it tight. "If it makesh you feel better? I did have it all worked out sso you'd jusht be dead real quick. You know? Not shuffer."

Jake laughed and flat watery wine bubbled back up his throat making him cough.

"And Moses?" he said, clicking his lips and gagging to get the wine out of his windpipe.

"I'll be honesht, I didn't want it to end. I wanted to make it worth my while."

Silence.

Jake felt a morbid curiosity. He couldn't quite hold an image of a bloody and torn Moses for long enough to make it seem real, and, as if Freesia could sense this, she took a large swig of wine, placed the bottle on the floor, and told him what had happened.

"He wash alive for two daysh, Jake. Nearly made it to three. He wash like a horshe; he wash sho fucking sstrong. After I'd ripped hiss mouth out with the bladesh," she made a slurping, clacking sound, "I wrapped hihs head in cling film, took nearly a whole roll, wrapped it up from hish neck to under hiss shnot bubblin' nose. All that blood jusst shquashed inshide there and squeeshed itss way around the back of hiss neck and down hish back. He bled for agesh out of a little gap at the back of hish neck. I'd already tied him to your chair at this point, found shome washing line in your ssink cupboard. I had to be careful. I wash driving nailss into his shinss one at a time and they were kind of shliding off the bone and sshifting all over the plashe. I wash worried that the nailsh might shnap the line and he'd get up and kick the sshit out of me. But that wass about the only time I thought he might have a go.

"Your ssink cupboard was full of goodiesh, Jake. Like you shaid." She smiled. "I found a pair of shecateurss and while he was ssleeping, ooh, the morning after I think, I shtarted to chop off hiss fingersh. When I shtarted on the firsst one, that'ss what woke him up. He kind of tried to shcream and he sshuffled a lot, but I managed to push the blade through the gap near his knuckle and I lopped hiss little finger clean off. He shtopped sstruggling then. Like he was reshigned to it."

Jake looked at his own hand and a faint nausea swept over him. He made a guttural *yukking* noise.

"After the third finger, I'd got it shussed sho that I knew what I wass doing. His lasht two fingerss came of real eashy, just a crunching grishle noishe really. Then I got shome toilet cleaner and poured it over hish nub of a hand. It wass hilarioush, Jake. All that bright blue Toilet Duck pooling out over where his fingerss used to be and mixing with clotsh of blood. It wash like ssome sstrange modern art painting. But you know what?" Her eyes were full of excitement.

Jake said, "But he didn't move."

"Yeah. He flincshed a few timess, but that wass all. And hish eyess, they followed me round the

239

room and he wash alwayss watching as I did theshe thingss to him. He looked curiouss. Can you believe that? He looked shurprissed and curioush at what his own inssidesh looked like. I wonder if he'd ever even sseen his own blood before. I mean, that'sh the feeling I got from the expressionss on what wash left of his face; that he'd never even bled before."

Jake was still curious. He wanted to know, more than anything, why Moses had taken his punishment as a mere curiosity. He needed to know how far Freesia had pushed him. He needed to know if, at some point, any point, Moses had shown remorse. If he'd cried, or whimpered or shook his plastic covered, blood filled head.

"What else?" Jake said. "I want to know how he died."

Freesia jerked her head back in surprise.

"Don't look at me all weird," Jake said. "I just want to know."

"Well," she continued, "I wass kind of playing a game with myshelf at that point and *only* ushing thingss I found in that cupboard under the ssink. There wash a craft knife, shome glue, cotton ballsh, brillo padss, a dishwasher tablet, a blender, an iron, casherole dishes, paintsstripper, shoe polish, and dental flossh."

"Shit," Jake said. "You used all those things?"

"Yeah. It wash a good game, Jake. I ran the craft knife down hiss bare forearm, shplitting his shkin and muscle, then I peeled it all back around the bone and I could see it all ssquishing and twitching ash he flexshed hish arm. He shtill looked curiouss, shtaring down at the inshides of hish own arm like that. Then I poured the paint shtripper into the hollowed out mesh and we both watched as red and white froth bubbled up and... God, that shtunk really bad, sho I lit shome incenshe sstickss, but, well, they shmelled a little old, Jake. You really aren't domessticated are you?"

"No, I am not domesticated."

"I showed him hiss fashe in a mirror and hiss eyesh were all over it like he wash examining whether he'd had a good haircut or not, which gave me an idea. Sho I plugged the iron in and waited agess for it to get real hot."

"What? That iron doesn't work."

"Yeah. I know," she said, and tutted like it was Jake's fault she'd wasted her time waiting for the broken iron to get hot. "I jusht ssmacked him in the front of hiss face with it inshtead, mashed hish nose up and ssplit all hiss cheek open. He wass falling apart by that point. Physhically, I mean. Jusht bitsh of him, all over."

Jake sat up straight. "Did you use the blender? I bought that to make smoothies."

"Ha. No. I didn't. After the iron," she shot an accusatory glance at Jake, "I didn't want to washte any more time. Oh the dishwasher tablet wass funny though. I pulled the cling-film out below the gash in his cheek, near where half hiss noshe was peeled off and hanging, and I dropped it in. It wass hilarioush, Jake. God I wish you'd sheen it, man. It wass all bubbling and frothing, and little white fleckss of powder were shwimming around inshide the plasstic.

Moshes looked more annoyed at that than anything.

"I shtuffed the cotton ballsh in between his toess, poured methylated shpirits over them and lit them. That shtunk ash well as hiss big, hairy toess crissped up. I shqueezed the shoe polish into hish eyess, right up under his drowssy eyelidsh, pushing it in with a plasstic shpoon. He looked like a beaten up panda bear. Did you know that shoe polish iss flammable ash well, Jake. It wass marvelloush."

Freesia was physically twitching now, her foot tapping, her fingers drumming her bare thighs. Her eyes, what Jake could see from the side, were reflecting the light from a gap in the sheet.

"How did he die, Freesia? I mean, after all that, how did he *actually* die?"

"I shliced the cling film up the sside with the craft knife, cutting deep into hish jaw and cheek again, and all that frothing blood and blobsh of congealing flesh and fat jusst shlid off to the floor. I could shtill shee his eyess moving about under hish burnt shut eyelidss, and they crinkled as they moved, and I jusht shaid, 'Well, Moses, I've run out of thingsh to play with now. Sho I'm going to kill you.' And I shwear, he tried to ssmile. I could shee under all that mess, hiss face twitch upwardsh, shaw the muschles inshide hish open cheek tighten. And he jusst said, real quiet and, I shwear with a hint of a laugh, he jusht said, 'Without my hat?' Which I thought was weird, ash if he'd thought there wass no way he could've died without hish hat."

"But *how*? How did he die? I need to know, Freesia."

"I put a bin bag over hish head and tied it up round his neck with dental floss and tape. Then I shtood back and watched the black plashtic crinkle in and out for a good couple of minutes until it didn't move any more. Weird thing ish, I wash ssad that he hadn't held out longer."

Freesia slid her hand to Jake's groin and pushed.

"But he is dead. I mean, gone?"

Jake's scrotum tingled.

Freesia moved in close to his face and whispered. "Yeah. He'ss gone in all shorts of directionss. You think I could carry him out in one pieshe?" She fluttered her mouth against Jake's neck, and his penis grew large. He closed his eyes and smiled.

"Don't worry, Jake, It'sh all cleaned up now. Four dayss remember?" She unzipped his trousers and ran her warm hand inside as her tongue flicked around the edges of his mouth. "You *are* going to need a new carpet though. Your'sh iss gone," she whispered.

"Mmm. Okay," Jake said, as he felt a cold rush of air around his cock.

"Now, let'sh fuck." Freesia said, sliding on top of him and pulling him into her as he watched the three tiny black angels staying perfectly still above them.

When Jake woke up, he was on his own lying in a cold, wet patch in Freesia's bed. He rolled onto his back, not sure whether he should be smiling or not. Above him, two tiny black angels rotated in opposite directions.

"Weird," he said to himself, wondering if he'd

imagined the third angel. He might have even wondered if Freesia fucking him had been real as well, if the evidence wasn't all over the bed and his trousers and his stomach and his face.

He went back to his den. Picked up clean clothes. Went outside. Showered under the solar camping shower array, which was at best just slightly warmer than freezing. Dressed. Went back to Freesia's to see if she was there. She wasn't.

On his way back through the warehouse, where the table was being set up by Jerome and, surprisingly, Momma Jane. Bob walked over with a stern look on his unshaven face.

"Hey, Jakey," he said. "I take it you know Freesia's back."

Jake couldn't help but smile. "Oh yes," he said. "I spoke to her last night."

"We need to talk," Bob said, walking away.

"What. About Freesia?"

"Kind of. Yes."

Jake felt like a guilty teenager who's parents somehow knew he'd had sex. He followed Bob out of the warehouse and onto his barge, where he sat down at the table, and wondered what kind of turn things could take now. Moses was dead. In pieces. Gone. He wasn't a threat any more. All Jake could think was that Bob was going to rip into him for fucking Freesia right under the families' noses. In his head he heard himself arguing that surely that kind of shit went on all the time in this kind of place. In his head, he also heard himself losing that argument when Momma Jane and Jessie might be levelled at him. Had the police found out? Had they been to the house? Freesia said that Moses hadn't made any noise at all, and that she'd disposed of his body. He felt confident that she knew what she was doing. He now had no carpet for Christ's sake. Moses already had a knack of being invisible; surely when he was dead and in pieces he'd be even more invisible. Maybe the postman had posted a new DVD and noticed a strange smell that aroused his suspicion and he'd had called the police. But Freesia said she'd cleaned the place up and, well, Jake reasoned that...

The cabin door swung open and slammed into the side. Zeek came bounding through, his hind legs slipping on the floor and skittering lumps of dirt away to the sides.

"Shit," Jake said, pulling his legs up onto the seat. "Fuck. Shit. Zeek. No. Fuck off. Shit."

Zeek crashed headlong into the seat below Jake's feet then jumped up under the table and nudged a frantic head into his ribs and chest and stomach, making an excited low grumble.

Jake sighed. "Dick head," he said. "I thought you were gonna tear me apart."

Zeek stopped and cocked his head to one side. Jake rubbed his palm across the dog's solid bony skull, and Zeek let out a loud bark that made Jake jump.

"Zeek," Bob shouted, as he came in with Freesia.

Zeek barked again and nudged his powerful snout into Jake's thigh.

"He's after my jewels, I think," Jake said.

"Zeek. Out." Bob said, and Zeek scuttled back the

way he'd come in the same fast forward, uncontrolled fashion with which he'd come in. Bob closed the door behind him. He leaned on the table, tilting it with his weight, and stared at Jake, a worried look on his face that Jake was sure he hadn't quite seen, ever. Freesia stood a little way behind him, her eyes cast down to the floor, her hands behind her back.

"We have a problem, Jake," he said.

Jake looked at Freesia who caught his eye for a tiny moment before looking at the floor again.

"It's Emma," Bob said.

"Emma?" Jake felt relieved that he wasn't going to get a dressing down about fucking Freesia after all. "What about her now?"

Bob stood up and started pacing, tiny shuffling steps. "We think Luce has her."

Jake felt his insides flatten.

"What? Luce has Emma?"

"Yes."

"Oh for fuck's sake. How? I mean, how do you know?"

"Freesia told me."

"What? When?"

"This morning. Earlier."

Jake leaned forward. The table tilted back towards him.

"She told you this morning?"

"Yes."

"Oi," Jake shouted at Freesia. She looked up. "You knew this yesterday. I mean, you knew all this before you fucked me last night? *While* you were fucking me last night?"

Bob stopped pacing and looked at Freesia. She shrugged.

"You fucked him?" Bob said. "Last night? Here?"

"Yeah she did," Jake said. "In her room."

"Fucking Starmouth," Bob spat. "You seen anything of Momma Jane this morning, Jake?"

"Yeah, she was setting the tables up with Jerome."

"And she didn't try to kill you?"

"No."

"Starmouth, you stupid bitch. Shit. Well, at least we don't have that on our plates as well."

Freesia looked almost relieved. But not quite.

"Emma," Jake said.

"Shit, yeah. Luce has Emma," Bob said, waving his hand at Freesia like a stage direction. And as if she'd taken it as a stage direction, she stepped forward.

"I'm pretty sure. I went to her house," she said.

"Emma's or Luce's?" Jake said.

"Emma's. For two days I went and she wasn't there. I'm sure Luce has her."

"Bullshit," Jake said. "Just because she wasn't home doesn't mean that crazy witch has her. You're guessing."

"No," Freesia said. "I'm ssure."

"You can't be sure. You can't be. You're guessing." Jake felt like he was trying to convince himself.

Bob spoke. "Well, Freesia has me convinced. I believe her."

"Oh great. That stupid bitch," Jake said, raising his hands to his head.

Freesia examined the palms of her hands.

"Freesia?" Bob said.

"No, Emma. And yes, Freesia. You... Arggh idiot."

"I'm shorry, Jake," Freesia said, her voice cracking. "I didn't think telling you wass the right thing to do. We want you to shtay here now. Bob doess," Bob glanced at her. She continued, "I didn't want to tell you and have you jusht run off. I thought that Mosses being gone would be enough."

"You stupid idiot," Jake said, flopping his head onto the table and gripping his fingers in and out.

"Hey," Freesia shouted, "You got a fuck out of it. You got to fuck me. Ishn't that what you wanted? To feel me from the insside. Come on. You didn't do sho bad."

Jake shouted into the table, "Fuck off. Shit. I don't know. No. Hang on." He lifted his head, looked at the ceiling and sneezed. He pushed his fingers into the bridge of his nose then sneezed again.

"Hey guys," Bob said. "Luce has Emma. Let's get back to that bit. I'm not giving you a lecture," he pointed at Freesia, "again about having to do it out in the yard." He shook his head. "Look, it's maybe not so bad."

"Not so bad?" Jake said, his eyes wide.

"Well, shit. Emma or no Emma, Luce was always going to be pissed when she found out Moses had been killed. I'd kind of accepted that. Took *that* bullet? I was kind of hoping you'd be here when it all kicked off, Jake."

"What? Me? What?"

"Look. We've dealt with Luce and Moses before." Jake waved his arms in despair.

"Jake," Bob said. "This isn't old news. How do you think I lost my shadow? How do you think I lost Seth? This tit for tat bullshit has been going on for years. We're a hotbed for being harvested out here."

"It'sh been happening for yearsh, Jake," Freesia said, stepping closer.

Bob put his arm out to stop her. "But it's been getting brutal, Jake. More and more of us just popping off, as it were. And pretty much all that are left are the one's without any grunt. I mean Christ, they're the family and I love them, but, they're the ones that even death can't be bothered with. There's only really me and Freesia left."

"And you now, Jake," Freesia said.

Jake spoke. "Ah, come on. You recruiting now?" He stopped. Looked at his hand and thought how strong it had become so quickly. He laughed. "You *are* recruiting. That's hilarious. You think I'll be useful to you. So you," he pointed at Bob, "*groom me*, and mend my hand, and you," he pointed at Freesia, "stop Moses killing me then fuck me. You know what's really interesting?"

Silence.

Jake continued. "I want to shake my head, but I just can't be bothered. I want to say that I've had enough and just walk out. But I'm kinda getting fed up with that too."

"So?" Bob said.

"So, I don't know. Get me a drink."

Freesia ran to the door as if she'd been told it was okay to go out and play in the rain.

"Zeek, no," she said opening it a bit and stuffing her foot in the gap. "Zeek. Sshit."

"Let him out," Jake said.

Zeek bolted out, skidded across the floor then bounded up beside Jake and placed his face on his thigh. Jake rubbed Zeek's head, felt the pulse in his skull, felt the thin, wiry fur prickle under the gaps in his fingers.

Jake looked at the ceiling and sneezed. His eyes stung.

Freesia came back out, pushed past Bob and slammed a bottle of absinthe down onto the table. She half smiled her best half smile.

Jake didn't smile any kind of smile. He picked up the bottle and stared through the sloshing green liquid. Zeek looked up at the bottle and whined. Bob looked at Freesia as if she'd brought the wrong bottle. Freesia shrugged.

Jake swigged. "Ooh ya bugger," he said, making a fuffing noise as he exhaled through pursed lips.

"Jake?" Bob said. "Seriously. Do you think I would give so much of a shit about you if I didn't see a bit of me in you?"

Jake swigged.

"Come on man," Bob said, moving in and taking the bottle and swigging. "Between me, you and Freesia, we might even be able to take Luce out of the equation."

Jake looked up, his eyes massive and red. He

sneezed. Zeek barked.

"And Emma?" he said, grabbing the bottle back.

Silence.

Bob's mouth moved in tiny increments but he didn't speak.

Freesia spoke, quiet but also angry. "You don't even love her, Jake."

Silence.

Jake is watching TV after school. Benji walks into the living room and he's limping. He's lifting one back leg and dragging the other. Behind him, on the dark green carpet are dark red ovals of blood.

"Benji?" Jake says. "Benji?"

Benji stops and looks up at Jake and Jake puts his chip sandwich down on the table and stares at the dog. He gets down on his hands and knees and just as Benji falls on his side, he pushes his hand under him and lifts him back up. Jake stares at the dog and at the blood bubbling out from his back legs and then he sneezes and Benji jumps and falls onto his other side. Jake rushes into the kitchen and grabs a handful of tea towels. He rushes back and wraps them around Benji as best he can. He sneezes again but this time Benji doesn't jump. Jake lifts Benji's face to his and looks at it. Jake sneezes again. The dog's head thumps onto the carpet and Jake thumps onto his backside staring at the grey and white thing that used to be his dad's best friend.

When his dad comes home and dumps his work gear on the floor, Jake points to Benji.

"He's dead, Dad," he says.

And Jake's dad crouches down beside his once best friend and runs an oily hand down his flank like he's checking to see if the dog really has gone. He leans his head into the short grey fur and leaves it there for a moment.

Jake sneezes and his dad jumps.

Jake looks into his dad's eyes that are all red and full of tears and his dad looks back at his son's eyes that are all red and full of tears, grabs him at the shoulders then kisses him hard in the centre of the forehead.

In the garden, before the rose bushes had grown so huge in the corner, Jake says how he was sorry he always hated that dog.

Jake's dad pulls him in close and kisses him on the top of his head.

"You never *really* hated him, son," he says into Jake's hair. "You hated the sneezing. That's all."

Jake never sneezed after that.

Jake sneezed.

"You know what? Let's ask the dog," he said, one hand rubbing his eyes, the other Zeek's head.

"What?" Bob said. "Jake, seriously. What?"

"Zeek?" Jake said. "Should I stay here?"

Silence.

"Zeek. Should I stay here?"

Zeek whimpered and nuzzled his head under Jake's arm then stayed there.

Freesia was playing with her hands, examining her fingernails. She breathed heavily.

"Zeek?" Jake asked. "Should I go and help

Emma?"

Zeek pulled back, lifted his head and, wagging his tail so that his whole back end moved, barked into Jake's face.

Jake sneezed. He rubbed his hands over Zeek's back, then stood up.

"Bob. Freesia. I'm gonna go help Emma," he said.

Freesia stopped playing with her hands and the flaps of her mouth quivered ever so slightly.

Bob opened his mouth then stammered. "No. Shit, Jake. Come *on.*"

Jake started to walk out. He rubbed his hands across his eyes and his nose, then sneezed.

"Jake, come on, man," Bob said. "It's not worth it."

"The dog says it is," Jake said.

As Jake walked out into the open air, a fine mist was descending and he let it settle on his itching eyes.

"I'm coming with you," Bob said.

"Whatever," Jake said.

Freesia stood next to Jake and looked at him.

Jake saw something like pride in those deep, brown eyes, then she said, "No, Bob. Let him go."

Jake walked away with the conversation behind him dwindling into 'let him go', 'suicide', and 'maybe for the best'.

Chapter Fifteen

During his walk down a cold country lane, Jake hadn't quite decided what he was going to do.

"Do you think she really has her?" his shadow said as it flickered across hawthorn hedges in the early morning sun.

"Why would they lie to me?"

"I don't know. I'm not sure."

Silence for a few steps.

The girl hummed, then said, "If she does have her, what are you going to do?"

"Hadn't really thought about it," Jake said, realising he really hadn't. "It just seemed like a good excuse to get out of that goddamn warehouse."

"I like it there."

"I know. You said. But I felt trapped and lonely."

"Lonely? But there were lots of people there, Jake. I like Jessie and her shadow."

"I know. You said that too. I guess I just feel less alone when I'm on my own."

"That doesn't make any sense," the girl said, huffing. "It's a stupid thing to say."

"Not really. I just didn't belong there. That's all."

"Oh. And you belong with Emma. Is that it?" The girl sounded angry.

Jake laughed and kicked at some loose stones sending them skittering across the road into the hedge on the other side.

"No way," he said. "We don't belong together. Never did really."

"But," she said, then paused. "You *are* going to rescue her aren't you?"

"Shit. Sorry. Well, I hadn't really thought of it as a *rescue* before," he said, looking into the sky at thin orange clouds. "Rescue makes it all sound a bit big."

"Jake," the girl squealed. "It *is* big. And what are you going to do after you rescue her?"

"Jesus," Jake said. He stood under the canopy of a bus stop. "Stop asking me questions about stuff that hasn't even happened yet."

"You really are silly, Jake. You don't plan anything do you?"

"No. I really don't."

On the bus, Jake wished he'd spent at least a few more hours at the warehouse. As more and more old people got on the bus, the noise became unbearable. The smell of tea and flowery perfume more and more pungent.

"Must be free pensioner bus pass time," he mumbled to himself.

"They all get free bus rides?" the girl said.

"Yes. All of them."

"Even really nasty old people?"

"Hadn't thought about it really," he said, staring out the window as another queue of pensioners shuffled in. "I guess so, yes."

"That's stupid. Some old people are the most horrible people there are. Spiteful old codgers."

Jake laughed and the woman next to him

squirmed herself into her chair, letting Jake know she was there, and that she was not pleased with him talking to the window.

"Old people," he said, tutting and squirming himself.

Jake wasn't entirely sure why he went home first. He had almost decided to get off the bus a little early and check on Emma's house, but, as if he were going for drinks after work, he wanted to go home and freshen up. His hand smelt. His hair was lank and greasy. His trousers clung to his thighs. His ears felt waxy.

He opened his front door, peered inside, then stepped into the dark living room. It smelled of incense, bleach, damp, and ozone. His feet echoed on the bare floorboards. He looked down at where his carpet used to be, surprised that the wood was actually cleaner around the door than the carpet had been. The TV was still on and hummed faintly with a black screen and tiny blue square in the corner. He walked over to the kitchen and opened the curtains then turned around to look at the room again. He expected to see some sign of something. Bloodstains. Broken furniture. Empty bottles of Toilet Duck or bent nails. Pieces of Moses. There was nothing. The room looked cleaner than it probably ever had. He ran his hand across the back of his chair and it felt soft and smooth. All the books on the bookshelf were neat and stood up, a far cry from the messy, half sloped piles they used to be. And there were no takeaway leaflets scattered randomly.

"I should marry this woman," he said.

"Don't be stupid, Jake. You say a lot of stupid things lately, Jake," the girl snapped.

"I was joking," he said, filling the kettle and switching it on.

"Oh," the girl said. "It's hard to tell sometimes."

"Yeah. I get that a lot."

While the kettle boiled, Jake checked out the bedroom. It looked the same as before, a little untidy. The alarm clock lay on its face on the cabinet, cupboard doors open with piles of clothes creeping out at the bottom. The bed was unmade and crumpled. Jake realised that Freesia must have slept in it. He ran his hand over the sheets then sniffed his palm confirming that she had indeed been sleeping in his bed the last few nights. He felt his insides flutter at the thought of her lying there and wondered if she'd been naked. He pictured Freesia and Emma lying there together in the exact same spot, their bodies like ghosts inside each other. He sniffed at his palm again then went to check the bathroom.

"Ah, crap," he said, staring at the mirror. It had been smashed, but all the pieces were still in place. It was so badly cracked that he couldn't even make out any individual part of his face. He shifted his head around and forward and back, but nothing, he was just a big smudge of cracked and broken pink. From the cracks spreading out in all directions, the mirror looked like it had been hit three or four times. If it was Freesia that had broken it, it hadn't been accidental.

In the kitchen, he made black coffee and drank it

whilst staring out the window.

Then he showered in warm water that actually made the shower gel and shampoo lather up into thick white froth.

"I can't believe it's only been a few days. I didn't realise I missed bubbles this much," he said.

"You like bubbles?" the girl said.

"Yeah. I guess I do."

"I remember bubbles, Jake."

"You do?" he said, spitting out water and rinsing himself.

"I think I do. Yes."

"When this is all done, I'll make sure you get plenty of bubbles then, eh?"

"What?"

"I don't know. Damn. I'm not sure I know what I meant."

Jake felt stupid as he towelled himself dry. For the briefest of moments, he somehow thought the little girl could be real.

He sat in his chair rubbing his hands on the arms, aware of how his bad hand didn't actually feel that bad any more. It looked normal as well, a little pale in places, a little blotchy in others, but mostly it looked like it had never been broken. He hunted down the side of the chair cushions for the remote but didn't find it.

He stared at the blue square on the otherwise empty screen and at the yellow icon showing an arrow pointing into it.

"Well," he said, "let's go find Emma."

"What?" the girl said. "Now?"

"Yup. Now."

"Aren't you going to collect some stuff? Like weapons and things?"

"What?" he said. The thought hadn't crossed his mind since he left the warehouse. "No. I just hadn't really thought... Besides," he said, standing up and staring close at the blue square and the yellow arrow, "Freesia probably used everything."

As Jake approached Emma's house, he was struck by how neat and tidy it looked from the outside. He hadn't been there for nearly seven years, eight maybe, since they broke up. The old wooden windows that he'd once spent a week painting had been replaced with very smart UPVC double-glazing and each pane was split into six smaller panes, giving the windows that country house look. He thought it looked kind of odd, all the other townhouses, butted up on each side, had plain UPVC or wooden windows. The front gate was still the same narrow, one person wide, ornate cast iron one that used to leave rust marks on the concrete below when it was wet, but now it was bright vivid green with a shiny hammered metal look.

Jake looked up at the top windows. He expected he might see Emma looking down, shocked that he had finally come back to the house after leaving all those years ago. He expected too much. The windows were empty and lifeless, like tired multi paned eyes.

As he opened the gate, he felt a tiny flutter in his chest. It felt odd to be back, especially knowing that

Emma wasn't there.

"She's not here, Jake," the girl said.

"I know," he said, pushing at the bright red front door that was, surprisingly, the same colour that Jake had painted it in the week after he'd finished the windows. "I just needed to check." He lifted the jaw of the brass lion doorknocker, then put it back. "How do you know she's not here?" he said, looking down at the shadow that spread out across the grass then bent up the wall to the lower edge of the window.

"I can't feel that other shadow. That man that you..."

"Okay. Fine," Jake said, "you seem to be getting good at knowing when other shadows are near or not." He pushed at the door that led into the alley at the side of the house and it swung open. "You never used to know that well. That they were near I mean." He stepped into the cool, dark tunnel. The girl didn't answer.

"Jesus," Jake said as he stepped into the garden.

"What is it, Jake?"

"This garden is immaculate."

Outside the back door was an area of sandstone crazy paving, the gaps filled with tiny pea-sized pieces of bright white gravel. Just beyond that was another stretch of the same beach-like gravel, edged with dull grey cobbles that sat beside large rocks that sat beside lush green plants that hung over the edges. All over, there were tall elegant grasses and broad, flat leafed plants and herbs. At the bottom of the garden, dark green ivy grew up and over the fence.

"Wow," Jake said, gently kicking a heavy cast

iron bucket that seemed to serve no other function than show, "Looks like a bloody magazine photo."

"It *is* beautiful," the girl said. "Nowhere to play though. Not a nice garden for children."

"No. Not for children."

Jake peered into the house through the patio doors, his hands cupped around his face.

"Wow," he said.

He pulled the handle and the door slid open.

"Ah crap," he said. "It's open."

"But she isn't here, Jake. I know it."

"Crap," Jake said again.

He checked the bottoms of his shoes before stepping into the cool room. It smelled of fresh carpet and coal.

"This place is immaculate," he said, looking around at the white leather couch and the thick cream carpet. On the wall above the open fire was a huge flatscreen TV that spanned the whole width of the chimney breast.

"Is she rich, Jake?"

Jake laughed. Stopped. Then swallowed.

"No, she's not rich. She has the exact same job I do. Almost. Shit, I mean damn, she has a lot of nice stuff." Jake shook his head. "She's *such* a snob."

He checked the kitchen, all black worktops, stainless appliances, stainless matching kettle and toaster, a six-hob oven with a curved glass cooker hood. Apart from the fridge, everything was in exactly the same place as when he'd lived there. But everything was new, not a trace of DIY cupboards, worn linoleum tile effect floor or single taps with rust under the plastic knobs.

"Christ," he said. "What has she been playing at?"

"But it looks so nice," the girl said.

"Hmm. I guess. Doesn't feel like home though. Not like when I lived here and it felt like home."

Jake went upstairs, past the black and white photos of old New York Central Station with the light beaming through the windows and onto passengers.

The girl continued to talk.

"You don't like this house do you?" she said.

"No. It's like a show home."

"A show home?"

"Yeah, a picture perfect house that people show you round to show you what a picture perfect house should look like."

He opened the door to the front bedroom, looking around before entering.

"Why wasn't it like this when you lived here?"

"Never had the money. Or the time. You know? There was just never... It just wasn't *us* to be like this."

The pink bed stood against a backdrop of dark chocolate brown, with a small set of cupboards built in overhead. He stood staring at the bed, imagining all the times they'd sat there talking about the future. All the times they'd made love and actually meant it. All the times Emma had complained that the windows let in too much of a cold draft, or that the bedclothes made her itch, or that the carpet was too thin and cheap and...

"Jake?"

"Yes?"

He left the room and closed the door, hunched his shoulders forward and stood at the top of the stairs looking down to the oak flooring at the front door.

"Were you happy here, Jake?"

He trudged down the stairs, realising that the handrail was still exactly as it had been before, the same warm, worn, silky feeling as it slid through the palm of his hand.

"For a while, yes," he said. "It was my first house. Our first house. We loved this place."

Back in the living room he sat on the sofa, sank deep into the corner, and rested his cheek against the cold arm. He stared at the huge, blank TV.

"*She* never loved this house. Did she?"

"She did. I'm sure of it. She wanted it to be nicer, but we just couldn't afford it. Really, we couldn't afford to get bogged down in loans for new furniture or kitchens or," he sighed. "Maybe she was right."

"About what Jake?"

"I never had any conviction she said. She said I never had any dreams or commitment. She said that I didn't seem to care about anything."

"Why did you leave her? Why did you stop loving her, if you loved her so much to begin with?"

Jake sighed again. "She left me. She kept the house of course. But, well, you know, we just split up."

"Why?"

"It kinda happened really quickly. She started to get angry all the time. She left for work without me in the mornings, only ever spoke to me in the evenings to tell me what a loser I was. In the space of about a month it all just fell apart."

"Do people in love really do that? Do they stop loving each other so quickly? I don't think they should."

"She just kept poking and prodding at me like she was testing me. It all happened so fast. I think maybe she was right. I can't remember her calling me a loser exactly, but, well. She was right."

"Jake, you're crying."

"Shit, am I?" He pulled his head from the settee and rubbed at the under sides of his eyes with his thumbs. "All the years I was in love with her and it came to nothing *so* quickly. I didn't know that could happen. With hindsight, I guess, there must have been something that made her so mad so quick. But at the time, I just didn't want to think what that might be. You know? So I just rolled over."

"Jake?"

"Yes."

"Do you think you love her? I mean, do you really want to get her back? I won't mind."

Jake smiled. "Of all the people in the world, the only one that makes sense is the shadow of a little girl."

"Just tell me one thing, Jake."

"Okay."

"Do you still love me?"

Jake looked down at his hands and clicked his thumbnails together. "God yes," he said. "Always."

He put his hands on his knees and pushed himself up.

"You and me against the world, eh?" he said.

"Told you," she said, and Jake could hear the playfulness in her voice.

Jake walked down the road with confidence in each step. He clenched his fists in and out, stretching his fingers of both hands then feeling the way his nails scraped against his palms. Despite the huge black clouds, stalled in the distance, the sun was warm on the back of his neck.

"Jake?" the girl said.

"Freesia told me."

"What. How did you know what I was going to ask, silly?"

"You were going to ask me how I knew where she lived. This Luce?"

"Yes. How?"

"Freesia told me that night we... One night in the warehouse."

"Yuk. Don't remind me. Horrible man."

He watched her shadow crinkle along the pavement, sheer across lampposts and bins. Watched the way her arms reached out towards dozing cats on fences. Watched the way she moved further away to run her shadow fingers over piles of leaves.

"You seem rather playful," he said.

"I am. Everything feels fine, Jake. I feel like I just woke up."

Jake laughed. "Me too."

"See those clouds, Jake?"

Jake looked up at the bruised sky just as the sun behind him faltered. The girl flickered on the patchwork concrete.

"Oh, I see them all right. Storm clouds. Big, fat, heavy storm clouds full of rain."

"I think they're for you, Jake."

"We'll see," he said. "When it starts to rain, we'll see."

On the corner of Little Cedar Grove, Jake stopped. His face was sweating, his knees hot, his feet sore. He looked down to the far end of an unremarkable street, terraced houses, tiny front gardens, small cars, narrow pavements.

He walked on, crossing the road to be on the even numbered side.

"Eighty-four," he muttered. "Eighty-four."

Outside number eighty, he stopped and leaned on the low front wall. A net curtain twitched. He continued to lean. He looked along towards eighty-four. It looked like a very normal house on a very normal street.

Doubts crept into his head. What if Freesia was lying? What if, for some reason, this was all a strange trick to get him out of the warehouse, out of harm's way, get the family out of harms way, in case Moses came back who couldn't possibly come back because Freesia had killed him then tidied up his house and left no trace of any body that Jake believed, that the family believed, had been hacked into nothing and disposed of. Now Jake was wondering if Moses really was dead or if that big nasty angry clever man was waiting for him behind door number eighty-four. Or if at that very moment the family back at the warehouse were enjoying the food he'd collected and laughing about the stupid man that came and went and never came back and they're all throwing party streamers and wearing shiny hats, celebrating the day that Freesia killed Moses and Jake went away and everyone lived happily ever after.

Chapter Sixteen

"This is it?" Jake said, staring at eighty-four Little Cedar Grove.

Apart from the glossy, black front door, the house looked like any other 1920's semi-detached house with badly maintained, wooden window frames and mock Tudor eaves that were dull grey instead of white.

"What did you expect?" the little girl said.

"Dunno," Jake said. "A castle? A bunker door leading down to the gates of hell? An abandoned hardware shop taken over and re..."

"Jake. Shush."

Jake glanced at each window in turn, then at the door.

"She's in there, Jake. Inside the house."

"Emma?"

"Yes. Her. And someone else."

"Luce?"

"I don't know. It feels horrible in there. It's not nice."

"I didn't expect it would be *nice*."

He felt the girl quiver.

"I'm scared, Jake. It's *messy* in there. Cold and dark and messy."

"What do you mean *messy*?"

"I don't know. Messy. Like at school if all the

children were playing in the playground and then a big nasty dog came in and everyone starts screaming but you can't hear them because they're all screaming at once and the dog is barking and biting at the children's feet and their hands and everyone's just running around trying to stay together in little groups. Jake?"

"I've got to go in."

"Please don't. Jake?"

"Just be quiet. We'll be fine. Just stay close to me and absolutely silent, okay?"

"No. Jake. No."

Now it was Jake who shushed the little girl and, as if she'd never existed, she shrank into nothing.

Jake pushed the front door open and cold air, colder even than the air outside now that the clouds had covered the sun, seeped out. It smelled of damp plaster and incense.

Inside, the hall was dark, the bare plaster walls pock marked all over with salty white patches like fine expanding cobwebs of crystal. The skirting boards were also pock marked with tidal patterns of black mould that spread out onto the bare floorboards. On the right of the hallway were stairs. Jake looked up them, letting his eyes become accustomed to the dark. At the top of the stairs, nothing. He looked down the length of the hallway, past two doors on the left, to an empty, door-less opening to the kitchen where, even from where he stood, with the cold air still seeping around him and out, he could see and hear fat raindrops on the single pane of glass above a cheap white plastic kettle.

He looked into a mirror on the wall beside him, a grey, dusty mirror that barely reflected his face. He was surprised to see how wide his eyes were, how alive he looked, even in smears of grey. He didn't feel alive. He felt empty and tiny and scared. He felt like he was being watched, and he stood in absolute silence, breathing through his mouth, listening for any noise that was different enough that it wasn't the rain.

He pushed the door closed behind him figuring it would be better to close it now than have it slam shut in a breeze. There was a rush of adrenaline as he walked in slow, heel to toe movements, over to the first door. He tilted his head towards it and listened. Nothing. He rested his shaking hand on the handle and inhaled, then started pushing it down. The handle squealed, the spring inside pinged and grumbled in an annoyingly increasing pitch. *No matter now*, he thought. If there was anyone in there, they'd see the handle moving. He pushed the door open then grabbed at its edge with his other hand to stop it swinging backwards into anything.

Inside, at one end of a long thick table, a woman was slumped over, her blonde hair spread out like seaweed across the table top. Fine threads of incense smoke floated around her. She clenched her outstretched hands into fists.

"Emma?" he said, forgetting completely any idea that he was trying to be quiet.

With what seemed to be immense effort, Emma lifted her head and pulled her hands into her chest.

"Jake," she said. "You came."

Her face was a mess. One side was swollen around a closed eye that looked like a slit in meat. Her jaw was fat and low. On her forehead was a huge white lump, ringed with purple lines.

"Jesus," Jake said. "What the fuck happened?" He moved towards her.

"Jake. No," she said, holding up a hand. "You shouldn't have come."

"Er," Jake said. "Clearly I *should*."

"No. It's what they wanted." She shook her head, her hair sticking to her bloodied face. "You stupid, *stupid* idiot."

"Yeah. I get that a lot," Jake said, frowning. "Now come on."

"No. I can't. If I move she'll do this all again. I can't."

The other door, at the side and behind Emma, opened and Jake's heart jumped, his throat closed, he swallowed, Emma flinched. Someone came in wearing a dark blue raincoat. Hood up. Head down. The coat was covered in small white dots and rain. The figure raised its head, then raised its hands to the hood and paused.

Jake looked at the round face deep inside the hood, at the young, bright amber eyes that stared back, at the tiny nose tilted up at the end and at the shiny purple lips twisted up on one side in a smile. Jake realised that he too was smiling. He stopped smiling and frowned.

"Luce," he said.

Luce pulled her hood back with bright purple fingernails and her silver hair floated down around her perfect face. She smiled at both sides of her mouth and pushed her hair behind her head.

"Jake," she said, her voice soft. She clapped her hands together in front of her lips then spoke again, her voice muffled behind her thumbs, "I knew you'd come."

Her eyes drifted to the floor at Jake's feet, her thin eyebrows twitched, her smile was still visible at either side of her hands. Jake felt hot and prickly. He was angry with himself for feeling aroused and intrigued by this perfect porcelain doll and her consuming persona.

"Good," Jake said, trying to sound authoritative. He stepped forward to the table, his chest out, his arms straight, his fists clenched. "Then you'll also know why I'm here, Luce."

Luce rubbed away some more of her hair, then, as she slowly unbuttoned her raincoat, she spoke. "Oh, I know exactly why you're here," she said, pulling off her coat and draping it over the chair behind Emma, making her flinch and bow her head. "I'm not sure *you* do," she said with a look of genuine confusion. "Do you?"

"I'm here," Jake said, leaning his knuckles on the warm, thick wood of the table, "to take Emma back." He smiled at Luce, but his mouth twitched uncontrollably.

"Do you like music, Jake?" Luce said, moving over to a CD player on the wall shelf.

"I'm here..." Jake said.

"Classical, Jake? Pick your poison."

She wore a green top with straps that reached up

over her pale shoulders and as she turned to the side, one strap dropped and Jake saw the lacy cream top beneath. Saw the shape of her breast. He saw three, dull brown freckles on her shoulder that looked like Orion's belt in a pale sky of flesh. She prodded the CD player and it started to play music. Loud.

"Oh shit," she said. "No, that won't do."

Emma looked at Luce, her one good eye wide, her other weeping pale pink fluid.

Jake gritted his teeth as a very loud female voice screamed over heavy, industrial music. He grabbed one hand in the other and massaged it as he remembered that day at the Big Screen. Luce prodded the CD player again. Each prod made her breast crease up and down near her shoulder. Jake shook his head and bit his lower lip. He shifted from side to side on the outer edges of his feet to displace the tightness in his trousers.

"Enough," he shouted.

Luce froze, lifted her head, raised one finger then said, "Kidney Thieves. Fantastic. A bit too loud for right now?" She bent closer to the CD player and prodded again. There was silence. A clinking shifting sound. Then piano. Light airy piano. Jake watched the muscles in her arms as she placed her fingers on the edge of the shelf.

"Ah," she said. "Clint Mansell." She turned to Jake. "Drink?"

Jake stared. The gentle piano and the incense smoke and Luce, made him feel nauseous and weak.

"Sit down," she said, waving a hand at the chair nearest him.

Jake pulled the chair out, his eyes never leaving Luce, and he sat with his elbows on the table. He huffed. He sounded defeated. He didn't mean to.

Luce pulled a chair around and sat next to Emma.

"Emma has told me all about you, Jake," she said.

He stared at Emma. Her face, all puffed up as it was, showed regret.

Luce pushed her fingers into her temples and closed her eyes and Jake felt cold in his feet, like his toes were dipped in icy water. He felt the little girl cower. He felt the cold move like needles beneath his kneecaps.

"Enough," he shouted, slamming the table with the palms of his hands. "I just want Emma back."

Luce's face was blank, her glowing amber eyes wide, her purple lips straight.

"Well," she said, her hands ghosting piano on the table to the tune on the CD player. "I really don't want to string this out. But, did you ever get an exciting gift that arrived late?"

She ran her hand over Emma's hair. Emma looked at Jake, both eyes weeping.

"I'm sorry, Jake," she said, slurring. She shrugged and turned to look at Luce.

"Do you know?" Jake said. "I think," he pushed his fingers into the bridge of his nose, "I reckon I could be over at your side of the table in a heartbeat." He stared at Luce. "And I'm thinking," cold up his thighs, "that my hands, even my fucked up one, could be around your neck, I mean thumbs pressing your windpipe. And I could count how long," cold in his hips, creeping to his spine, "it takes for your pretty *do me* eyes to close."

Luce ran her middle finger along her throat and shuffled in her chair. She closed her eyes and lifted her face to the ceiling.

"Go on," she said. "Then what?"

"Then I'll fuck you. I'll fucking fuck you."

Luce laughed.

"God yes," she said, looking at Jake and blinking, "I'd like that. But then, it won't be as good now as it would be after you hear what your beloved Emma has to tell you. God, after that, you'll feel like you could fuck the whole world." She stopped and her face screwed up, all tight lips and knotted brow. "Shit this is taking ages." She grabbed Emma's hair and yanked her head back making her gasp. "Tell him how you came here of your own free will."

Emma grumbled, making a sound like she was swallowing thick mucus.

"Tell him," Luce shouted into her face. "Then maybe I'll let you watch us together. You'd like that, Emma? Like to watch Jake fucking me while you sit and wonder about how your face is all a fucking mess and how my face is all pretty and covered in sweat and smiling and gasping."

"Fuck you," Emma spat. "Fuck you."

Luce clapped her hands and her other strap fell. Jake stared at Emma.

"Oh yes," Luce said. "Tell him that bit about you being a lesbian slut."

Jake's stomach tightened.

"Tell him," Luce said playfully. She kissed Emma on the side of her face. Emma swatted her away.

Luce carried on in a childish, playground song. "Tell him how you came here," she laughed. "How you came here of your own free will then *came* here."

Emma screeched and her hands shot up to her face like she was in sudden pain.

"Tell him," Luce said, her voice low and nasty. "How you screamed my name as I pushed my face between your thighs."

"No," Emma said.

"But all those nights?" Luce laughed. "I know I didn't mean nothing to you then. I *know*."

Luce looked at Jake. She seemed able to turn her face from scorn to innocent beauty in a heartbeat.

"Oh," she said. "Are you upset, Jake? Your precious little girlfriend is broken." She clapped again. "I broke her. I knew you'd like that."

Jake's face was a gravity pulled sack of loose flesh. He shook his head side to side.

The piano played.

Jake thought how easy it would be to get up and leave.

"I'll be honest. I didn't really feel it. You know? Really feel it?" Luce said.

"I'm going now," Jake said, standing up. "And I'm taking Emma."

Luce pushed her fingers into her hair and shook her head wildly. "Shush, Jake," she said. "Please. Quiet. Sit down. That's not the best part. I thought it would be. I thought that would really get your goat. But then. Oh wow. You've got to hear this, Jake."

"I don't care," Jake said, leaning on the table again. "I'm taking her anyway."

Luce pulled her hair out to the side then thrust her hand to the ceiling.

"But this is the bit where the postman arrives with the present you've waited for for *so* long, Jake. It has *got* to be worth the wait." She slapped Emma in the side of the head. Jake grimaced but sat back down. Luce poked a fingernail into Emma's face, just below her swollen eye. With each word she spoke, she prodded. "Tell him why you went back to him after all that time and latched on to him. Why you used him like a sad lap dog."

By the time she had finished the sentence, her fingernail was dripping weak, red fluid. Emma groaned. Luce leaned in close and hissed something into her ear that Jake didn't quite catch.

"The shadow, Jake," Emma said into the table. "Your shadow. I knew you had one. I saw you changing everyday at work. Saw the way you looked at people and how you stared at the floor all the time like you were looking for lost change in an amusement arcade. And I saw the stupid maps you drew, Jake." She looked up. "And I just needed to know."

The piano played.

"I had to know," she continued, "if that shadow of yours was a little girl." She sobbed, a guttural swallowing noise, then said, "So I came back to you, Jake. Every single chance I got I just tried to know more."

"Know what?" Jake said, leaning forward, expectant of an answer.

"If it was a girl."

Luce waved her hands in the air and screamed.

"Okay," Emma said. "I wanted to know if that little girl was ours."

Jake poked out a lazy finger, more into the air than at Emma. "Ours?" He looked at Luce, then back at Emma. "What do you mean, *ours?*"

Emma sighed. "It all made sense, Jake. A young girl. Seven years old."

"What?" Jake said. "Seven? How did you know she was seven? I don't even really know that."

"I was guessing, Jake. I was always guessing. From what my shadow told me when he'd been crossing over her and talking and stuff, you know. Just guessing. Trying to fill in the blanks."

Jake shook his head.

"Seven years ago, Jake. When you left me."

Jake scowled.

"Okay," Emma said. "When I pushed you out. When I suddenly decided I didn't want anything to do with you any more."

Jake rubbed his thumbs into his screwed up eyes.

Emma's voice became flat and monotone. "I had an abortion, Jake. I got rid of our child."

For a moment, Jake wasn't in the room. His body felt twisted up like an old twig and he floated down a rough stream.

Luce clapped her hands in front of her mouth again and smiled her wide smile. She was staring right at Jake, studying his expression. Jake's face was blank. He was still floating.

"Jake?" Emma said.

"Jake?" Luce said.

Jake was back in the room.

He shrugged.

"Jake!" Emma screamed at him.

Luce opened her hands and placed them on her cheeks, her amber eyes wide, her purple mouth open, her pink tongue flicking across her top teeth.

"Figures," Jake said.

"Figures?" Luce said, her face screwed into a ball. "She kills your child, throws you out the house, comes back, treats you like shit, has a lesbian love thing, with *me,* and all you can say is 'figures'?"

Jake placed his hands on top his head, his fingers locked, and shrugged again.

"Yeah, figures. Do you think that I wasn't expecting something like this, Emma? You stupid bitch. My whole life I expected this, something like this, and well, just so happens it was you all along, Emma. I'm not disappointed." He shook his head and stood up.

"Jake?" Emma said, pleading for something.

"What? You want me to be angry? Want me to cry and sob? Would it make you feel better if I just kicked off and spun around the room knocking shit over and smashing things up? Is that how you saw it?"

Emma's lips smacked together as she said, "I...just...I..."

"I don't feel anything, Emma. Really. I'm leaving now and I changed my mind. You can stay here."

"Jake?" Luce said. "If you leave now, I will kill her."

Emma looked up at Luce then at her own

quivering hands. "No. Jake?" she said.

Jake sat back down. Emma breathed in then exhaled. Jake's head tilted to one side ever so slightly.

"Do it," he said.

"Jake?" Emma said.

"What?" Luce said.

"Do it," he said. "Kill her." He tilted his head the other way and his neck creaked.

"Jake. No," Emma pleaded. "She will. I know she will. She's not kidding Jake."

"I know."

For a brief moment, the only movement in the room was the incense smoke lifting in thin streams. Then Luce reached over to the side of the CD player and pulled out a long thin knife. Emma panicked. She tried to stand up but Luce grabbed her hair, smashed her face into the table then pulled her head over the back of the chair.

"It's not like in the movies, Jake," Luce said, examining the blade as she turned it in her hand.

Emma was reaching back trying to grab Luce, her legs kicking at the underneath of the table with dull barely audible thuds like random heartbeats.

Jake shrugged again. "We're not in a movie, Luce," he said.

With the blade through the side of her neck, Emma grabbed at the protruding end, her fingers slicing open along the pink-grey metal, her nails clicking. Luce turned her body to the side and the knife slid out the front of Emma's throat. For as long as it took Jake to blink there was nothing, no blood, no movement from Emma. Just a cold breeze on his side and the smell of fresh rain. Then Emma began flailing, her screams gurgling and whistling through the front of her neck, her fingers reaching and grasping and holding and tearing at the spaces in her throat that she was trying to hold together. Then she fell sideways onto the floor, leaving the table covered in a forest of blood.

"Jake?" Luce said, wiping the blade on her thigh.

"Hmm?"

"Jake? Are you okay?" Her voice was soft, caring.

"Put the knife down," he said.

"Ah. Yes, of course." Luce placed the knife back on the shelf next to the CD player. She ruffled her hair and folded her bare arms across her chest. She looked down at the floor, then back at Jake. "Jake? Don't go."

"Are you nuts? Of course I'm going." He felt the cold in his feet again, then another breeze from the open door beside him and a faint smell.

Luce started to walk around the table towards him, her arms still folded, a half smile on her lips as she bit them. "No listen, Jake. I'm serious."

"Don't," Jake said. "Don't come any closer."

Luce stopped. She looked past Jake to the window, then at the door to his side.

"I have a proposition for you," she said. Now it was Luce that tilted her head to one side, her silver hair spreading across the front of her shoulder.

"No. You're not taking the little girl," Jake said.

"No, Jake, I mean, well, yes."

"I'm going."

"I know. You said. A few times. But you're still here. Because you want to be."

"You don't know what I want."

"No. But I know what *I* want. And I know what you can get out of it. Just, hear, just listen to me, Jake." She rubbed her hands down her stomach then lifted them, blew through them like she was about to cast some lucky dice, then folded her arms again, pushing her breasts up into neat, tight mounds.

Jake sniffed.

"I like you, Jake. There's something about you that I didn't expect. Something I can't quite put my finger on. Look. I want the little girl."

Jake huffed.

"No, listen. In return you can work for me."

Jake snapped his head back and scowled. "Fuck off. You *are* nuts."

"Argh. Stupid man. Listen."

"I'm not giving up the girl. Not now."

Luce stamped her foot. "I need you, Jake. Everything about you just screams of what I need. You killed that man at the warehouse." Jake raised one eyebrow. She continued, "You spent time over there, with them, with the family. You didn't bat a fucking eyelid when I killed Emma. In fact, you told me to do it. I'll be honest, I thought I might get you when you found out we'd slept together. For some stupid reason, I really did think that would fuck with your head. But oh, Jake. Killing her like we did. That was *so* cool." She stopped as if listening for something or waiting for a response. When neither a sound nor a response came, she carried on. "And Moses? I'm not angry about Moses. Tell you the truth he was beginning to slip up. If you hadn't killed him when you did I may have done it myself. You did me a favour."

"Hang on," Jake said.

Luce was still talking. "I've never even seen him bleed before, except at my hands when he wanted it, and you came along and just killed him. Poof. Gone."

"No. I didn't kill him."

"It's okay, Jake. Do I look angry? I told you, I'm not." She beamed a huge smile.

"Jesus. Look. I...didn't...kill...Moses."

Silence.

Luce twitched her nose.

"But he *is* dead. I know he's dead. There's no *way* he'd be away from here for more than a couple of days."

"I didn't kill him, Luce," Jake said, palms to the ceiling. "Am I not making sense or something?"

"Well. No. I thought you cut him into little pieces and spread him all over everywhere."

Jake felt another breeze on his neck, and cold up to his knees. Luce looked out behind him again. Jake heard the soft patter of fat raindrops.

"No," Jake said. "And will you please take whatever the hell that thing crawling up my fucking legs is off me," he said, making flicking motions like he was shooing away flies.

"But if you didn't kill him, Jake, then who did?" She raised her hands and moved towards Jake as if trying to stop something.

There was a loud crack in Jake's skull. White pain behind his eyeballs. He turned around.

"Freesia," he said, as he fell to the floor.

Chapter Seventeen

Jake opened his eyes. His legs were spread out in front of him on a dark, stone floor. Between his thighs was a black spread of blood. He sniffed and a warm, thick clot, slid from his nose to the back of his throat. He pushed air out through one nostril and watched a drop of blood shine as it fell through light then land in the dark pool beneath him. He felt something cold on the back of his neck and reached to it. His hands didn't move. Blinking like he was trying to stay awake, he pulled both arms again and felt the bite of metal on his wrist bones.

"Ah, fuck," he said, licking his dry lips.

He lifted his head and as he rolled it slowly around, he felt something like a cold wet towel wrapped around his neck. He closed one eye against the sheer white light shining straight at him then looked over to the side where his hand hung in an old, iron shackle chained to a rusty eyelet on the rough wall. He wanted so badly to reach up and squeeze the pressure out of the bridge of his nose, but instead he screwed his face into a tight ball. Opened his mouth, shut it, then wiggled his jaw side to side. His face made tiny creaking noises and another thick clot of blood slid down his throat. He tried to look out past the light but couldn't see anything so he hung his head down where it felt most comfortable, to where the tight throbbing pain in the base of his skull stopped.

"Are you there?" he whispered.

No answer. He could still feel the little girl, just. He smiled.

"Good girl," he said.

He heard footsteps on the floorboards above him, then a raised voice. Luce or Freesia. He couldn't work out anything they were saying. They were arguing. That much was certain.

"Now that I would like to see," he said, imagining the two women face to face, spitting and cursing at one another.

There was a sudden cold all the way up his spine, like he'd fallen backwards, naked onto ice, and a noise in his head like a million steel ball bearings rolling down a metal scaffold tube. He winced at the cold and the pain and the noise. The marbles spoke all around the inside of his skull, crashing and screeching and pinging.

"I'm sure you'd just love that," the voice said, ebbing and flowing.

Jake smacked his teeth together at the front then spoke, "You were upstairs. You were the one trying to crawl up into me."

"Yes. Hello, Jake. I'm Abe." As the steel balls spoke that last word, it was as if they'd all run to the bottom of the tube and gurgled away into a sloping resonating nothing.

"Abe," Jake said, mimicking the sound that Abe had made, his voice starting high and descending into a hushed rumble. Then, in his own voice, he said, "Not interested." He shot a thick glob of congealed blood out of one nostril and it plopped onto the floor. With one nostril clear, he could smell again. The air smelled damp, but tinged with the clean smell of fresh blood.

"You brought her here," Abe said. His voice was softer, like the scaffold tube was being slowly tilted left to right, the sound inside rippling like soft metal waves.

"Emma?"

"Ah. Of course," Abe said with a tinny chuckle. "Maybe I should have said *them*. Emma. Freesia. And I know the little girl's here too."

"You leave her the fuck alone."

"Oh I intend to. I'm on my best behaviour, Jake. I'm on guard duty."

There was an almighty crashing din in Jake's head as Abe laughed.

"Doesn't stop me hunting around inside you though," he said. "She's canny this little one of yours. Canny and scared. I've never had this much trouble teasing a lost one out like this before."

Above, a door slammed and Jake couldn't decide if he could hear soft footsteps moving away, or if he was imagining it.

"You're not having her," Jake said. "No one is. She's mine."

Abe made three quiet clinking noises and Jake got the impression he was thinking.

Clink.

Clink.

Clink.

"That's not *exactly* true now, is it, Jake?" he said.

"I mean it," Jake said. "You've seen what I'm capable of."

Abe laughed, but softer this time, like a cable being over tightened. "Listen to Jake," he said. "Now he's all that. Doesn't sound like you. Not one bit. Sounds forced."

From behind the light, Jake heard a door open, felt the air around him shift.

"Abe," Luce said. "I told you not to talk to him."

Abe spoke, sounding distant. "He was annoying me, Luce. He was sounding off. I think he thinks he's clever."

"And you're annoying me," Luce said, stepping to the side of the light where she was illuminated at last and Jake could look at her again.

She was still wearing the same green top and pale cream vest, but she had pulled the straps back up. Jake guessed he couldn't have been unconscious for too long.

"How's the head, Jake?" she said, kneeling down but staying out of reach of his legs.

"It'd hurt less without this parasite bouncing around inside it like a broken tin toy monkey drummer."

Luce laughed. "He's like that. But I will say this. He's no toy monkey."

Luce pulled over a chair and sat with the back between her legs, facing Jake. She reached out and moved the light.

"There," she said. "Better?"

Jake blinked. "Much. Yeah. That's great."

"Turns out," she said, looking at the floorboards above, "that it was Freesia that killed Moses."

"Well, I did try to tell you."

"And you want to know why?"

"No. I want to know..."

"For love. She did it for me. Do you know what it's like having that kind of hold over people? It's a blessing and a curse. That stupid bitch. I mean, I knew she was capable of killing. But to go behind *my* back? Without *my* say so?"

"How long have you known S*tarmouth*?" Jake said.

"Quite a while as it happens. Yes, we go back some time."

"I knew it. Fucking knew it."

"You did not."

"No, I mean, the second I saw that ruined faced whore upstairs, it was like a light bulb exploding in my head. She set this whole thing up, didn't she?"

"Well, turns out she did, yes. Again, without my knowledge. Shit, Jake, It could have so easily gone south. Do people still say that? That things go south? She was just like a bull in a china shop, no, a blundering elephant escaped from a circus. I'm still considering killing her, but, well, we'll wait and see. She's in my bed now, resting. We had quite a row."

"Is Bob in on it?" Jake said. He needed to know. He was hoping that Luce would say no.

"Good God no," Luce said, waving a hand dismissively. "God no. Not Bob's style at all. I think if he'd have got wind of what Freesia was up to, she'd be in more pieces than Moses right now."

"She should be. Just how much of this crap is her fault. How far back does she go?"

"Oh, me and her have been fucking for months. You think that mouth is only good for men? Just think about it."

Jake thought about it but was interrupted as Luce spoke.

"I guess she kinda got the impression that me and Moses weren't gonna be in it together for much longer. She must have known how pissed off I'd been getting with him. I kept mentioning how he was becoming weaker and softer and...less edgy. Love does that to you, doesn't it, Jake?"

"Huh?"

"Makes your mouth loose. No pun intended. You say things you shouldn't and don't even realise you said them. Anyway, Freesia, she gets the idea into her head that if she kills Moses, then, with me and her being lovers, I do hate that word, lovers, ridiculous. I was in it for the short sprints. Yes, so, if she kills Moses there'd be this handy opening that she could fill. Ah, I'm doing it again."

"Yes. It's almost childish," Jake said, smiling. "So. She kills Moses. You get angry that he's dead, 'cause, and I'm guessing out loud here, I'm guessing you still have, had, a need for him. Freesia...*Starmouth*, she panics and tells you that *I* killed Moses."

"Yes. Not a great plan. She should try not to think so hard."

Jake was annoyed that Freesia could have been so stupid and that she was so easily willing to throw him under a bus just so she could be with Luce. Then he remembered Emma and how she hadn't been entirely blameless.

"How did Emma end up here?" he said.

"I went to her house and invited her out for coffee. She said yes."

Jake rolled his eyes. "Figures."

"So, now." Luce twirled her finger in the air like she was mixing clouds, "Emma is sleeping with me, and Freesia isn't really where she wanted to be in all this so she goes off in a huff."

Jake shook his head. "So, you turned it all back around by using Emma on me *and* that stupid bitch Starmouth."

"Yes. Aren't I good?"

"Yeah, good is one word." Jake nodded his head side to side as he spoke. "Emma gets banged by you. Starmouth comes back to the warehouse and tells me Emma's here. I decide to come rescue Emma. Emma's out of the picture. I'm guessing out loud here," he said and smiled, "you were going to kill Emma all along. Starmouth and Luce live happily ever after."

Luce pushed herself back on the chair, her fingernails glinting in the light, dust motes sparkling down in front of her barely illuminated face.

"You left out you and the girl on purpose," she said. "Other than that? Yes. Spot on."

"Yup. We're still here."

Luce stood up. "I want the girl," she said.

"And I told you no."

"You're in no position to argue. I could kill you in

a heartbeat. Take the girl that way."

"No. You'd have done that already."

"I didn't kill Freesia yet."

Jake flexed his hands in the shackles. "Yes."

"Look, Jake, my little proposition still stands. There's no way I want to let you go. I see something in you that I only ever saw in Moses a long time ago. And something else. It's that something else that's really gnawing away inside my head. So here's the deal. I get the girl. You get..."

"Blah, blah, blah. You said already. Shit. For all your charisma and, frankly, filthy charm, I'm just not sold on the idea."

Luce stamped her foot.

"I get the girl. You get me," she said.

Jake looked her up and down, from her feet to the very top of her downcast head, her eyes looking up at him. She turned the chair around and sat down on it the right way. She placed her palms flat on her knees.

"I wasn't always like this," she said. "Bitter and angry and stealing shadows and killing people. But death has a way of doing that to you. Don't get me wrong, it's not like I suddenly decided, oh well I have a perfect right to kill because it happened to me and now I know death. Nothing like that. It was quite the opposite for a while."

Luce closed her eyes. Jake watched and listened.

"My husband, Steve. We were in love. Yeah, I know what I said, but this was real. Then he died. He had a tumour on his brain. When he was diagnosed, I laughed. I actually laughed and told him that was why he kept putting things in the fridge that he shouldn't, like razors or TV remotes or even plants. Then he laughed as well, but his eyes didn't laugh quite as hard as his mouth. You know? Then we cried for, oh must have been two days.

"I kept telling him it would be okay, that he'd be fine and there'd be a way to fix him. I honestly believed he'd be okay and I just kept telling him that. Then, one morning, I woke up and just knew, I just knew right there that he was gone. The bed felt different. Even before I reached over and ran my hand across his forehead and rubbed sleep out of his eyes with my thumbs, I knew he was dead. I kissed his cold lips. And deep down, I hoped that maybe somehow God would find a way to let him feel that kiss.

"But I don't think God was listening. I just kept replaying all the times I told Steve he'd be fine and how I'd been so wrong. How I'd lied to him every time. He died, and I kept wondering if he went to sleep the night before smiling and thinking that maybe the next day would be the one where the doctors said he'd be fine and I could reach over and just say 'see, told you' and kiss him.

"I started drinking. A lot. And I don't mean accidentally, like it crept up on me. It was a conscious decision. I just drank as much as I could until I'd fall asleep, then I'd get up and do it again."

Luce stopped. Jake was silent. He thought he should say something. Urge her to go on. He didn't say a word.

She took a deep breath, eyes still closed.

"So, I'm taking the kids to school in the car, and we're driving down a country road, and a rabbit runs out and, just like that, I've killed it. I hear it thump and bump under the car and I see it behind me in the mirror as a brown-red streak. And I'm thinking, shit, I didn't even brake. I didn't swerve. I didn't even blink. I just didn't react. I saw the rabbit come out into the road, I knew it was there but I just did nothing. And that scared me. I'd driven the kids to school a hundred times before, but that rabbit, it made me realise that I was really still drunk, and I was drunk enough that I was just switched off to everything. So I stopped the car at the side of the road and looked round at the kids in the back, at their worried little faces, and I could see every single emotion they'd ever felt at that exact moment. Like they were scared for the rabbit and me.

"And I said to them that maybe we should walk the rest of the way to school, and they smiled and I remembered how much I loved them.

"When I opened my eyes I knew something was wrong. The front of the car was in a ditch. There was a smell I never quite understood. I tried to turn around to see if the kids were okay, but my neck hurt so bad that it wouldn't move and I could feel heat running down my shins and I knew there was pain but it was as if it was too hot to even register. And I knew something really bad had happened. The back of the car felt empty. That was the feeling. That there was nothing back there any more. That my kids, sitting behind me, were empty shells."

Luce's eyes were wide open and she stared

through Jake into the past. He hadn't even noticed the point that she'd opened her eyes, but, all the amber was gone and they looked grey like an empty evening sky.

For a long time, the only sound was that of Jake's bubbling nose.

Luce's eyes filled back to amber like someone had dropped liquid gold onto the surface of two tiny ponds.

"So here I am, Jake," she said. "And I didn't know then what I know now. That while I was sitting there inside a crushed car, trapped with my dead babies, that what I thought was steam or smoke lifting away and rolling over the hedgerows was in fact what was left of my children. My Lost Dark."

Jake mouthed the words sorry, but no sound came out.

"So, that is why I can be such a bitch," she said, smiling. "And why I want that little girl of yours."

Jake's eyes stung. His vision blurred.

"What if it's not her, Luce?" he said, expecting her to fly into a rage. She didn't.

"But what if it *is*? Just what *if*?"

"Jesus, Luce. I can't. I can't just give her up."

"Jake, it's not like that. You're not giving her up. You'll be setting her free. Come *on,* Jake."

"I don't know."

"There's nothing to know. Look, if it isn't her, I'll give her back and the deal still stands. And believe me, that is not an easy thing to do. To give a shadow back. It's a pain in the arse. So I'm kinda...shit...what am I saying?" She stood up, then said, "I'm going to go get a drink. A small one." She turned to leave the cellar. "Abe," she shouted.

Jake felt as if a huge, smothering cloak had been lifted, and he knew that Abe had left him.

"Jake?" the little girl whispered when Luce was out of the cellar.

"I don't know," he said.

"But, you can't let me go. Not to her. I won't let you. I won't."

"But, what *if*?"

"No. There is no what if, Jake. I'm yours now, and I want to be yours forever."

"Oh come on. Listen to yourself. It doesn't make sense that you're with me all the time. It's just wrong."

"No. No it isn't wrong. It's right."

Silence.

Jake closed his eyes tight.

The girl spoke again. "I love you, Jake. I really do."

"I know you do, but listen to yourself. You're just a little girl. I'm a grown man. It's just wrong."

"I won't go to her, Jake. I'll find a way to be gone forever. If you won't love me, I'll be gone forever."

"Come *on*. You're being stupid now."

"No, Jake. I'm being childish. I'm being a little girl. I am *not* stupid."

Jake was on the edge of telling her that maybe it could all work out, that maybe *he'd* find a way to keep her, but he already felt lost. He knew Luce wasn't lying to him, about her husband, about the accident, and about the girl. A sob suddenly rose up from his chest, and cool tears dripped onto the floor, shining in the black-red blood like miniature ponds.

"It'll be fine," he said. "I promise. It'll be fine. Okay?"

There was no reply.

"You hear me?" he said. "I promise I'll find a way that makes everything good."

Silence.

Then the girl shouted, so loud that she sounded not unlike Abe had before. "I'm not stupid, Jake. I'm not." Then her voice became calm. "You're a bastard."

Jake was shocked at the directness of the girl's statement.

"No. Please." Jake was sobbing more, his chest heaving up and down, the shackles biting harder into his wrists with every movement.

"Bastard, bastard, bastard."

He felt the girl crawl away into nothing again. He took a deep breath, held it, then whistled it out through tight lips.

Luce came back through the door. Abe was clearly visible at her feet as she crossed in front of the light.

"Now, you're not going to kick me are you, Jake?" she said.

"No."

She moved closer and crouched down on her heels between his legs. She held out a small tumbler.

"Drink?" she said.

"What the hell is that?" Jake said, staring at the

green liquid as it rippled against the edges of the glass.

"You look like you need it," she said. She was so close he could taste her breath, sweet, smoky, warm.

"Yeah, but..."

"It's absinthe, Jake. That's all. Thought I'd treat you."

She pushed the glass up to his mouth and tilted it. Jake felt the cold on his lips, then the harsh burn in his throat as he drank it all. Luce stood up and stepped back, tilting her head to examine him.

"Nice?" she said.

"I could get used to it," Jake croaked. He tried to smile, but wasn't sure it appeared as a smile.

Luce placed the tumbler on the floor and clapped her hands in front of her face.

"Oh, Jake," she said. "So you've thought about our little arrangement then?"

"Yes. I think, I just, well. It just seems to make sense somehow. I mean, I just. Yes."

"That's great," she said, bobbing up and down on her toes. She sat down. "I *would* like to know one thing though, Jake."

"Hmm?" Jake wasn't sure where this conversation was going. He'd said yes, agreed to her little proposition. The deal was done. If anything it was himself that had more questions.

"That bit of you that's missing," Luce said, chewing her bottom lip. "The bit I can't quite grasp. The *why you are Jake* bit."

"What?"

"I told you my story, Jake. How I got to be me,

today. How I changed. There has to be the same with you?"

Jake was confused. "Er. No. I don't think there is," he said.

"Jake. I need to know. I just do. Why all the destruction? Why are you so willing to just give up on everything? Destroy everything of any value or that's close to you so quickly?"

"I didn't know I did?" he said, bemused by her analysis of him.

Luce sighed. "This isn't going well, Jake. I told you my reason. Now, you tell me yours. Dead parents? Child abuse? Age? Is it an age thing?" She sounded mocking. "Too old to sleep with pretty young schoolgirls now?" Her voice went back to her questioning tone. "Are you ill? Do you have cancer like my husband did? What? Come *on.*"

All the images that Luce had suggested flashed around in his head like a bizarre cartoon strip. He knew it was none of them, but he was trying to cling to any one of those pictures. To find a reason.

"I'm completely self-destructive?" he said to himself. "Shit."

Then, the only movement he made, was a rocking motion with one arm. A gentle swinging, swaying, rocking, swiping movement.

Jake is ten. He walks into the Saturday morning Kids Club in the village hall and there's Catherine, sitting at a small table near the door.

"Hello, Jake," she says, smiling her cute, so mature, fourteen-year-old smile.

Jake holds out his hand to show her he has money.

Catherine reaches over and takes twenty pence, her warm fingers rubbing over his palm for a tiny moment. She turns a spiral-bound notebook around, and Jake ticks a box next to his name. Then he ticks another box in the column 'chips'. Catherine reaches over to his hand that hasn't moved and takes another twenty pence. Jake looks at the last of his money and looks down at the book and at the empty box in the 'pop' column. He bites his bottom lip and scratches down another tick. He smiles. Catherine smiles, takes the last of his money and puts it into a shiny red tin. She closes the tin and locks it, putting the key in her shirt pocket.

"Cool," she says. "I'll be going to the chip shop at twelve. You can come if you like and help me carry all the food. There's ten so far eating." She blows a big pink bubblegum bubble and as it pops, the smell of warm, chewed blackcurrant hits Jake.

"Okay," he mumbles, looking down at his worn trainers and his too short trousers.

He walks over to a large box and pulls out two metal roller skates. He fiddles with the undersides of them then sits on a pile of old blue rubber mats and puts the skates on, tightening the leather belts so they won't slip. He stands at the edge of the wooden hall floor and waits for a gap as kids roll past.

He skates around and around and around, smiling and laughing as kids fall over. He skates over to the cassette player and turns up the volume and all the kids make more noise and skate faster and the hall is getting hotter and hotter and Jake is sweating and feeling light-headed and he looks up at the clock and it's only 9:30 and he keeps skating and he's doing that thing in corners where you slide one leg under the other to go round fast and he does this for quite some time until his knees really hurt and his ankles are sliding around in his too big trainers.

He sits back on the mats. Drinks a plastic cup of orange juice. Takes off his skates, then drinks another plastic cup of juice, this time blackcurrant. He looks over at Catherine who is scribbling something in the back of the notebook, her tongue poking from her lips.

He leaves his trainers next to the roller skate box and pads through into the Quiet Room.

The Quiet Room is empty. He walks over to the trestle table in the centre and pushes it with his hand. It hardly moves. He leans his weight on it and it doesn't buckle in the middle.

"Yes," he says.

From a white painted, badly chipped, louvre doored cupboard, he pulls out three boxes of dominoes. He puts them on the floor.

He looks at the clock. 10:30.

He places the dominoes end up on the table, one after the other. Straight lines. Curves. A figure of eight. When he's used up a box, he uses the empty box as a step and sets up more dominoes so that they go up and over like steps. He stands back to see where he wants the course to go next.

Two older kids, the big kids, come in.

"Whatchyadoin, Jake?" Ben says.

"A domino rally," Jake says, his smile wide.

"Cool," says the other kid, the one with tiny, thin, too close together, eyes. "How long'd this take?"

Jake looks at the clock. 11:30. "Oh. Not long," he says.

Then, as Jake is crouching down to place another domino, the kid with the eyes, he pushes Ben hard in the centre of his spine. Ben shouts, "Oh no!" and makes a dramatic, foot wheeling swan dive motion towards the table. Jake makes a clucking noise in his throat. Ben stops pedalling close to the table and stands there laughing. Jake's shoulders are moving up and down and he's wondering why he's breathing so hard but doesn't feel like he's breathing.

"Close eh?" Ben says, and laughs harder. He turns to leave and as he takes a step forward, he swings his leg back behind him and kicks the table.

Jake is clutching his head in his hands and staring as every domino crashes down at once, some spilling onto the floor.

Ben and the kid with the eyes slam the door behind them, and Jake can still hear them laughing.

Jake misses his chips and pop as he sits in the cupboard hugging his knees.

The week after, the exact same thing happens, only this time, Jake tries to shield the table with his body and outstretched arms. This time, when Jake is pushed into the table, there are three big kids laughing and pointing at him.

Another week and Jake skips roller skating and starts to set up the dominoes early so that he can set them going himself before... A basketball slams right into the centre of the table and Jake is already crying by the time it rolls away back out the door.

The week after that, Jake sets up maybe half his dominoes. He's checking the door every few minutes. The kid with the eyes walks in and smiles. Jake smiles back and nudges the table himself. The kid's eyes actually grow larger and his mouth turns down as the dominoes scatter to the floor. He leaves the room.

Another week, and as Ben and another big kid, not the one with the eyes, walk in, Jake puts his hands under the table and lifts it high into the air, tipping it on its side, the dominoes launching up then skittering along the floor and into the skirting boards.

Ben and the other big kid don't laugh.

The week after, Jake is almost done and no kids have come in at all. He's on his last box of dominoes and has set up one of the largest domino rally layouts he thinks he's ever seen, even on TV. And no kids have even looked through the door. He looks at the table. Looks at the three dominoes in his hand. He places one finger close to the first domino and stares down the beautiful line that curls away into a blur making him cross-eyed.

Then he stands back. He takes another look at those dominoes, snaking and swirling and stepping over bridges and fanning out in elaborate diamond patterns, then he picks up a plastic backed folding chair and slams it down hard into the table. His eyes are wide, his nostrils flaring.

Catherine rushes in. "Jake, what the hell are you doing, Jake?"

"Fuck off!" he shouts and slams the chair into the table again. Even after all the dominoes are gone, he just keeps smacking at the table as it lies flat on the floor. He throws the chair down into the broken wood and scattered dominoes, and smiles.

Luce blinked.

"Jake?" she said.

"Yes," he said, worn out from the effort of telling his story.

"That's it?"

"Yes."

"Dominoes? You systematically fucked up your whole life because of some dominoes?"

"Fuck you, Luce," he said, rattling his chains.

"No, I mean, come on. I was not expecting that."

"You asked."

"No, I mean, Jake. That is *so* fucking cool." She clapped a few times then held her hands to her chest.

Jake smiled. He thought that Luce might not be impressed. But he'd learned to trust that she was nothing if not genuine.

"Will it hurt?" he said.

"Yes."

"Will it," he screwed his face up, "will it hurt the girl?"

"Oh, no. No. I don't want that. She's my baby. Do you know how much that means to me?"

"No."

"Oh, Jake, I'm sorry. I forgot."

She stood up, walked over, lifted his head in her soft hands and kissed him full on the lips. Jake groaned. She slipped her tongue inside his mouth, absinthe on absinthe and Jake groaned again.

"Jake," she said, smoothing his hair back with her thumbs. "This is going to be *so* fucking cool."

Jake licked his lips then ran his tongue around the inside of his mouth.

Chapter Eighteen

Luce reached over to a table and picked up a piece of short, fat, chalk that looked like a miniature trig point from a mountaintop.

"I'm not a witch, Jake," she said, eyeing the chalk.

"I never said you were. I might have said bitch."

"Might have?"

"Yeah. Might still."

"Jake," she said, pretending to look sad, "I get that a lot. But I'm not. A witch, I mean."

"No, I can understand. It's the pointy hat."

Luce looked up at her forehead.

"Chalk, Jake. Good old English chalk. It's what I do. It's what I do best."

"You're going to draw round me aren't you?"

Luce laughed. "Ha, you almost made me miss Moses for a moment there. He was a retarded wisecracking ass-hole when it came to the drawing. But no, I'm going to draw around her." She waved the chalk at Jake's feet.

"I tried everything, Jake. After Steve then after the crash. I tried all sorts of weird stuff. I think that's where the witch thing came from. You should hear the children round here. 'Witch witch, what a bitch, a witch with jogging trousers, where's your hat, witch? Yeah," she rolled her eyes, "poetic bunch."

"So they *think* you're a witch?"

"Oh come on, Jake. Woman living on her own in a run-down house with a front garden overgrown as high as the window ledge, never shuts her curtains. They're kids, Jake."

"But what about Moses? Surely people saw him."

"Oh, Moses had this thing. He was even harder to see than shadows. He was..." she looked up at the floorboards, "he was unique."

"Unique. Right," Jake said. He rattled the chains. "Are you going to let me out of these damn things?"

Luce walked over and unscrewed the shackles. Jake pulled his hands to his chest and massaged them.

"I thought you'd have asked ages ago," Luce said.

Jake grimaced. "Cramp, ouch, fuck, cramp," he said. "I didn't want to spoil the atmosphere. I'm surprised you didn't offer to undo them ages ago."

"Yeah, well, I didn't want you to kick me in my pretty little face."

Jake huffed and stood up.

"Shit, I never want to be locked up like that again."

"Never?" Luce said, raising an eyebrow.

"Jesus, Luce," Jake said, waving his tingling hands towards her. "The chalk."

"God you sound as desperate to get this all wrapped us as I did two hours ago."

"I've only been down here two hours?" He looked at his wrists.

"Three."

"Three. Where's Emma?"

"She's still upstairs." Luce stared hard at Jake, and

he thought she was maybe trying to work out if he was going to try to get away.

"And that backstabbing bitch Starmouth?"

"She's in my bed. She snores bad."

"Hmm," Jake said.

Luce clutched her chest. "The chalk," she said. "I was telling you about the chalk."

"Go on."

"It was an accident. I'd tried everything to try and contact my children. Ouija boards, tarot cards, runes, blah de fucking bollocks, blah. I needed to know, Jake. I mean, well, I was being selfish and I wanted to know if they were angry with me. I wanted them to tell me it was okay and that none of it was my fault. I wanted Steve to forgive me for being stupid and I wanted my children to tell me they still loved me. I went to see a lot of psychics. God they're awful. They are so awful, Jake. And they hide and pretend that all the shit they come out with is okay because they're doing it all for you. They're all fucking liars out to make money off the bereaved. No... You want a real witch, go see them fat faced, flowery dressed old bastards."

"Luce, you're drifting."

"Chalk. Yes. Then I saw a really short five-minute documentary thing on TV about a guy, and he's drawing round stuff."

"Stuff?"

"Yeah, He'd go out with a box of chalk and he'd draw round shadows of bikes, or lampposts or cars. And people are all 'oooh, that's graffiti' and he's like 'no, it's chalk' and they're like 'oh, okay, cool.' And he just drew round shadows of everyday objects. But next day, his outlines are still there. So there'd be an outline of a pushbike across the pavement, but no bike. Or an outline of a lamppost's shadow, right next to its real shadow. Until it rained, the shadows would always be there.

"And that's when I had a real moment of clarity. Turns out, we've been doing it forever, Jake. Cavemen drew round the shadows of their hunters to make sure they would come back safe. Druids traced the shadows of stones and trees to preserve their natural energies. Everyone forever has always done it. They captured a moment in time and it never went away.

"And then, I read something, somewhere in a magazine at the hospital when, later, when...about Egyptians who believed that your shadow was part of you, that your shadow was as important as your name, or your heart, or your soul. They called it the Sheut." Her face was a storyteller's, wide eyes, raised cheekbones. "They believed that a person couldn't exist without a shadow, nor a shadow without a person. God, Jake, it all just made sense right then. And one night I came back here with this guy and well, he was worn out and drunk, so I brought him down here and it worked. I drew round his shadow with nothing more than pavement chalk. Come here."

She hooked her arm under his and pulled him to the corner of the cellar where the light didn't penetrate.

"You feel them?" she said, her voice a draft on

his neck.

Jake stood still. "No. Nothing."

"They're all there, Jake. All wrapped up in the corner. All bundled in like years of cobwebs."

Jake heard and felt nothing except cold and damp in the still air.

"An army, Jake," she said. Then she whispered, "They're my army."

Jake remembered everything all at once about what the girl had said about the Army of the Dark. He pushed Luce away.

"The party," he said. "In the dark. That was you wasn't it? That was them. You set up the whole Party in the Dark thing."

"Not the first time I've done it," she said, placing her hand on his shoulder. "It just makes perfect sense doesn't it? Get as many people as possible all in the exact same spot."

"And harvest them," Jake said, reaching out to the wall and resting his hands on the stone.

"Can you imagine how many people at that party were just like you, Jake? All drawn together by a simple promise of a party. In *the dark*."

"Ah crap," Jake said with a sudden realisation. "Probably everyone."

"Not quite all of them no. But close enough."

"All those people with spare shadows or new shadows, or, even maybe on their fifth or God knows what number shadow." Jake bowed his head and chuckled into his chest. "Hundreds of people all with shadows that didn't belong to them. Luce. That is quite clever."

"Thank you," she breathed into his ear.

"People died, Luce. Lots of people died." He snapped his hands away from the wall and turned to her. She was playing with her hair, her face calm. "Some of them just disappeared," he said. "Gone. Vanished. I mean, come on, Luce. It was a mess. I was there."

Luce narrowed her eyes and through a tiny straight mouth she said, "I was looking for my babies."

Jake turned back to the wall. Once again, a simple explanation of her actions made him understand, and he felt as calm as Luce looked.

"There are a lot of shadows in there somewhere," she said.

"In there? In the wall?"

Luce shrugged. "I think so, yes," she said, rubbing her thumb on his shoulder. "I don't quite know how, or whether they're in it, or behind it," she shrugged. "But they're all there somewhere."

"These are all the shadows that *you* captured?"

"My army, Jake. But there are others as well. Abe tells me about the others." She took her hand away and then ruffled her hair at her temples with her fingertips. "There are loads more in there than *I* captured. Hundreds, I think. And I don't know how they got there. It scares me sometimes."

Jake laughed hard at the wall then turned to Luce who was pulling strands of hair up and letting them float down like thin fractures of silver against the black, one after the other. Over and over.

"That scares you?" Jake said. "That's great. I like

that."

Luce began twirling the strands of hair around her fingers. "Yeah," she said to herself. "Abe says they were already there."

"In the wall," Jake was beginning to understand the concept of hundreds of shadows all bunched up in the corner of the cellar. He ran his fingers around the edges of the bricks as if looking for a way to open a secret entrance.

"Yes, Jake. In...the...wall." She bit the side of her lower lip. "Except...not in the wall."

"Okay. So in there somewhere. Like a doorway. Let's just say that. Like a doorway. And you just, what, you summon them all up when you need them?"

"Abe does it for me. But I couldn't tell you how. They do know me. They know who I am."

"And after they've run amok, they just come right on back like homing pigeons?" Jake couldn't believe that those poor lost, captured shadows would want to come back.

"Most of them, yes. But some attach to people while they're out there. I guess they see an easy way out."

Jake thought he understood, but asked more questions anyway.

"So, they harvest shadows for you and bring them back here, so the army just gets bigger."

"I don't know. I don't know how many there are. I know there are still lots. I think some must come back. Others stay out there. Abe says that there are all sorts in there, that you can't measure them by their number."

"All sorts?"

"I don't ask. Really, Jake, I don't ask."

"Yeah. I'd be worried if I lived on top of this mess." He realised as he spoke that this was exactly what his little girl must have felt, out on the doorstep to the house. "The girl," he said.

"Hmm. Yes. Come on."

"No, I mean. She won't end up in there with them?"

"Jake. No. You know that won't happen. You *do* know that."

Luce left him by the wall, his head swaying, his arms reaching out.

"Jake, come back over here," she said. She was already standing next to the light. "What a beautiful accident, eh, Jake? I can capture shadows. And I can keep them."

Jake wandered back into the light and Luce shifted it about.

"Oh God, Jake. This will be so fantastic. This, I, this will be *so*..."

Jake felt like a child, like he was trying his best to audition for a school play. He held his arms out wide and looked at the floor.

"This okay?" he said.

"No," Luce said. "Have you been watching *The Wizard of Oz*? You look like a spastic scarecrow."

Jake pulled his arms into his sides and shrugged. "I was going more for Jesus," he said. "On the cross."

"Jake. It's not *you* I want. It's, well, ahhh, Jake.

313

You know. Shit."

Luce was waving her arms around and shuffling her feet. She had become angry and agitated. Jake took a deep breath. Luce adjusted the light some more.

"There," she said. "Now. Don't move."

The little girl spoke, clearly and without any hint that she was scared, "It was me and you against the world, Jake. Me and you."

Luce looked down at her feet as if Abe had said something to her.

Jake looked down to his side but couldn't see any sign of the girl.

Luce moved in close, careful to keep herself out of the light. She crouched down next to Jake.

"Hey, sweetie," she said.

She ran her finger around the perfect black form that was the little girl, tracing her outline. Then she lifted her finger to her mouth and kissed it, placed it under her nose and inhaled.

"Oh my God," she said, her eyes glassy and wet. "My baby." She blinked, and a single tear squeezed out and rolled from her face, glinting in the light.

"Luce," Jake said. "Keep that Abe away while you do this. I don't..."

Luce looked confused. "Of course. Shit, Jake."

She moved in even closer and pushed the tip of the chalk into the wall at the base of Jake's feet. He felt the girl shaking like she'd been out in the cold too long.

She spoke to him, her tiny voice barely audible over the minute sound of the chalk scratching over the wall. "You and me against the world, Jake," she whispered.

Jake looked at the side of Luce's face as she continued to pull the chalk around somewhere out of sight. He imagined how easy it would be to kick her soft cheekbone, to push her to the floor with his heel then grind her pretty face into the concrete with his boot until her eye sockets cracked and her jaw bone split and her windpipe popped open. Then just as suddenly, he imagined what it would feel like to hold her naked body against his. To place his hands into the small of her back and pull her in so close that there wasn't a single gap between their flesh.

"Jake," Luce snapped. "Stop moving."

Jake tried to stand even more still than he thought he already was.

"Will this hurt?" he said, as Luce raised her head to his waist height.

"Probably," she said, her voice muffled by her hair hanging down over her mouth. "God she's so beautiful, Jake. I can almost feel her already."

"Will it hurt us both?"

"No. Just you."

Jake whistled air through his lips.

"Why is it taking so long?" he said.

"I want to get this right. I've never been so nervous."

"You mean you can get it wrong?"

"Oh no. Not any more. Not now. She's staying so still, Jake. She wants this. I'm sure of it. So sure. It's like she wants to be with me."

Jake felt weak and there was a tingling down his

left side like pins and needles.

"Not long now. God she'll have the most beautiful face. I know it."

His side, between his hips and his ribs, felt like it was on fire, as if the flesh were being stripped away and pieces of him were falling to the floor. He felt his knees creaking under pressure. He closed his eyes against the pain and there was a noise in his head like the silence after a car crash and he could smell burning, burnt bone, flaming, compacting, crushing.

He heard Luce say, "Hey, sweetie."

Then he was on the floor on his hands and knees, staring at how his fingers were splayed out and wondering why he couldn't move them. His eyes were burning and his throat was cold and tight and he felt a ripping in the very base of his stomach and cried out something unintelligible at the floor and tried to move his hands away from the vomit that was streaming from inside him pulling his whole body into a squeezed and racked tube but his hands wouldn't move and the sick splashed in bright yellows and vivid greens and reds and blues and washed and lapped up over his fingers and settled in his knuckles then his elbows gave way and his face hit the stinking puddle so that sick was forced out at the sides or up into his nostrils and mouth and he tasted the tiny bitter lumps of his own insides on his tongue while he snorted out thick bile from one nostril then rolled over onto his back so that he felt the cold sick seep into his hair as he rocked his head forward and back and closed his eyes and when he opened them again Luce was right over him with her bright silver hair dangling down so close that it tickled his nose which he found even more nauseating then the sick and blood and he sneezed in her face and watched the sick and saliva sparkle as she bunched her whole face up against it.

Then he felt fine.

He breathed out a lungful of air, and it was as if he'd just recovered from a bad hangover. He groaned.

Luce stood over him and stared straight down. It looked as if she was smiling so hard that she couldn't open her mouth to speak. When she did, her voice was cracked and soft and distant and warm.

"I found my baby, Jake." She cupped a hand over her mouth and started to sob. "I got my baby girl back."

Jake felt empty inside. It was the exact same feeling he'd had when he'd sold the fishing gear after his dad died. Only this was now and hurt more than he remembered.

Luce stepped away, and Jake heard her walk out through the door. She made tiny, excited, squeaking noises. Jake lay in his own sick, staring at the dust motes hanging above him like stars.

Jake's head was still throbbing when he entered the room upstairs. Luce was by the CD player, prodding it. As soon as music started, she prodded again. And again. She turned around. Her face was red, her eyes wide, her shoulders high.

"Oh, Jake," she said.

Jake opened his mouth.

"You look stinky," she said. "Mr. Stinky. Go and shower."

Jake walked over to the chair at the end of the table.

"No, Jake," Luce said, pointing. "No. Go take a shower."

"Is she okay?" Jake said.

Luce prodded at the CD player then switched it off. She looked down at her feet and lifted her heels one at a time as if examining new shoes.

"My little sweetheart is just fine. Aren't you, sweetie?"

Then her face screwed up.

"What's wrong?" Jake said, a sudden panic washing over him.

Luce turned in small circles, stepping out from the table, then over to the window, then small circles back again. "She's fine. I know she is. She's here, Jake. I can feel her. I can smell her. It worked out just fine."

"But?"

"But, well, she's kinda quiet. That's all." She waved her arms into the air. "I guess it's just the shock of it. That'll be it. Just shock."

Jake thought about how when the girl first spoke to him, that she never shut up. He felt a pain in his chest, like a solid hot block of heartburn. He stared hard at the floor around Luce and was sure there was something there, that his little girl was there, but faint. Whether she was scared, or confused or hiding he wasn't sure. He looked down at his own feet and there was nothing. He felt weak and light headed. Drunk. The pain in his head seeped down his neck and into his shoulders.

"Oh, Jake," Luce said. "We'll worry about getting you a new shadow soon enough."

"We'd better," he said, swaying side to side as if the movements might magically conjure a new shadow.

"Just go shower," Luce said, waving him away.

Jake showered using half-empty bottles of what must have been Moses's stuff. He washed his hair in his shampoo and dried himself on a damp towel that must have been his as well, it didn't feel like Luce's. He closed the toilet lid, sat on it, put his head into his hands and cried. Silent, motionless cries. He hadn't even considered finding new clothes, so he dressed back into his own clothes. He wiped the steamed mirror and stared at himself. He looked just the same as he ever did in a steamed up bathroom mirror. Tired. He felt relieved. Then he smiled but didn't actually know why. It was as if his own reflection smiling back at him was the only genuine smile he'd ever seen.

In another room, he heard bedsprings creak and remembered Freesia. Then he remembered Emma and how he'd just walked through the room and not even glanced at her body. Surely she was still lying there, dead and probably cold by now. He remembered Moses, and Bob, and Momma Jane, and Jessie, and Den. All the faces and the voices all mixed up inside his head, all vying for some sort of recognition. Jake shook his head and the little girl's face was there, smiling, then frowning, smiling then frowning.

"There are clean clothes you know," Luce said as Jake entered the room. "Moses had lots of shirts. Bit big for you, but clean and well ironed."

"I'm okay," Jake said. "There's no way I'm wearing any of his stuff."

Luce sat watching the incense smoke spiral upwards from a recently lit, scarlet cone.

"We can burn all his old stuff," she said. "Start again, Jake."

Jake sat down at the corner of the table next to her. He lay his head down and reached his arm out. He expected Luce might reach over and place her hand over his. She didn't. He closed his eyes and started drifting to sleep. He felt like he'd been pushed down a hill and hit all the rocks on the way to the bottom. As his mind drifted, he could hear Luce talking to the little girl.

"Come on, sweetie, you have to talk to me. I'm your mum. Remember me?"

Jake opened his eyes and stared down the table towards the window. Outside was even darker than before.

"I know, honey," Luce was saying. "Me too. And then maybe the zoo. Ah, okay yes, oh my sweet, sweet baby."

Jake closed his eyes again.

"...just something I have to do for you," Luce said, somewhere on the edge of his consciousness.

Her voice sounded like an old record running slower. "I...want...to...give...you...a..."

Jake opened his eyes and sat up. There had been a huge bang that he'd heard whilst he was asleep, a huge thud that he knew had been real just seconds before he'd opened his eyes.

"Ah crap," he said. "Luce?"

He stood up and looked down. Luce lay on her side on the floor, her knees pushed up into her eyes. She was pressed up close to Emma's sticky red body.

"Jesus, Luce," he said, bending down. He pulled her hair away from her face and placed his hand on her shoulder to pull her over onto her back. She was twitching and shivering. Her breathing was shallow. Thick red blood streamed from her nose.

Jake leapt back as something flashed into his head. Then he sat on the floor and placed his hand back on Luce. He put his other hand on the top of her head.

He closed his eyes and she was there.

"What did you do?" he said to the little girl.

"It wasn't me, Jake," she said. "Are you angry?"

"Yes, I'm angry. You've only been gone a few minutes and you've hurt Luce. Why?"

"It wasn't me."

"Then what?"

The little girl laughed. "She tried to tell me my name." She laughed again. "Silly, Mummy."

Jake rolled Luce onto her back then lifted her up and pulled her close into his side.

"You stupid little girl," he said. "You could have killed her."

"But I didn't."

"Is this how it's going to be from now on? There's no need for any of this."

"I don't like her. I hate her."

"But she's your mum. Your mummy. Isn't she?"

"I think she is, yes. But I don't *like* her, Jake."

"But maybe you will. You just need time."

"I spent all my time with you, Jake. I wanted you. Not *her*."

"You're being silly again."

"Jake," she squealed. "I told you before."

"Okay, okay." Jake calmed himself down so as not to upset her any more. He held Luce's face in his hands and tried to rub away the blood, smearing it around her lips and cheeks. He looked down onto the tops of her closed eyes, willing her to open them.

"Come on, Luce," he said. "You're okay. You'll be okay."

Luce murmured, "That little bitch."

"No, Luce. Quiet now." Jake was shocked at the anger in Luce's voice. "It was an accident. Believe me. I know. You really shouldn't have tried to give her a name."

He heard the girl laughing even harder, but faint and distant, and she was humming a nursery rhyme, "Ring a ring of roses. A pocket full of posies. Atishoo. Atishho." Then she laughed again.

Luce's eyes quivered then opened, and she looked down at all the blood that was hers and Emma's.

"It wasn't an accident," she said.

"Of course it was. Come on, Luce, let's get you back up."

"No, Jake," Luce struggled and nudged herself

closer into Jake's side. She clearly wanted to stay put for a while. She looked up at Jake and her eyes were dark and tired, her face red, her teeth bright white inside her lazy mouth. "She *asked* me to tell her her name."

Jake smiled.

"Jake?" the little girl said.

"Yes?" Jake whispered.

"Hmm?" Luce groaned.

The little girl said, "Be quiet for a while, Jake. I want to talk to Mummy."

"Okay, I will," Jake whispered.

"Jake?" Luce said.

"Mummy?"

"What?" Luce said, loud and angry.

"I'm sorry, Mummy. It *was* an accident."

"Was it?"

"Yes. I forgot. I was so excited about us, I just forgot."

Luce smiled. "Okay, sweetie. It's okay. I'm sorry I shouted at you."

"That's okay."

Silence.

"Mummy?"

"Huh?"

"Are you still my friend?"

"Oh, of course I am my little baby. Mummy is your best friend in the whole world."

"And you *do* love me, don't you?"

"Yes. Very much. I love you so, so much."

"Can you feel this?"

"What? Feel what? No."

"I want to show you something, Mummy."
"Is that..."
"It's my hand. Hold my hand, Mummy. I want to take you somewhere."

Chapter Nineteen

Luce felt her arm lifting and then her whole body tilted forwards and she was in the air for a fraction of a second being pulled by her arm and teased and stretched and she felt tiny strings of Jake behind her being teased away into nothing like wet cobwebs and the ceiling became black cloth that she was floating towards face first with one arm dangling below her and the other reaching out to where there were no stars in the black comforting blanket that wrapped itself around her face until her vision was nothing except nothing dripping with the smell of tar that pushed into her nostrils and formed into thick gloopy balls in the back of her throat and she was terrified like she hadn't been in years but her screams made no sound except that she could hear the very faint rumble of something like a distant storm drawing closer through the black fog then it hit her in the back.

"Hey, Mummy," the little girl said, louder, clearer than Luce had ever heard her before. "You can open your eyes now."

Luce opened her eyes to blue sky and green trees disappearing all the way into the distance. After the darkness she'd just been dragged through, it was such a shocking contrast that she gasped and realised that there was no tar blocking her throat.

"My God," she said. "Sweetie? Where are we?"

She felt the girl squeeze her hand, and over the smell of damp rock and leaves and fresh air, she smelled her. She looked down at the girl and only then realised that they were standing on a very narrow ledge a very long way up a cliff face.

Tears streamed down Luce's face. "My God," she said. "Baby." She tried to crouch to the side to touch her daughter, to run her hand across the freckles and kiss her sweet round face, but she realised that she was gripping a cold iron railing, and that to let go would be suicide. She shuffled sideways and tried to reach over so that she could place her hand on her daughter's beautiful straight blonde hair.

"Don't let go of my hand, Mummy," the girl said, looking down.

"Oh but sweetheart. I want to hold all of you. I want to..."

"And don't let go of the railing either. It's dangerous." She looked up at her mum and smiled, her lips wrinkling, her freckles squeezed together on raised cheeks. "Up here." Luce felt emptiness in her stomach and somewhere deeper down, like her womb was aching. "But I want to hold you. You're, you... You're real."

"I'm real," the little said, shrugging. "I know." She laughed.

Luce slid her right hand along the railing, feeling the rough scratchy surface pulling at her palm. "If I can just move..."

"No," the girl snapped.

Luce stopped moving. If the ledge hadn't been so

narrow and her body was not pushed back into the stone behind her, she would have stamped her feet in frustration.

"But, I found you. You're here and you're real. I have to..."

"Isn't it pretty, Mummy?"

"What?"

"Here. This place. Isn't it just wonderful?"

Luce relaxed and stared out into the distance through a fine drizzle to where bright sunlight crept across dark green hills. A sparkling blue river wound its way down a valley and disappeared over a white cliff into mist.

"What's your favourite bit, Mummy?"

Luce narrowed her eyes. She wanted to point but nodded her head instead.

"Over there, near the waterfall, where the water just disappears out of sight. See?" she said.

"Yes."

"And those large birds circling over the pine trees. It's so beautiful."

"It is. I like the waterfall too. I like the way it just disappears, how you can't see where it goes."

"Hmm. Yes."

"I'd like to go see it one day and see where it goes. I think I could."

"Hey," Luce said, feeling brighter after taking in the beautiful scenery. "Maybe we could go together."

"Hmm. No. I don't think we could."

"Oh?"

Luce inhaled the stench of something rotten. For a

tiny fraction of a second, her nostrils were filled with the smell of a dead animal. Then it was gone.

"Why have you brought me here, sweetie?" she said.

"I wanted you to see how beautiful the world was, Mummy. How it can be so full of precious things."

Luce felt sad. "It is beautiful. It is."

"And I wanted to hold your hand one last time, Mummy."

"What?"

The stench rose up the cliff. Luce felt it crawl up her body as a warm thick odour, before it crept into her lungs.

"What *is* that smell?" she said, looking down past her feet and the shrubs that clung just below.

"Look harder, Mummy. Down there."

Luce blinked and when she opened her eyes again she could see clearly. It was as if she was looking into the split body of some huge dead animal with dark grey maggots writhing around in darker black, rotting flesh. She swallowed and the taste of the rot slid down her throat.

"What the hell is that?" she said, still focusing on the moving mass as it heaved and slid around hundreds of feet below.

"Not that, Mummy. They. What are they?"

Luce felt her heart crash into her chest, felt and tasted the rot in her throat as it rose up to her tongue.

"They're my friends. Some of them. There are so many Lost Dark down there."

"Oh God," Luce said as a sickening realisation swept over her. "Who?"

"A lot of them are very sad and don't know why they're there. Some of them loved each other so much they just threw themselves down there just so they could be together forever."

Luce felt faint and dizzy. Her breathing was fast.

"Please just tell me," she said.

"Some of them are very angry as well," the girl said. "They tell me a lot of things, Mummy. Luce. Do you know what it's like to love someone so much..."

"God yes." Luce felt panic. Something she hadn't felt for a long time. She gripped the rail behind her.

"...and then to throw yourself off a cliff and die together..."

Luce couldn't take her eyes off them. She was sure she could see individual figures, misshaped and molten, crawling up higher on the waves of bodies below them.

"...and they were so happy, even after they were dead..."

Faces began to form. Ripped shadows with dark black O's for mouths and angry, slanting eyes filled with desire.

"...and they thought they could be together forever, Luce."

"Oh shit no," Luce said. She tried to close her eyes but the best she could manage was a tight squint; she didn't want to let the things out of her sight.

"And they were torn apart. The men watched and cried as their best friends in the whole world were taken away. And the women would kneel down with each other and cry black tears for days and days and ask why their lovers had been stolen, or why their children never came back."

"Sweetie. It can't be. Tell me."

"Can you see them all, Luce?"

"Yes, I can see them," Luce snapped. She knew who they were. Deep down, she knew. She wanted to be told. She gripped the girl's hand tight.

"You're hurting me, Mummy. You're squeezing my hand too hard. Luce."

"Sorry. God I'm sorry. I never..."

"That's my army. Down there."

Luce was shaking. "I need to go back now, sweetie. You hear me? I want to go back to Jake."

The girl laughed. "He doesn't want you. He wants me. We were meant to be together."

"But I'm your mother. And I want to go back. Now!"

The girl giggled and swung Luce's arm forward and back.

"Do you hear me?" Luce screamed. "I'm your mother damn you. Take me back right now."

The girl hummed *Ring a Ring of Roses*.

"Now!" Luce screamed again, as more and more shadows began to creep upwards like fingers reaching out of a rising black sea of hatred, crashing and crawling up the white cliff.

"You took them away, Luce. For your army. You killed those people down there again. You split them up and ruined their forever. And they're not happy."

Luce's back scraped against the rock as she slid down it. She gripped the iron railing. Her arms began to twitch. Her muscles tightened. She let go of the girl's hand and grabbed the railing with both hands, pulling herself as upright as she could manage.

"Abe," she cried. And as she did, the seething mass lowered itself. Then it bubbled up again higher than before and the stench became stronger.

"He won't help you, Luce. He can't."

Luce was trying to work out how far away from Abe she really was, if there was a physical gap between here and him or something else. She tried to imagine Abe crawling through the same black void that she had been teased through. Images flashed in her head of the cliff and the house and the cellar and Abe and Jake, but none of them made sense.

"They can't reach me up here. They can't," she said.

"No. They can't. They never get this high."

"And you won't push me. I'm your mother. You hear?"

"I can't push you, Luce. I'm not strong enough."

"Then you take me home, right now. You hear?"

"Luce?"

Luce looked at the girl and her face was that of a little girl in complete control. The little girl reached around behind her shiny red dress and started to fiddle with the bow of a bright blue ribbon. Her tongue stuck out as she concentrated on the knot. Then she smiled as it came undone and hung loose on each side.

"I used to have a beautiful red ribbon for this dress. But I dropped it over the edge there. When Jake was here with me."

"You brought Jake here?"

"Yes. And he saw how beautiful it was. All of it."

The little girl pulled one end of the ribbon.

Behind her, Luce felt the railing slide in her palm.

"What the hell?" she said, trying to look behind her.

The girl pulled the ribbon some more, holding it out in front of her as she did.

The railing slid between Luce's hands, her tightened grip making no difference to the ease at which it moved.

"No," she shouted. "Please no. I can't hold... No."

"I'm sorry, Luce. But it was never about you."

The girl continued to pull the ribbon, and Luce felt the rail disappear from her right hand. She screamed and tried to push herself back further, her fingernails clawing at the moss and stone.

Luce stared at the girl as she held out the whole of the ribbon. She felt herself tilting forwards as the ribbon swayed and fluttered in the wind rising from below. She felt her fingernails wrenching up and heard them crack and split as she tried to grab the rock. She tried to scream but no sound came out. As she fell forward her body hit the shrubs just below her and she spun around. She watched beautiful bright green leaves flutter up past her and then watched her daughter standing in her beautiful red dress holding out the shimmering blue ribbon. Her daughter let go of the ribbon, and Luce fell faster, and the little girl became smaller and smaller against the bright white canvas of rock until she was gone and all that Luce could see was a thin shining ribbon of blue, twisting and floating on the wind rising up from below.

Chapter Twenty

Luce slumped in Jake's arms. He pulled her in closer to his chest. Her head fell forward.

"Luce?"

Nothing.

"Ah crap. Come on, Luce."

Nothing.

He pulled her head back into his neck and looked at her face. Her eyes were closed. Her nose clotted with black clumps. Her mouth open.

"Luce. No."

He knew she was gone. Her body felt hollow, a shell.

"Come on. I've done this. I got through this."

He ran his hand down her bare shoulder and onto her arm but felt nothing.

"Jesus, Luce. Come *on. I* tried to give her a name and I pulled through."

But he knew that Luce wasn't going to pull through anything.

There was no Luce.

Nothing.

He rested his chin on her head, then reached up and pressed his fingers into the bridge of his nose.

He tried to cry.

Nothing.

Jake is staring at three full boxes of dominoes. The lids are all slid back so that he can see the black rectangles beneath. He stares at the trestle table and walks over. He pushes it and it doesn't move. He leans on it and it feels solid. He can see exactly where he wants this domino rally to go, see the curves and the straight. He can hear every single click and clack as the black rectangles fall on each other and the momentum continues through figure of eights and up steps and into cascades of beautiful triangles and he hears the soft click and clack of the very last few dominoes as they reach the end and he watches a double blank black rectangle teeter on the edge of gravity. For a moment that last domino rocks back, like it doesn't want to go. But it does. And it clicks onto the table and Jake stares and thinks how beautiful the dominoes look, even laid out flat, all just kissing one another at each end. And the domino rally is finished and there's nothing. Just silence. Nothing.

Jake smiles, slides the box lids closed and places the dominoes back into the louvre doored built in cupboards.

Jake slid Luce to the floor and brushed her hair back away from her face. He stood up and looked at the two of them, Luce curled up and foetal behind Emma. He tilted his head and stared. He tilted his head back the other way and stared. Luce and Emma lying in each other's blood as one. And right then, he couldn't decide which of them he'd loved the most.

He thought about all the times he'd spent with

Emma. The house, the beds, the holidays, the closeness, the Party in the Dark. He thought about their lost baby, and if it was good enough that it was dead before it had been alive. If maybe it was lucky. He shook his head.

He thought about how wonderful he and Luce might have been together. The time they could have spent together. The house. The cellar. The death. The fun. The fun of having Luce all for himself, knowing that she could have made him cry with pleasure and break him into pieces, only to put him back together again.

"Figures," he said.

He moved over to the CD player and switched it on. It clicked and whirred. He didn't recognise the piano tune that played, but he sighed and it felt comfortable. Then he saw the end of the knife. He pulled it out by his fingertips, moved it to his other hand. He examined his pink-red thumb and forefinger. He couldn't even remember whose blood it was on there.

He sat down at the end of the table and pushed the tip of the blade into the wood. He twisted it and pulled it, making white marks. He stood up and dragged the blade along the whole length of the table, then back down. He leaned over, grunting and breathing heavily as he scored and scratched and gouged until every last inch of the table was covered in scratches like a carved map of his anger, fear, regret and loneliness.

He sat down again and stared at the knife. He held it to his wrist and felt the warmth in its tip on the pulse of his body. Then he looked up at the window. The rain beat down harder, popping and thudding. It talked to him. He listened. He started to draw the knife slowly across his wrist, watching as it dug in. He felt the sting of it as his flesh snagged and caught. But he didn't bleed. He stared at the bare white mark across the ridges of his tendons, then at the bare white marks of the scratches on the table. The rain spoke to him and told him how he could have had Luce all to himself. The rain laughed at him. It whispered to him that he might as well kill himself now. It told him he was utterly alone.

He pressed the blade onto his wrist and wondered just how much killing himself would hurt.

He gripped the handle tight and wondered if it would hurt more than being totally and utterly alone.

The rain stopped.

His eyes widened.

"Freesia," he said.

He stood up and rushed into the hallway. He ran up the stairs, the knife sliding along the banister on its side. "Freesia," he shouted. There was no answer. He pushed open a door. The toilet. He ran down the corridor and pushed open another door. Inside was a bed covered in boxes, newspapers, and photographs. A desk with a black candle and two dragons and a piece of white chalk. A pile of teddy bears and action figures. He left and crashed through another door. The smell of Freesia hit him. It was warm and soft and vile and sickly, and he was over to the dull grey double bed in one stride. He stared at the crumpled sheets and at the sepia, tide mark stains in the middle, at the duvet lying on the floor crumpled and stinking of her, of them. Of all of them.

"Fuck," he said.

Freesia was gone. *Bitch*, he thought. *I really wanted to kill something. Bitch.*

Back downstairs he lit a fresh incense cone and sat down. He watched the smoke billow up, frantic at first like it had a purpose, then it settled into slow waves of smoke that flattened out like the anvils of a storm cloud. The rain had started again. He listened to its soft pitter-patter as he held the blade to his wrist. He held the tip close to his palm and thought, *yeah, I'll do this properly now.*

He pushed the tip of the blade into the grey-blue vein.

"Hey, you. I'm down here at your feet."

Jake dropped the knife on the table and stared at the tiny indentation in his wrist. He stared at the table. He stared at the window and at all the tiny orange globes of rain reflecting the streetlights outside.

"That's you?"

"Yeah. Hello." The little girl giggled.

Jake laughed.

"You came back," he said.

"I came back, Jake. I came back for you."

"Wow, that's great."

"Really?"

"Really."

"You're not mad are you?"

Jake looked at the knife. "No. I'm not mad." He rubbed his eyes. "Luce is gone."

"I know."

"I thought she'd be okay. I mean, she only tried to give you a name."

"No, Jake. It was more than that."

"Was it you? Did you kill her?"

"No, silly. Well, not really. I took her to Giddy Edge."

"What? Why?"

"I showed her all those shadows, Jake. All those Lost Dark."

Jake laughed and wiped at his mouth.

"Oh that *is* grand," he said. "I'm guessing, and its just a guess, but I'm guessing those shadows weren't best pleased to see her."

"Ha. No."

"She was your mummy."

"She was. Once." She huffed. "But I didn't like her, Jake. I like you."

"Phew. Good. That's good then."

There was silence, then the girl said, "They tore her to pieces. I saw her turn into tiny, tiny pieces. Like a million red raindrops."

"Shit."

"Jake!"

"Sorry. I mean, er, damn. Are you okay? I mean, seeing that. Your mum?"

"I think I enjoyed it."

"Oh, Christ."

"It's okay, Jake. *I* didn't kill her. It wasn't *my* fault. Not like when she killed me. When it *was* her fault." She paused. "She deserved it," she said.

"Hmm. I guess. So you're really back. With me, I

mean? Attached."
　"Yes. Silly. I always said I would be."
　"Wow. That's great."
　The only sounds were piano and rain.
　Jake's face hurt with the effort of smiling.

Chapter Twenty-One

Jake stood at the window watching the heavy rain that was turning to sleet. It seemed to reflect the orange streetlights less now. Cars drove by, illuminating it like dazzling diamonds that streaked into the dark tarmac.

"Are you looking for her?" the girl asked.

"Freesia? No. Not really. I'm sure she's long gone by now. Long gone, somewhere."

"Does it worry you, Jake?"

"No. Not as much as you might think. Not right now."

Jake watched a taxi pull up. A young couple got out and wandered up the drive of the house opposite. They were laughing. The girl stumbled in high-heeled shoes. The man had his arm through hers, and as he led her to the door. They laughed. They lingered for a while on the doorstep and neither of them seemed to mind the cold, hard rain. The man opened the door and waved the woman inside. The light from their hall glowed peach, then the door shut.

"Seems not everyone is bothered by the rain." Jake said.

"Where's Abe?" the girl said.

Jake gripped the edge of the windowsill and placed his forehead on the freezing cold glass. He closed his eyes then spun around and leaned back onto the windowsill with his backside and hands.

"I'd forgotten all about him," he said. He walked over to where Luce and Emma were, staying close to the table edge, and craned his head sideways so that he could see the bodies without, he thought, exposing his own body too much.

"I don't..." the girl said.

"Shh. Quiet."

Jake listened for any sign that Abe, or any other shadow, was down there, huddled somewhere, pressed up close against the cooling flesh of the women. He kept thinking that at any moment there would be that terrible din of metal on metal inside his skull. As the bodies came into view, he moved his head in all directions, trying his hardest to spot any shadow at any angle, but the floor around the bodies was flat and dull and empty.

"Jake," the girl whispered.

"What?" he hissed.

"I don't think there is *anything* here at all," she said at a normal volume.

"I know," he said, still hissing, then louder, "I think Abe is gone as well."

"Jake?"

Jake crouched down and looked at the closeness of the bodies. He wondered what it would feel like to slide his hand between the two of them, if one would be colder than the other.

"Jake?" the girl said, impatience in her voice.

"What?"

"Do you think Abe went with her? With Freesia?"

Jake stood up and looked back at the window. He looked at the door for any sign that it was moving in a breeze.

"I don't think so," he said. "I think Abe was too good for her. I get the impression that given the chance, he would quite happily kill her for what she did."

"You mean if he thought it was her fault about Luce?"

"Maybe." Jake looked around the room. "Freesia must have gone before Luce died. She must have."

Jake tapped his thumb on the side of his forehead.

"But he's not here," the girl said. "I know he's not."

"Do you think Luce left him with her? I mean as some kind of...insurance? Jesus. What if she left Abe with Freesia not just to guard her, but to maybe store him there. In case Luce needed him back? If anything went wrong with..."

"I don't think Abe needed *storing*," the girl said.

"Abe and Freesia." Jake shook his head. "If they *are* together I have no idea what that means. I can't decide if it's really, really funny or really, really dangerous. Maybe both."

"Do you think they'll go back to Bob and the family and Jessie? Do you think they'll try to hurt Jessie?"

"Look, I don't know."

"Jake?"

"Yes?"

"I'm glad I'm back with you."

"So am I," he said, smiling. "It feels right."

He picked up a silver picture frame from the shelf. It was the perfect 'family by the lake' portrait, Steve with one arm around Luce, around the back of her thick black hair, the other arm slightly raised as if he'd just set the timer on the camera and was running back to be with his family. Luce was resting one hand on a young girl. She had long straight blonde hair, a perfect round face, amber eyes and freckles all over. She was smiling and holding a bunch of red flowers in her lap. To the left of the girl was a boy a little older than her with thick black curly hair. He held her other hand in his, and was looking up at his mum and smiling, and even from the angle of his face, his eyes were large and round and amber.

"That's your brother?" Jake said, placing his finger on the boy's face.

"Yes. That was my brother. I lost him after the accident."

"After the accident. You can remember all that?"

"Yes. I can remember everything. Do you know what it's like to not be able to close your eyes? To see everything?"

Jake pressed his thumb and forefinger into the bridge of his nose, shook his head, and laughed.

"You knew everything all along," he said.

"Yes, Jake. Sorry."

"Should I ask you why you didn't tell me?"

"You can ask."

"Why didn't you tell me?"

"I didn't want to scare you."

Jake laughed. "You are precious," he said. "You

didn't want to scare me?" He paused. "Actually, to be fair, I think you're the only person I know who hasn't scared me. Apart from the Giddy Edge thing of course. Oh and the name thing."

Jake put the picture down and adjusted it so it sat neatly on the edge of the shelf. He looked back at the bodies of the women, then out the window.

In the hall, he looked at himself in the mirror.

"Jake?" the girl said.

"Hmm?"

"Do you want to know my name?"

Jake frowned. His reflection frowned back. "Not if it's gonna hurt. No."

"Oh, Jake it will be fine. My mum, Luce, called it out as she fell. She told me my name, and now that I know it, I can tell you."

"Oh please, God yes. Tell me."

"Hello, Jake," she said. "I'm Bethany."

"Bethany." Jake smiled into the mirror. "That sounds absolutely fine. I was going to call you Jennifer." He laughed and the light filtering through the glass panels in the door shifted up and down his face.

He reached over to the stand in the corner and picked up a wide-brimmed hat. He looked into the mirror again, put the hat on and adjusted it so that shadow covered his face. He stared at the two pinpoints of light in his eyes and smiled.

"It's you and me against the world," Bethany said. "It always was. Always."

"Bethany?" Jake said, opening the door and stepping out into the cold rain that thudded into his new hat.

"Yes, Jake?"

"Let's go find your brother."

Made in the USA
Charleston, SC
30 May 2013